THE REAPER
RESCUES THE GENIE
NOCTURNE FALLS, BOOK NINE

KRISTEN PAINTER

THE REAPER RESCUES THE GENIE:
Nocturne Falls, Book Nine

Copyright © 2018 Kristen Painter

ISBN: 978-1-941695-37-1
Published in the United States of America.

Welcome to Nocturne Falls, the town that celebrates Halloween 365 days a year. The tourists think it's all a show: the vampires, the werewolves, the witches, the occasional gargoyle flying through the sky. But the supernaturals populating the town know better.

Living in Nocturne Falls means being yourself. Fangs, fur, and all.

Death is what grim reaper Lucien Dupree knows best. Or rather, he did until his reaping powers became tragically unreliable. Now he's living in a self-imposed exile to keep humanity safe. Sure, it's a lonely existence, but it's the best thing for everyone. Except him.

Retired genie, Imari Zephara, has found her happy place in Nocturne Falls. Well, as happy as she can be considering the alternative returning home would bring her. Then a dark force rears its ugly head and throws her life into turmoil. Suddenly the only way to save herself is to join forces with death, who turns out to be a pretty amazing guy.

But Lucien's defective powers might not be enough to overcome centuries of jinn tradition, meaning Imari's life would no longer be her own. All he wants is to give her the chance to choose her own future. Hopefully, one that includes him. What more could a guy a wish for?

Dedicated to my readers,
who are obviously the best.

Death was Lucien Dupree's life.

Or it had been for more years than he could count. But then, once a grim reaper, always a grim reaper. Retirement didn't really exist, not in the human sense of the word, anyway. The powers were permanent and dependable.

At least, they were supposed to be.

As it turned out, they weren't, and he'd been forced into retirement. He'd accepted it, yes, but there had been no other option. His most important power had become unreliable, and that made *him* unreliable. So the job he'd given up his human life for centuries ago was gone.

Just. Like. That.

He'd bowed out of all future assignments with the understanding that if things changed, he could return to work.

Things hadn't changed. Not in decades. He no longer had hope they would.

Because of that unexplained shift in his abilities, his life now was a more self-imposed exile than the easy, carefree days the word *retirement* conjured up. What else could it be? He was a reaper who could not control the most important of his abilities.

Something he'd discovered in the most horrible way possible.

He squeezed his eyes shut at that memory and leaned his head against his chair, ignoring the book in his hands. He wasn't really reading it anyway. He'd tried, but there wasn't much that could distract him from the pit of despair he quite often sank into.

Tonight was one of those nights.

He was, in a word, miserable. But why use one word when there were so many others that did the job equally well? Despondent. Wretched. Morose. Hopeless.

"Lucien, stop moping."

He didn't need to open his eyes to know his grandmother had entered the room. Her words, kind as they were, only served to worsen his mood.

After all, she was the ghostly proof of how broken he had become.

But being the good grandson he was, he opened his eyes, fixed a smile on his face, closed his book, and brought his gaze to hers. "Yes, *Mémé*."

She peered at him, the hallway behind her visible through her translucent form. "I was going to bed. But I could sit up with you for a while if you want. Talk a little, maybe?"

Her kindness widened his smile effortlessly, and

2

he shook his head. She was such a good woman. "Thank you, but I'm fine. I need to go check on things at the club." He didn't. The club almost ran itself. But it was the escape he needed.

She pursed her lips. "You don't look fine."

"I was just thinking about Kora." That was only a half-lie, and an easy one to tell because it was so believable.

Hattie sighed with understanding. "That child. Where is she now?"

He shrugged. She was nearly impossible to keep track of, but the last he'd heard, she was in Istanbul. Hopefully staying out of trouble, but that was unlikely.

"Are you going to send Greyson after her again?"

"Only if she asks for my help. Which she hasn't. I'm not sure she will again after Rome."

"But you saved her life."

He stared at his hands. At the hands that wielded unpredictable death. "Technically, Greyson saved her life."

"And you paid for his efforts, so that allows you to take credit." She shook her head. "She needs a spanking."

He snorted. "Best of luck with that." But he admired that Hattie was fearless even in the face of the willful vampire who was his daughter. He put the book on the chairside table and stood. "I love you, *Mémé*."

"I love you, too, Lucy."

Only Hattie Dupree could get away with calling

3

him that. It was one of many things she could get away with. Like the lace doilies and dishes of hard candy in the living room. If she asked him for the world, he would have bankrupted his vast wealth to get it for her, but she'd never asked for anything, except to live with him after…the incident.

He would have thought she'd have asked for her life back, even knowing it couldn't happen, but she didn't seem to hold that against him. Maybe because he'd managed to return her soul to her? He wasn't sure, but they never discussed it. She just went about her life as if she'd always been a ghost.

As if he wasn't responsible for her undead state of being.

Grandmothers were interesting and wonderful that way. Now more than ever, she had become his heart. His soul. The one good thing in his otherwise bleak existence. "Sleep well, *Mémé*."

"You, too. Good night, sweetheart." She floated away down the hall toward her quarters in the enormous underground levels that made up their home.

He almost sank back into his chair, but tonight the club really did call to him.

Insomnia was the business that had helped occupy him in the years since they'd moved to Nocturne Falls. It was an exclusive, supernaturals-only hotspot that gave him some leverage in town. He didn't need much. Just to be left alone. The club's popularity bought him that. So did some of his other financial contributions in town. The cost was worth it to him, though. And highly effective. In fact, only a handful of people knew he owned the club or that he resided in Nocturne Falls. That's exactly how he wanted it.

Of course, the Ellinghams knew, but he didn't mind. They were the family who owned the town, and they were a reasonable bunch of vampires. He had deeply conflicted feelings about vampires. There were some very good ones, such as the Ellinghams and Greyson Garrett, the vampire who worked for him on an as-needed basis. Then there were some dreadful ones, such as his ex-wife.

His lip had curled without him realizing it.

He sighed out the bitter taste in his mouth and took solace in the fact that Pavlina was no longer around to torment him. And not because of anything he'd done. His hands were clean of that death. She'd just made too many enemies and had paid the price. But he wasn't going to dwell on her. That would only drag him down deeper.

Tonight, he needed to be lifted up. He needed to sink into the energy of the one thing he would never have again. Humanity.

Because, despite serving only supernaturals, the patrons in his club still had a great deal of their human sides left. The vampires not as much as the shifters, for sure, but the witches were essentially just humans with very special gifts. The fae *looked* mostly human if you didn't focus on the ears.

In his club, he could inhale the warm breath of life, revel in the laughter and joy of his patrons, and remind himself that there was still good in the world.

He could imagine that he too was human again.

He wasn't. He never would be. But even a reaper could dream.

His mood made him reckless. He had so little to lose. Most nights, he was content to lurk in the secret hallways that surrounded the club and watch the patrons through the one-way mirrors that lined the walls for that very purpose. But tonight, watching wasn't going to be enough.

So after throwing on a dark suit, a dark shirt, and a thin pair of black leather gloves, he slipped through a passageway that led from his home to the always reserved area of Insomnia's VIP section.

It was always reserved because no one was allowed in it but him. Even if he only used it once a year.

The music's pulsating thump vibrated through his bloodstream, forcing him to be present. Forcing him to let go of the past. It was a good thing to lose himself like this sometimes. To forget the past and live in the moment. Too hard to do often for someone like him, but he needed this tonight.

He walked to the railing that separated the elevated platform from the club a few feet below, but kept slightly behind the sheer silk curtains that hung from the corners of the private box.

The place was busy. That pleased him. He didn't need the money, which was part of the reason he paid his employees so well, but he wanted the popularity. He wanted the power that gave him to remain secluded. And he wanted to see the people who made up this curious town.

Especially because he almost never left his home. It was in everyone's best interests that he not mingle. He was too dangerous, too unpredictable.

And he didn't want another unintentional death on his hands. Literally.

He gripped the railing, letting the pulse of the music flow through the metal and into him. He didn't dance. He had no idea what rhythm was, but the throb of the club music felt like a heartbeat, and *that* he understood.

He liked it. Better that *thump, thump, thump* than the deafening silence of nothing.

The lights strobed and flashed over the crowd of dancers. He imagined the colors, but it had been so long since he'd actually seen them he had no idea what they might actually look like. The ability to see color had been stripped from him when he'd gotten his first assignment as a reaper.

His division was known as the War Angels. It was partially a misnomer. They weren't angels at all, but merchants of death. But the war part was correct. He and his fellow reapers swept the battlefields of the world, taking the souls of the casualties, both soldier and civilian.

All of the War Angels had been stripped of their color vision. It was supposed to be a mercy, to prevent the burnout from seeing so many wounded. So much blood.

He would have liked the chance to choose for himself, but that was an old wound and not one he spent much thought on anymore. What was done was done.

A server approached. Trina, a fae woman who was one of the shift managers. She was also one of the few who had permission to engage with him. "Good evening, sir."

"Evening, Trina."

"Shall I get you the usual?"

He paused a moment. His usual was a single glass of good cognac. Tonight, his usual didn't feel like it would be enough. "Bring the bottle."

"I'll be right back." She was familiar enough with him that her expression showed no shock or surprise.

If he wanted to drown his sorrows, that was his business.

He watched her work her way through the crowd and back to the bar, but she was only partway there when another woman caught his eye.

The woman was very, *very* pretty. Even without his ability to see color, he understood that her dark hair and dark eyes made for a mesmerizing combination. The men around her seemed as captivated as Lucien was.

She was standing with a group of female friends near the edge of the dance floor. He recognized a few of them as regulars. They seemed to be trying to persuade her to dance with them. She kept shaking her head and laughing off their requests.

At last, her friends gave up and went off to dance without her. She stayed where she was, arms crossed defensively in front of her, making eye contact with no one. The smile that had been present for her friends left when they did.

He understood. They'd already talked her into

coming to Insomnia tonight. This wasn't her usual place. He would have known. He would have remembered seeing this particular woman before.

She seemed to want to leave but acted like she felt some kind of obligation to remain. Maybe it was one of her friends' birthdays. Or hers? No. Not hers. She wouldn't celebrate like this.

Trina returned with his bottle of cognac and a single glass. She poured for him, but left the glass on the small table. She'd been trained well. "Can I get you anything else, sir?"

He tipped his head toward the woman across the dance floor. "Do you know who that is?"

Trina stepped closer to the railing and followed his line of sight. "I don't recognize her. I can ask around."

"No, it's not important. Is she drinking anything?"

"She asked for tea, but that's not on our menu."

Tea? What sort of woman came to a nightclub and wanted to drink tea? His curiosity was aroused. "We don't have tea."

It was a statement, not a question, but Trina answered him anyway. "No, sir."

"We serve coffee."

She sort of wobbled her head back and forth. "Yes, but that's because we can't make Irish coffees without it."

He snorted softly. "Stay here."

It only took a minute to return to his apartment and raid the kitchen for a tin of his best Assam loose leaf. He entered the VIP box again and set the tin on the table. "Make her a cup of that."

9

Trina nodded, took the tin, and went to do as he'd bidden.

He left the railing and sat on the plush white leather sofa where he could stretch out his long legs. Tea. How odd. Almost as an afterthought, he remembered his cognac. He tugged his gloves off so the liquid could benefit from the warmth of his hand and lifted the glass, holding it up so the light shone through it.

He knew the color of good cognac. Hadn't seen it in ages, but it wasn't a color he was soon to forget. He imagined this cognac had that deep amber hue. A sip confirmed that it was his usual, but the bottle already displayed that it was a very fine brand. The liquor's burn lit the length of his throat with a pleasant heat, and for those few moments, he thought he remembered what normal felt like.

But just thinking that brought back all the reasons why he wasn't normal.

He frowned and tossed back the remaining cognac. That was no way to treat such a fine beverage, but correctness was the last thing he cared about. A recklessness came over him. Why should he care what was proper?

He poured himself another.

Obliterating part of his brain, now there was a thing to focus on. He lifted the glass, but reason returned and he made himself sip it. He wasn't an animal. He was just a miserable sot of a being who had no real reason to carry on.

Save for his grandmother.

An outsider might guess his daughter would be reason enough, but Kora had been poisoned against him by her mother to the point that his child regarded him as a bank account and not much more. He knew Kora blamed him for her mother's untimely end, but he'd had nothing to do with it, despite his deadly touch.

Besides, Kora was an adult, no matter that he considered her still a child. Had been for nearly a hundred and fifty years. She was a vampire to boot, one of the rare few born that way, but that had only served to make her even more her mother's daughter.

Lucien blew out a thick breath. His life was a complete and utter dung heap.

Save for his grandmother.

He lifted the glass, filled a third time now, in a toast to her. And stopped dead.

Standing at the entrance of his private VIP area was the beautiful tea drinker.

She lifted the cup in her hand, one of the clear mugs used for coffee by the looks of it, and nodded. "Very kind of you."

Her voice held the slight lilt of a foreign land, but not one he could immediately place.

Before he could answer, Trina came rushing up the steps. "Ma'am, you have to leave. This is a restricted—"

"It's fine, Trina."

She glanced at him, her expression at last showing surprise. "Yes, sir."

She retreated, leaving him with the woman.

The woman smiled, glancing at her tea. "You must be someone very important."

He shook his head. She smelled like night-blooming jasmine and sandalwood, and this close, he realized how wrong he'd been to think her merely pretty.

She was staggeringly beautiful. Unreal, almost. More perfect than he'd imagined. She had to be supernatural to be that flawless.

"No," he said, astounded he could find the capacity to craft a response in her presence. "I'm no one."

She laughed, a sweet, joyful sound. "That's not true at all, is it?"

Was she playing with him? Or did she know the truth? His lack of interaction with anyone besides his grandmother, and occasionally Greyson, had left him deficient in reading people. And he wasn't one of those reapers who could see a person's aura. A War Angel didn't need to know how good or bad a person was, and there was no time for that assessment on the battlefield anyway. "I…" But he was at a loss as to how to answer.

She took a few steps toward him and sat on the far end of the couch where he was. "I'm being forward, I know, and I sincerely hope you don't read anything into this, but the crowd is…" She sighed and looked toward the dance floor, her smile fading.

Then her gaze returned to him. "The tea is very good."

"It's Assam." He understood about the crowd. He wasn't a fan either, mostly out of necessity.

She smiled again. "I know."

What was she? Not a vampire. No fangs. No pointed ears, either, that he could see. A witch, then? A supernatural of some kind, for sure, because nothing about her seemed exactly human. And humans weren't allowed in Insomnia. His gaze dropped to the glass in his hand. Perhaps he'd had enough to drink.

"I'm Imari, by the way."

"That's a lovely name." Imari. He knew that name somehow. She worked here in town, but he couldn't quite place her.

"Thank you." She stuck her hand out. "And thank you very much for the tea."

Maybe it was the cognac. Maybe it was because of how off center she'd knocked him by speaking with him so boldly. Or maybe being this close to this much beauty had rattled him. But for some inexplicable reason, he reached out and took her hand in his.

Without a glove on.

The second their hands touched, his world imploded. Fear. Panic. But she held on to him, oblivious to the danger. Yes, his gloves were off, but she remained very much alive. How was that possible?

He peered into her eyes, trying to ascertain that he wasn't reaping her soul in that very moment, and froze. How was this possible? He was seeing something he shouldn't.

Color.

Namely, Imari's eyes. And they were the same deep, rich golden brown of the cognac in his glass.

He stared at her like he'd just been shot. That wasn't a reaction she was used to, but then, she didn't talk to many men. Not outside of the spa where she worked anyway. And most of her clients were women, but besides that, there just wasn't much talking in her part of the spa.

That was one of the great benefits of being a massage therapist. Most people wanted quiet during their session. She was good with that.

And it wasn't that she didn't like people—she did. She liked people a great deal. Most people, that was. Time and experience had caused her to pull back from a lot of social interaction. Now she just wanted to fly below the radar and enjoy a life of her own choosing. She had a few girlfriends in town, and that was good enough for her.

Despite all that, she had to ask him, "Are you okay?"

"I—the color of your—yes, I'm fine." He slipped his hand out of hers, and the shock in his eyes changed to something dark and a little frightening. Then he blinked, and it was gone.

Fine? He didn't seem fine at all. "Are you sure you're all right?"

He didn't immediately answer, just kept staring at her with his penetrating gaze. Then the lights from the dance floor flashed over them, and for the briefest of moments, she thought she could see the bones of his face. As if his skull had suddenly become visible.

She blinked twice. The image vanished.

That couldn't have been what she'd seen. Could it? But she wasn't one to ignore signs or omens. He was connected to death in some way. She'd felt it in her bones the second she'd spoken to him. Granted, she had some practice in that area, considering her betrothed was an ifrit. The ifrit were a particular kind of jinn, a dark, humorless lot primarily relegated to guarding the world that all jinn called home, the Chaos Realm.

And despite being betrothed to Khalid, she'd met him only once, and then, according to custom, there had been no words exchanged. Fine with her. She had no desire to speak to the man her parents had chosen for her to marry. Even less desire to actually marry him.

Fortunately, she was *not* an ifrit, and like most of the jinn who weren't ifrit, she had a keen ability to suss people out. To understand who they were and what they needed. It was a big part of what had made her so good at being a genie and so adept at her current job.

Her current job was important, too. It helped shield her true identity from the world. Because while a genie was a much-sought-after creature, massage therapists were rather plentiful. And even though a large handful of people in town knew she was a genie, they also thought she was retired. Out of wishes, as it were. Best they thought that. For them and for her. It kept them from asking and kept her from lying to her friends.

She swallowed and got to her feet. "I've overstayed my welcome. Which might not have been a welcome to begin with, now that I think back. Excuse me." She headed for the steps.

"Imari," he breathed out.

Almost to the exit, she stopped, but didn't turn. She didn't want to see the skull again. Not because it frightened her, but because in some odd way it reminded her of the future she was desperate to avoid. Perhaps because she thought of her life with Khalid as a kind of death. "Thank you for the tea."

"You're welcome."

She glanced at him then to acknowledge his words. The skull she thought she'd imagined hadn't returned. The face she'd first encountered was still there.

That was the face that had drawn her to him. He looked so sad. Forlorn, really. As though he had taken the weight of the world upon himself. Or suffered a terrible loss. Maybe he had. It would explain the way he looked. And his connection with death.

He had been quite handsome at one time. The

THE REAPER RESCUES THE GENIE

traces of male beauty lingered in the strong lines of his face, but the gloom that hung over him made him seem tired and worn. Something in his life, no doubt. Some kind of trouble.

He also looked like he could use a friend.

But would he be the sort of man who would want to use her if he ever found out who she was and what she was truly capable of? She didn't want to think of him that way, but everyone wanted something.

She had to leave.

"I'm Lucien."

She smiled, more from compassion for whatever hurt had befallen him than because she was happy. "Thank you, Lucien. I really have to go. I've bothered you for far too long."

"You haven't bothered me. And you certainly didn't overstay your welcome. I enjoyed the company."

"Thank you again." With a nod, she darted down the steps and into the crowd. If his gaze was still on her, she couldn't tell. She found one of her friends, made an excuse for her early departure, and left the club.

Not until she stepped outside and stood beneath the starry night sky did she truly exhale. Her friends had driven, so she took her phone out and ordered a Ryde. The service's app said seven minutes. That wasn't too bad.

"Nice night, huh?"

Startled, she whipped around to see who'd spoken to her. A man hung in the shadows, smoking a cigarette and leaning against the worn brick exterior of the warehouse that housed Insomnia. The name Caldwell Manufacturing could be seen in faded white paint on the building's side. The whole idea was that you had to know about Insomnia to find Insomnia. She gave a little nod in response. "Yes, very nice."

He blew out a stream of smoke, then inhaled again. The ember at the end of the cigarette glowed red hot in the dim light. "Sorry, didn't mean to scare you."

"It's fine." She busied herself with nothing on her phone in an attempt to end any further conversation. The man looked familiar, though. Where had she seen him before? He hadn't been a massage client, she'd remember that. So where was he from? She didn't go out all that much, but she'd run to the Shop-n-Save for groceries yesterday. Maybe that was it. Yes, in the deli department. Or the frozen foods. Somewhere.

She snuck a look at him.

And now he was here, at the same nightclub as she was. The small hairs on the back of her neck came to attention, but she did her best to ignore them. Nocturne Falls was a small town. People ran into each other. It meant nothing.

Still, she watched him out of the corner of her eye.

"You're a good dancer." He peeled himself off the brick to stretch his thick, squat body, gesturing at her with his cigarette.

The small hairs went up again. He'd been in the club, then. But she hadn't spotted him there. And she could swear he was human, a species not allowed through Insomnia's doors. She answered with a tight smile before looking at her phone again. "Thanks."

Her Ryde was five minutes away.

In her peripheral vision, she saw him take a few steps in her direction. "But then, the jinn know how to move, don't they?" He wiggled his hips, laughing. "Belly dancing is in your blood, right?"

She scowled at him even as her pulse ticked up and alarm bells sounded in her head. She shoved her phone into her purse. "I don't know what you're talking about."

"You're jinn, sweetheart." He spread his arms out like he'd just made a very obvious statement. "You can't fool me. I know your kind inside and out. It's my job. And I'm the best at what I do."

She narrowed her eyes even as nervous energy caused a little tremble to run through her. She hadn't lived this long without handling the occasional creeper. It happened to all women. "Is your job harassing women? Because you're exceptional at that."

"Nah, that's not my job." He leaned in, his smile wide and ugly with smoke-stained teeth. "I'm a wish merchant."

Her blood went cold. A wish merchant. She froze to the spot. Panic raked down her spine. There wasn't a genie alive who didn't know what a wish merchant was capable of. How they could destroy a genie's life. She'd escaped one in Bangkok almost two hundred years ago and had considered herself lucky then.

She didn't feel lucky now. "Get away from me."

"Can't. Because you're about to make me a very

19

rich man." He grabbed her wrist. "At least, you'd better. Took me too damn long to track you down."

She opened her mouth to scream, but another voice interrupted her, a voice like daggers cutting through sandpaper.

"Take your hands off her, or I will put *mine* on you."

She and her assailant turned at the same time.

Behind them towered a blackness unlike anything Imari had ever seen. It was a shadow *and* an abyss, both there and not. In the form of a man. A black-hooded cloak snapped around the creature like a living thing, and within it, shapes pulsed inside the darkness. Hands. Mouths gaping. A nightmare come to life. With eyes that glowed like hot coals.

She could barely breathe. Her heart pounded, filling her head with the sound and making all other thought impossible.

The wish merchant released her wrist. His eyes were wide and his jaw slack as he backed away. He shook his head, then turned and took off running. No doubt he thought he'd just seen death. Wish merchants were a superstitious lot, and for that, she was eternally grateful.

As his footsteps faded, Imari tried to speak, but her mouth was dry from the tenseness of the moment.

Car tires crunched over pavement. Her Ryde was here. Headlights flashed across the looming figure.

For a second, she saw the face within the hood that held those fiery eyes. A skull.

Then the lights moved past, and just like that, her savior disappeared.

"Thank you," she whispered. Then she climbed into the car as fast as she could.

She didn't stop trembling until an hour after she was home. She lay in her bed, staring at the ceiling, and tried not to break down. She wasn't a delicate flower, but she'd come to think of herself as safe for so long that tonight had rattled her.

Hard.

A wish merchant. Here in Nocturne Falls. Never in a million years would she have thought that was possible. She considered this town a haven. A safe zone. And it had been until tonight.

That scum would find her again. He knew she was here now. There was no reason for him to give up until he'd gotten what he wanted.

She chewed on her bottom lip as her head started to ache. She'd have to leave. There was no other option. Not really. Sure, there were *other* options, but none she was willing to take. At least not the one that involved Khalid.

But what if she didn't have to go that far? She glanced toward the embroidered textile that covered the wall behind her vanity table. Just thinking about the possible escape that lay behind there intensified the ache in her head.

Even so, she threw the covers back and padded over to the table. She drew back the fabric, tying it up in a knot and out of the way to reveal the wall safe hidden there. A few quick spins of the combination unlocked the door.

She opened it, needing to see that the luminous, bejeweled bottle was still there. Still secure. It was.

Carefully, she took the bottle from the safe and cradled it in her hands. The weight of it always gave her comfort. The glass gleamed with iridescence, like an oil slick. Blues and purples and greens. Gems dotted the bottle's surface in a pattern like peacock feathers. Swirls of amethysts, emeralds, and sapphires set in gold filigree and speckled with diamonds and moonstones. The stopper was an uncut emerald encircled with diamonds and iolite set in more fancifully worked gold.

The bottle alone was worth a king's ransom. But to her, it was priceless beyond measure. To her, it was freedom. It had the power to become her prison, but she wouldn't let that happen. So long as the bottle remained in her control, that wouldn't happen.

And yet she was thinking about giving it away. To a man who could very well be the angel of death.

"I am a fool."

Hattie kissed the top of Lucien's head. "No, you're not, honey. You saw the man following her out, and you listened to your gut. From what you told me, you probably saved her life."

"I *am* a fool, and I doubt it was that desperate." But he'd kept Imari from being hurt. He allowed himself some comfort in that. Of course, he'd never see her again. Not after the display he'd put on. But showing off his reaper form was all he'd been able to think of to scare the cretin away without actually touching him.

Although, Lucien had been prepared to do that if things had taken a turn for the worse. He could have claimed it as a defensive killing, then. Hoped for some leniency from the council. There was little chance they'd allow him another accident.

"Honey, stop being so hard on yourself."

"I scared her away." It wasn't an answer, just a

statement of fact. And the idea of never seeing her again cut him deeply. The incredible Imari, who seemed not only immune to his deadly effects, but whose touch had brought color back to his world. Magnificent color. He hadn't known how much he'd missed it until he'd had it for those few brief seconds her hand had held his.

But the contact of her skin, of her warm, gloriously silky fingers in his, that had been the true revelation. Missing color was nothing compared to not being touched. And her touch was…exceptional.

Hattie set a plate in front of him. "I doubt that. Most supernatural women are made of stronger stuff."

The plate held two slices of bacon and a three-egg omelet filled with spinach, goat cheese, fresh chives, and diced tomato. It was one of his favorite things, and the rich aroma begged him to dive in.

"I'm not hungry," he grumped.

"Yes, you are. And even death needs to eat, so go on, have at it."

"*Mémé*, I am not a child."

She sat across from him, giving him the same stern look she'd been giving him for the last one hundred and twenty-three years. "Well, you could have fooled me with that pout."

He rolled his eyes. "I do not pout."

"No?" She sipped her tea. She didn't *need* to eat. She was a ghost, after all, but Lucien knew how she loved food, especially her tea and sweets, and in corporeal form, as she was now, she could eat and drink just like any living person.

There was laughter in her eyes. Laughter directed at him.

With a sigh, he picked up his fork. He ate, and while the breakfast Hattie had prepared was delicious, it did nothing to soothe the ache inside him.

She reached over and patted his arm. "I still think you did the right thing, Lucy. Even if you did scare her."

He shrugged.

"What kind of supernatural did you say she is?"

"I didn't, because I'm not sure. Witch, perhaps."

"What's her name again?"

He hadn't told his grandmother because he didn't want her to get involved. What would Imari think if Hattie tracked her down and tried to persuade her that Lucien was really a dear, sweet boy? Because those *were* the words she would use. He sighed. "Imari. But don't—"

"Imari Zephara?"

"I don't know her last name, but I doubt there are many other Imaris in town. How do you know her?"

"She's a massage therapist at the Nocturne Falls Spa."

His brows lifted. "And you know that because?"

She sipped her tea before answering. "Where do you think I get my hair done?"

"All right, but how does that—isn't the spa sort of an...*extravagant* place to have your hair done?"

Her eyes narrowed ever so slightly. "We can afford it."

"True enough. I wasn't complaining, just asking.

And your hair always looks lovely." He liked that she indulged herself so. She deserved it. A thousand times over. "Anyway, so you know her because of going there?"

Hattie shifted in her seat and put her hand on the newspaper that sat folded next to her place setting. "I do. We're not best friends or anything like that, but I know who she is. I've seen her once or twice passing through the salon." She turned her cup slightly on its saucer. "She's very beautiful."

Imari was that. He stared at his own cup of tea, lost in the memory of her golden-brown eyes once again, her sweet, exotic perfume drifting past his nose, teasing him to lean in and—

"Lucien. *Lucien.*"

He glanced up. "Yes, *Mémé*?"

But he recognized the look on her face instantly. The pursed mouth. The determined gaze. The just so set of her jaw. "No. Do not talk to her. Do not say anything to her about me. She doesn't know who or what I am, and I want it kept that way. You know how much I want to be left alone. If you say something and someone overhears, my life—*our* life—could be ruined. I won't stay in a town where I'm the object of fear and ridicule."

Compassion crinkled the corners of her eyes. "I won't say a word. I adore this town. I wouldn't want to do anything to jeopardize our being here."

"I know." Beyond that, it would kill his business. No one would come to a club where the owner might accidentally reap their soul. But he believed Hattie.

He knew she didn't want to move. She absolutely loved Nocturne Falls. It was the most normal life she'd had since he'd taken her first one away from her. "Thank you."

She gave him a curt nod, like she was a little miffed that he'd assumed she'd do something to endanger them. She unfolded the front page of today's edition of the Tombstone, smoothing it so she could read the headlines. "Your omelet is getting cold."

"Yes, *Mémé*."

He was halfway through his breakfast when his phone vibrated. Hattie allowed the paper at the table, but didn't like phones. Of course, he rarely got calls. Unless it was Kora.

That got him to check the screen, but it wasn't her, it was Greyson. He answered. "Yes?"

"Lucien, I need to come by and see you."

"What's wrong?"

Hattie mouthed, *Kora?*

Lucien shook his head and mouthed back, *Greyson.* With a nod, Hattie returned to her paper.

Greyson answered Lucien's question. "I was asked not to discuss it over the phone."

Lucien frowned. That sounded cryptic. Maybe it was Kora after all. "Fine. When?"

"In about half an hour."

"I'll be here." He hung up. Wasn't like he'd be anywhere else.

"What was that about?" Hattie asked.

"Greyson has some kind of business he can't discuss over the phone."

"Hmm. Probably something the Ellinghams need."

"Probably." But what would the Ellinghams need from him? Then a cold thought hit him. What if Imari had relayed the incident at the club to Hugh or Sebastian? She didn't know Lucien was the owner of the club, but they'd know from her description that he was the one who'd scared her.

What would they have told her about him? He hoped nothing. But there might be a reprimand coming his way. So be it. He could explain his side and let them know he'd saved her. And frankly, if she was upset at having her life saved, maybe it was best that he was never going to see her again.

Suddenly miffed, he pushed his plate away. "I'm going to my study."

Hattie looked up from the Tombstone. "All right. I'll bring Greyson in when he arrives."

Lucien left the table and stormed off to his study. It was a highly masculine space filled with dark paneling, rich leather, and thick Oriental carpets. It was also the one area Hattie was not allowed to improve upon. This place was his. His fortress of sorts. The art was of his choosing, and the walls were lined with bookshelves heavy with a mix of the old classics he loved and some new selections he'd yet to read.

Books were a great comfort to him. They helped him escape the pit of his life. But at the moment, he had actual work to do. That should be enough to take his mind off the disaster of last night. At least until Greyson arrived.

He sat at his desk, fired up his laptop, and opened the club's accounting software so he could go over the receipts for the previous night. It had been a very good evening. Hattie could afford to have her hair done anywhere she liked. And as often, too.

Checking the receipts didn't take much time, however, and he found himself doing a quick internet search for the Nocturne Falls Spa.

He clicked on the link for the website, then on the link for massage. There were no pictures of the therapists, only lists of the types of massages available. Swedish. Deep tissue. Hot stone. He grimaced. Who would want hot stones put on them? That sounded like medieval torture.

But the idea of Imari's hands on him...he drifted on that tangent for a few long, self-indulgent moments. He'd never had a massage. Not really. During his reaper sabbatical, a brief venture into humanity that War Angels were encouraged to take—and his even shorter and more disastrous attempt at marriage—Pavlina had once endeavored to rub his shoulders. He'd found her touch unbearably hard. All that untempered vampire strength. As if she'd been trying to pry his muscles loose from his bones. There had been nothing relaxing about it.

Imari would be different, of course. She had to know what she was doing. It was her job after all. If she was bad at it, the spa wouldn't keep her on.

"Lucien?" Hattie stuck her head in. She was smiling and holding a bunch of wildflowers wrapped in tissue paper and ribbon, no doubt a gift from the vampire who'd just arrived. "Greyson is here."

Lucien shut down the spa's webpage and nodded as he got to his feet. "Good."

Greyson entered. "Thanks, Hattie."

"You're welcome. Can I get you anything? Coffee? Tea?"

"No, I'm fine, thank you. I'll just be a few minutes."

"All right." She left them.

Greyson closed the study door.

Lucien sat back down. "Let me guess. The Ellinghams are cross because I showed my true form and scared one of their precious citizens."

Greyson made a face. "I have no idea what you're talking about."

That took the wind out of Lucien's sails. "You don't? Then why are you here?"

Greyson took a seat on the big leather couch. "I'm here because someone needs your help."

Lucien barked out a laugh. "Not likely."

"She does."

The feminine pronoun gave Lucien pause. "Who?"

"A woman by the name of Imari Zephara. She says she met you the other night. Well, she doesn't know exactly who you are—"

"Then how did she know to contact you about me?"

"She didn't. She only knew that I frequent Insomnia and thought I might know the man she met there. She figured if you were in the VIP section, you might be a regular."

"That's a stretch. I could have been anyone. A wealthy tourist in from Prague."

Greyson laughed softly. "You sent her tea. You made it clear you had some pull at the club. If you want to be anonymous, maybe don't throw your weight around so much."

"I'd never have gotten you to work for me otherwise." But Greyson had a point. Lucien really was a fool. "What does she want of me?"

"She's in some danger. At least she thinks she is. Seems a man has been tracking her and—"

"I saw him. Outside the club." It was a great relief to know she wasn't angry at him.

Greyson paused. "You followed her out?"

Lucien hated explaining himself. "She...intrigued me. What about the man?"

"Well, Imari is jinn."

"She's a genie?"

Greyson nodded. "And the man after her is a wish merchant. He means to capture her and sell her to the highest bidder."

The shock of that made Lucien's breath catch in his throat. "That's illegal. And immoral."

"It is. But you and I both know that what happens in the supernatural world rarely follows human law. Or a moral compass."

Both were painfully true. "Where do I come in?"

"She wants to give you her genie bottle for temporary safe-keeping. She thinks you're the only one the wish merchant won't try to steal it from. Apparently, they're a very superstitious bunch, and

31

she thinks you're the angel of death because of how you appeared and how terrified the wish merchant was of you. Wish merchants tend to avoid any kind of death omen whenever possible."

"Did you tell her I wasn't an angel of death? That I was a reaper?"

"No, the conversation never came back around to that. Does it matter?"

"Yes, it matters. I'm a grim reaper. There's a difference."

"I don't think she cares. She just wants to scare off the wish merchant."

Lucien made a face. This was all new ground for him. He didn't know much about the jinn. But he was certainly intrigued by Imari. "Her bottle? A wish merchant? I need more information."

"I'll tell you what I can, but I don't know anything else about the wish merchant than what I told you. As for the bottle, it's her life, and her freedom as long as it's in her possession. Whoever holds it, owns her and her magic."

"I don't want to own her."

"That's what she's counting on."

"She's counting on it?" Lucien snorted. "Why on earth would she trust me with it? She doesn't know me at all."

"Like I said, she thinks you're an angel of death, and as an angel, she also thinks you'd have no need for wishes and would do the right thing and give the bottle back to her when the wish merchant gives up and goes away." Greyson mumbled something else.

"What was that?"

"I, uh, might have also told her you were a stand-up guy."

"You *vouched* for me."

"I did."

Lucien rolled his eyes. What he didn't need were personal recommendations that resulted in him doing favors for people. Not that Imari was just anyone. She'd made him see color. But there was a reason he didn't interact with others. He didn't want to cut anyone else's life short inadvertently. And just because that didn't happen the first time he and Imari touched didn't mean it wouldn't happen the second time.

And there *would* be a second time, if the opportunity arose. Not because he wished to harm her in any way, but he was a weak man, and she was a beautiful woman. If he'd forgotten his head around her once, he'd do it again. Especially with how tempting it would be to want to see color again.

"So?" Greyson asked. "What do you think?"

What he thought and what he felt were two different things, but he was strong enough to follow his head and ignore his heart. "No."

Frowning, Greyson stood up. "Lucien, you owe me. What I went through in Rome for you—"

"For Kora."

"Same thing," he snarled, showing his fangs. "That woman nearly got us both killed."

"And you were paid handsomely."

"Not enough for nearly dying. Not that I'm asking for more money. But you know what I mean."

Lucien sighed, but he understood that Greyson spoke the truth. Kora had cost them all dearly. Not that she cared. "Fine, bring me the bottle."

"I can't. If Imari gives it to me, I become the owner, and I'm not taking on that responsibility. Imari has to give it to you herself."

"Then bring her here."

Greyson snorted. "Really?"

Lucien ground his back teeth together. "Not *here* here. To the club."

Greyson's brows lifted, and a dubious light shone in his eyes. "To the same place where the wish merchant almost nabbed her? Great idea."

"I can protect her. I can make sure—"

Greyson slapped a little card down on Lucien's desk. "That's her address. Be there tonight at nine."

Imari's nerves were taut with stress, but no massage could have helped her. She must have peeked through the curtains to look out at the parking lot a hundred times, but there was no sign of Lucien *or* the wish merchant. Yet. Although the wish merchant might very well be out there somewhere. Of course, Lucien was the only one she wanted to see.

Hmm. *Wanted* wasn't the right word. But she needed the protection of an angel of death, and he was her only hope. Wish merchants were terrified of the harbingers of death, as the one stalking her had demonstrated. They were all a superstitious lot, from what she'd been told, and it was something she planned to use to her advantage.

She'd never known an angel of death personally before Lucien. Not that she really knew him, but she had made his acquaintance. He was so much warmer than she would have imagined an angel of death. More solid too.

But then, so was Khalid, her betrothed.

She frowned and let the curtains drop before going back to the kitchen to tidy up. The dinner she'd made was one of her favorites. Just a simple meal of lamb stew and rice, but she'd only picked at it. Hard to eat when death's messenger was on his way to your apartment. Even if he was coming to do you a favor.

He was, wasn't he? Going to do her a favor? What had Greyson said? She finished her cleaning and sat on the couch, her fingers laced together, her legs crossed under her, and tried to think back to her conversation with him.

She stared at nothing, her focus inward. He'd said he'd gotten Lucien to come to her house. That was all she could really pin down.

She pressed her fingers to her temples. Maybe she should just leave town. It would be easier.

Except that it wouldn't. It would mean leaving her friends behind. And most of her things. Plus there was no guarantee the wish merchant wouldn't find her in her location. Why should she walk away from the happy, peaceful life she'd made for herself here? It would mean the wish merchant had won.

It would also mean that she was one step closer to a future with Khalid.

Leaving would mean, in essence, that the wish merchant was commanding her path without even owning her bottle. She'd had enough of being told what to do in her life. The wish merchant would not get that chance.

No, she had a plan. She got to her feet, hands

clenched at her sides. She was not backing down. Even if that meant giving away her freedom temporarily. It was better than permanently, she reminded herself.

Much, much better.

She started a pot of tea, mostly to distract herself, but also so that she'd have something to offer Lucien when he arrived.

A knock at the door startled her. Was that Lucien? She flattened her hand to her stomach. Who else would it be? The wish merchant wouldn't dare come to her door, would he? What was she thinking? The doorman would never let him up.

She took a breath and went to answer it.

It was Lucien. He looked exactly as he had in the club. A different suit maybe. But still a very expensive one all the same. The man dressed impeccably, right down to the leather gloves he wore. Maybe being so well dressed was an angel-of-death thing. It was bad enough getting a sign that your death was imminent, but she supposed it would be even worse if the messenger was an unshaven slob.

Her thoughts were going down a rabbit hole, undoubtedly because knowing who and what the man at the door was unsettled her. She did her best to ignore the rambling in her head and nodded. "Thank you for coming."

He frowned. "You should thank Greyson."

"I suppose I should." She imagined she had Greyson to thank for the leather duffle in Lucien's hand too. Wouldn't do for him to walk out of the

Excelsior carrying her genie bottle in his hands for all to see. She nodded again, her stress accelerating at his sharp tone. "I'll make sure I do."

She reminded herself that her nerves were only because of who he was. Then she almost laughed. Who wouldn't be nervous around an angel of death? But she'd also hoped he'd be in a good mood. That didn't seem to be the case. Coming here had upset him for some reason. "Won't you come in?"

His expression softened a little. "Thank you."

She led him through the foyer and into the living room of her condo. She loved living at the Excelsior. The building catered to supernaturals, and the amenities were excellent. Plus, the condo was spacious. And she liked space. Being confined was something else she'd had enough of. She gestured toward the couch. "Please, sit."

He took a seat, but didn't seem very comfortable in it. Being an angel of death, he probably didn't care for her bright color scheme. She loved color. But both times she'd seen him, he'd been dressed in black, white, and shades of gray. Perhaps that was part of his uniform? She knew nothing about his kind of supernatural. "Would you like some tea? I was just making a pot."

"All right."

Good, because it had been steeping long enough. She brought it over and poured it into two gold-decorated glasses. "Sugar?"

"Yes." He sighed. "I understand it's what's done, but I didn't come here for small talk and tea. Greyson said you were in trouble. And that it has to do with the man who followed you out of the club last night."

"It does." She added a cube of sugar to both of their glasses, then sat on the thick, tufted floor pillow beside the table. It put her lower than Lucien, but she hoped that allowing him a place of power would make him feel benevolent. "I owe you a very large and sincere thank you for that. He would have taken me."

"For what purpose?"

She thought Greyson would have told him more about the wish merchant, but perhaps Lucien wanted to hear her tell it. She didn't mind that or his directness. There was nothing to be gained by misunderstandings or talking in circles. "I'm a genie. He plans to kidnap me and either sell me or the wishes I can grant to the highest bidder. Probably he'll opt to sell the wishes individually. He'll believe that will make him the most money. If that's what he chooses to do, he'll keep selling them for as long as he can. Or until I manage to escape. Which isn't likely."

Lucien's eyes narrowed as if he was deep in thought. "You're jinn, obviously."

"Yes."

"What kind of supernatural is the wish merchant?"

"He's human."

Lucien frowned. "He wouldn't have been granted entrance into Insomnia, then, unless he was with a supernatural. My bouncers can't be bribed. I'll check the security footage to see who he was with, and they will be dealt with." He paused. "If the wish merchant is human, how would he control you?"

She laughed gently, lowering her eyes for a moment so he wouldn't think she was laughing at him. She wasn't, either. But his honesty about what he did and didn't know was refreshing. So many people tried to appear as if they knew it all. "You don't know much about genies, do you?"

"I don't know anything about them. Other than they can grant wishes."

"Then let me give you a quick lesson. We cannot use our wishes for our own gain. We may sell or barter our wishes, but at no time are we ever permitted to use them to harm humans."

His narrow-eyed gaze stayed on her. "And other supernaturals?"

She smiled. "There is a reason they leave us alone." That wasn't really an answer, but he didn't pursue it. She liked that, but doubted he was even marginally afraid of her.

He sipped his tea, then set the glass on the table and sat back. "And so you propose what? That I help you in exchange for wishes?"

A wisp of steam curled up from her glass. "Not exactly. And I hope that won't be a problem, because I don't have any wishes to give you. I don't have them to give anyone." She couldn't make eye contact when she lied. It was hard enough for a genie to bend the truth, even more difficult to break it entirely.

"Then just tell the wish merchant that and he'll be on his way." He got to his feet with sudden urgency. "You don't need me."

"But I do." She jumped up, blocking his exit. Panic made her heart race. He couldn't leave until he'd agreed to help her. "He'll put me back in my bottle and then…"

She stared up at him, hating that she was about to reveal such a great secret to him. Hating how vulnerable she was about to become. Again. She just couldn't reveal everything. Not yet. She waffled on how much to tell him. On what details would get him to help her.

Lucien glared down at her, clearly out of patience. "And then *what*?"

She made her decision. "And then I'll have another thousand wishes to my name. Years of being chained to whomever possesses my bottle. At their whim. Years of being hunted by men like the one at the club." Except that wasn't exactly what would happen. Being forced back into her bottle would result in her getting another thousand wishes, but it would also result in her finally facing Khalid. The marriage she'd been avoiding since she'd been old enough to know about all her life would happen.

Either way, the outcome wasn't good. Because in both instances, she ended up as someone else's property. The ache in her belly nearly made her sick. Anger wound up her spine. "I won't do it," she said. "I won't."

The anger jolted through her, pushing her. She grabbed hold of his lapels, pressing her knuckles into his hard chest. His warmth seeped into her skin. "Please help me. You have to. I need you."

The second she touched him, his eyes went wide, and he went very still.

It was as if a switch had been thrown inside him. Or a thunderbolt had struck him. Whatever was happening, it was a shock to his system.

He finally swallowed and glanced around. "Your home is...*very* colorful."

Was he mocking her? What kind of answer was that? She frowned at him then, disgusted, pushed him away and stalked to the window. She crossed her arms and stared down at the parking lot, looking for unfamiliar cars and trying not to believe that Khalid was her only hope. "Fine. I understand. You don't want to help me. Don't want to be involved. I guess helping me isn't as interesting to you as announcing people's impending death to them."

He didn't answer, and she didn't look at him. She couldn't, or he might see the tears building in her eyes. Instead, she flicked her hand at him, jangling the bracelets on her wrist. "You can let yourself out."

The moment her touch left Lucien, so did his color vision. But the images of Imari and her apartment were seared into his brain.

Her home was so dazzling, he wondered if Insomnia needed to be redecorated.

The walls were painted a deep raspberry, while the upholstery was navy, and everything else — the layered rugs, the plentiful pillows, the fabrics and tapestries on the walls — was patterned in every color conceivable. All around the home were touches of gold and brass. Accents of crystal and glass, all of it brightly colored, added sparkling life.

For the brief moment that she'd been in contact with him, he'd felt like he was standing in a jewel box in some far-away land.

With the queen of that land in front of him. The lights of Insomnia had done a disservice to her beauty. She was agonizingly lovely. Her large, cognac eyes, lush mouth, and abundant curls would have been too much on any other woman, but on her, they were each a piece of a bewilderingly perfect puzzle.

She fascinated him. How was it possible that she brought color back to his eyes? Made him feel so complete and so out of sorts all at once?

And this time, she'd done it without making skin-to-skin contact. Remarkable.

He wanted to feel that way again. To remember that life was not just a dull gray wash. To see more color.

He craved it, in fact. Or perhaps what he craved was her.

He cleared his throat, but she didn't turn from the window. That was fine. The view of her from the back was equally as pleasing as it was from the front. "I didn't mean I wouldn't help you."

That got her attention. She stiffened, but didn't turn. "You will?"

He had no choice. Greyson had called in a favor. Part of him wanted to deny her. She would disrupt his life. Make him want what he couldn't have. She already had. But he would find a way to deal with all of that. "I will. But on my terms."

She finally looked at him, gaze narrowed slightly. Her arms stayed crossed. "I have no wishes to give."

"So you said. I'm not interested in wishes. I have all the wealth and possessions I need." That didn't mean he wasn't without wants and needs, but his burdens were his own to bear.

She relaxed a little. "What then?"

"You tell no one that I am helping you. Not a mention of my name, not a reference to me or about who or what you think I am, not where we met, not even a hint that I am remotely involved."

She dropped her arms to her sides. "That's it?"

"For now, yes." He gave her a moment. "Can you do that?"

"Yes. I give you my word. And thank you." She glanced once more outside, then walked away from the window. "I have a few rules of my own."

This should be interesting. It wasn't often a grim reaper was given rules. Oh, people tried. They bargained and cajoled, begged and pleaded, but rules? Never. He almost smiled. But then, she didn't know what he really was. She thought he was just death's calling card, not death itself. Better that way. Protection for both of them.

Although, her courage in the face of an angel of death was still impressive. So much so, he couldn't help but comment. "You're not afraid of me."

She stopped a few feet away and looked at him. "Should I be? You're here to help me, not announce my impending doom. Or have I missed something?"

"No, you're right, I'm here only to help." Not words he'd spoken much in his life. Or possibly ever. "What are your rules?"

She smiled, but there was a darkness in her gaze. Fear. And something else he wasn't sure of. "I'm giving you my bottle for my protection, but you have to understand that it is my life. You must protect it."

"I will."

She laughed. "Asking the angel of death to protect my life seems odd even to my ears."

"Not that odd."

"I suppose not, given the town we live in." She brushed a strand of hair back. "Without that bottle…" She smiled weakly. "It's priceless. In every possible way."

"I understand, I assure you. So what's the rule?"

"Just that you must promise to protect it at all costs."

"I will. Is that your only rule?"

"No. You must also return it to me when this is over. No hesitation, no bargaining, no changing your mind."

"Done. Anything else?"

"Those are my only rules for now." She nodded. "I'll get the bottle."

She left him then, disappearing down a hall. To where, he wasn't sure. Her bedroom? He tried to imagine what that would look like. What colors she'd used there. But his imagination kept conjuring up images of her sprawled on a pile of silk pillows, her hair flowing out around her, one finger crooked to beckon him—

He shook himself. What was wrong with his brain? Was he color drunk? She wasn't going to beckon him or encourage him in any way. She wanted him only for the protection he could give her, and any thoughts to the contrary had no place in his head. "No place," he muttered.

"What was that?"

He startled, the odd feeling of guilt warming his skin. "I wasn't, that is, I didn't say anything."

She tipped her head, peering at him. "You said *something*."

"I don't recall." He shifted his attention to adjusting the bracelet of his watch, pleased he couldn't see her in full color. He could barely maintain himself with her in shades of gray. Did genies have the power to befuddle other supernaturals? He didn't know but didn't want to ask and point out what she was doing to him. There was no adjusting left to do, so he changed the subject. "That must be the bottle."

The object in her hands was exquisite. Even without color, he could see it was studded with gems and metal filigree.

"It is." She held it close to herself, making no move to give it to him. "And remember, priceless."

"I understand." He held his hand out.

She frowned.

He held out both hands.

She still didn't make any attempt to place it in his possession.

He dropped his attempt to retrieve the bottle from her. "You clearly don't want to part with this."

She sighed and shook her head. "Imagine the most valuable thing in your life. Would you want to give that up? Even if it meant protecting yourself from a fate worse than death? Or whatever your death equivalent would be. It's not a good feeling." She clutched the bottle closer. "Greyson promised me you were trustworthy."

It seemed like she was reminding herself of that, but he answered anyway. "I am."

He wasn't without sympathy. There was no way, under any imaginable circumstances, that he would ever give up his scythe. Retired or not, that tool was a part of him. It was also the only thing that could reap his life. He wasn't about to put it in anyone else's hands.

"That's good." She kept staring at the bottle. "But I can't do this. I'm sorry for making you come out here, but I just can't go through with this."

He understood. And he didn't want her to agonize over something so precious being in a stranger's possession. "You're not really in any danger in the Excelsior, are you? It's my understanding this is a very secure building. One of the Ellinghams lives here after all. Julian, I believe. With his wife."

"I know. And it *is* a very secure building. But wish merchants are crafty."

"You think he could get in here?" The man *had* gotten into Insomnia, but that had to be because he was with someone. No one who lived in the Excelsior would let a stranger in, would they? He doubted it, but it still remained a risk. One, apparently, she was willing to take.

She glanced back toward the foyer. "No, probably not. But I have to leave at some point. I have a job to do. I can't just not show up."

"Of course not." Even if that was an extremely unwise idea. "But you could take some time off."

"Maybe."

"What if he tries to grab you again?"

"During daylight hours? Not likely. And if it's after dark, I'll call for the doorman to come to my car and walk me in."

She was trying to convince herself at this point. He nodded with no real conviction. "You could do that."

She chewed on her lower lip like she was suddenly rethinking things.

"He did get into Insomnia, though." Lucien thought it was worth mentioning. He'd requested the video from his security team, but he hadn't opened it yet. An email from Kora about needing more money had put him in a funk before coming here. He'd chosen not to answer it. "And I said I would find the supernatural who brought him in and deal with them, and I will, so that won't happen again. But I can't speak for how things operate in this building. I'm sure it's highly unlikely, though."

Her mouth crooked into an unhappy expression. "Unless the supernatural who helped him also happens to live here."

"That's a possibility. Listen, I'll give you my number." Even as he said it, he realized how rare a thing that was for him to do. "If you change your mind, call me."

"Thank you. I'm sorry to have dragged you out here. I guess I was too scared by what happened at the club to think properly. Seeing you was probably enough to send him running."

"Perhaps. I am awfully frightening."

She laughed, and Lucien was almost convinced by

it. Her thumb worried one of the larger stones on the bottle. "He's probably not even in town anymore."

"All the same," Lucien said, "take my number."

"That's kind of you." She set the bottle on the coffee table, then found a pad of paper and pen for him.

He jotted his number down. "There. I wish you well."

"Thank you."

"I can see myself out." He gripped the handles of the leather duffle he'd brought more firmly than necessary. "Have a good night."

"You too."

An inexplicable sadness came over him as he rode down in the elevator. She wouldn't call. He knew that. She didn't want him to have the bottle. She didn't want anyone to have it. He understood.

But to never see her again left him feeling…empty. He had no reason to feel that way. He'd seen her twice. Exchanged a handful of sentences. They meant nothing to each other. They weren't even friends. Acquaintances at best.

But she made him see color. And she appeared to be immune to his touch.

And then there was the pitiful truth that he was a desperately lonely man. Maybe she'd come into Insomnia again. He might see her then.

How very pathetic of him.

The old anger rose up in him. Anger at his gifts gone wrong. Anger at the life of solitude that had been forced upon him.

There was no fairness in his life. Not even when he'd taken his sabbatical and attempted to live a normal life, he'd ended up with a wife who'd been unfaithful and a daughter who wanted nothing more than to spend his money and traipse around the world getting herself into trouble.

The elevator doors slid open.

He stormed out and past the doorman, acknowledging the man's farewell with a grunt as he made his way to the parking lot. He'd driven his Bugatti this evening, and he was glad he'd chosen it instead of the Land Rover Hattie used. A long, fast drive through the hills and mountains surrounding Nocturne Falls was just what he needed.

As he approached the car, a man appeared from behind an SUV in the next row.

The wish merchant.

Lucien went on alert, everything else forgotten.

The man nodded at Lucien. "What's in the bag, chum?"

Lucien ignored him for a moment, then thought better of it. For Imari's sake, he'd deal with this fool. "You're the wish merchant."

"That's right. What of it?"

Lucien let a little of his reaper form show through, feeling the bones of his face ache at the transformation. His voice took on a huskier tone. "Is your wish for death?"

The man's eyes widened, then his haughty expression partially returned. He snapped his fingers. "Adira."

A pretty but haggard-looking young woman stepped out from behind the SUV. "Yes, master," she whispered.

Another genie? Lucien wasn't sure, but the girl was some kind of supernatural. He sensed that much.

The man pointed at Lucien as he spoke to Adira. "I wish for him to be immobile."

She looked at Lucien, then blinked as she made a quick nod in his direction. Sparks of glitter drifted through the air.

Had she cast a spell on him? Used one of her wishes to do as the wish merchant had commanded? If so, it hadn't worked, but he decided to play along to see what he could learn. He went still, then rolled his eyes around in what he hoped looked like panic.

It did the trick.

The man smiled and snapped his fingers again. "Fetch the bag."

Adira nodded and scurried forward, approaching Lucien with her head low and unspoken words of apology in her gaze. She took the duffle from his hands and went back to the wish merchant's side.

"I wish us to be home," the man said.

With another burst of glitter in the air, they were gone.

Imari sat cross-legged on her bed, the bottle a few inches in front of her. She'd been sitting there, staring at it since Lucien left. And questioning her own actions. She should have given it to him. What was wrong with her? Greyson said he was trustworthy. And Greyson wasn't a guy who'd feed her a line of baloney just to make himself look good.

Lucien had saved her life after all. That was worth something. How could she doubt his intentions now?

She didn't, actually. No, when she dug down into what she was feeling, the truth was something different. She was petrified to turn the bottle over to anyone. That fear was as real as the metallic taste that had filled her mouth when she'd thought about putting it in his hands. As real as the ringing in her ears and the pounding of her heart.

She could not go back to being someone's possession again. No matter if that someone was the wish merchant or Khalid, it wasn't a path she ever wanted to walk.

A deep sigh slipped out of her as her heart grew heavier. No, she couldn't give her bottle—and control of her life—to someone. But what if the wish merchant didn't leave town?

It was great to think he'd seen Lucien and hightailed it out of Dodge, for sure. And it was possible. Except...wish merchants didn't give up that easily.

With that in mind, she took the bottle in hand and got off the bed. The safe was the best place for it. Staring at it wasn't going to change anything.

A sharp pounding on the door caused her to jump and nearly drop the bottle. Who could that be? It was late now. Nearly ten. The wish merchant? Her pulse increased again.

Her nerves were a jangled mess. She needed to be in bed. Asleep. Instead, she padded out to the living room, stopping to put the bottle back in the safe and give the tumbler a spin to lock it.

Then she went to the door. She glanced through the peephole and relaxed. Lucien. She opened the door. "Did you forget something?"

He pushed his way in. "You're not safe here."

"But you said yourself the Excelsior is a good—"

"The wish merchant is still in town."

The breath left her body. "H-how do you know that?"

"I ran into him in the parking lot. He's got a woman with him who does whatever he tells her to

54

do. I believe she's also a genie, but I'm not certain. At his command, she tried to freeze me in place."

"Was there any glitter?"

He frowned. "Yes. Why?"

"Genie spells leave a trace. What do you mean she tried to freeze you?"

"I let them think her spell worked, but it had no effect on me."

She pondered that a moment. "Our spells don't work on vampires since they're technically dead. Maybe you fall into that category too."

"Maybe. Whatever the case, he thinks he has your bottle. He had her take my duffle bag, so I assume he thought it was in there. Then he had her transport them home, wherever that is."

Imari felt ill. "That's not good. Not good at all. If he's already got a genie, he's unstoppable. No doubt that's how he got into Insomnia too. Probably wished to appear as a supernatural to anyone who saw him. What did she look like?"

"Like you. Dark hair, dark eyes. Pretty, but not like you. She seemed scared of him. He called her Adira. Know her?"

"No, but I've been retired a long time and there are a lot of us." She wrung her hands. "This is not good."

"You said that. Why does he need you if he has a genie already?"

"The genie in his control might be running out of wishes. Or he's got a buyer willing to pay for a genie of their own and he doesn't want to part with his."

Lucien grimaced, perhaps at how awful the whole

thing was. "Look, he's obviously not afraid of me now that he thinks his genie can control me, but you still need to pack a bag and leave. I am positive that as soon as he figures out the bottle isn't in that duffle, he'll be back."

She wrapped her arms around herself. "Where am I going to go? I don't want to bring trouble to my friends' doorsteps."

Lucien looked like he was trying not to answer. But something pulled the words out of him. Something unfamiliar, by the look in his eyes. Kindness? Compassion? She wasn't sure. "He knows where you live. He doesn't have that information about me."

She stared at him, a little dumbstruck. "Are you asking me to come to your house? To stay with you?"

"You won't be alone with me, if that's what you're worried about. Now hurry up."

His comment made her ask, "Who else lives there?" Was the angel of death married? That couldn't be. Could it? What on earth would his wife look like?

"We need to *leave*."

"Right." She ran to the bedroom, grabbed an overnight bag and threw some things into it, then zipped up the bag. He was bossing her around, but at the moment she was flustered and didn't mind that much. But he'd better not keep it up. She ran back to the living room. "What about the bottle?"

"Bring it."

She got it from the safe and tucked it into the bag with her clothes. "Ready."

"Let's go." He hustled them out of the building and to his car, his gaze sweeping the grounds, no doubt looking for the wish merchant.

"Nice ride," she said. That was an understatement. The Bugatti was top-end, one of the models that had only been produced in small quantities. In the case of this paintless beast, *very* small quantities. It was a welcome distraction.

With a nod, he opened her door for her, then jogged to his side and slid behind the wheel. They were on the road in no time.

That was when he finally spoke. "It's a Bugatti."

"I know. A Bugatti Veyron Pur Sang, to be exact." She ran her hand along the door panel. "Only five of these incredible machines were produced, and they were built specifically to be paintless in order to show off the Veyron's exquisite aluminum and carbon fiber frame. This isn't so much a car as a work of art."

He took his eyes off the road long enough to throw her a confused look. "How do you know so much about this vehicle?"

She laughed and stared through the low-slung windshield. "I'm a genie. What do you think most men spend their wishes on? Cars they'd never been able to have, that's what. It's my job to know about these things."

"Do you...like cars like this?"

"I think they're fascinating. And beautiful. Especially the vehicles that are made in such small quantities. They're more like sculpture than transportation. So yes, I guess I like them very much."

"Then you're going to enjoy my garage."

"How many cars do you have?"

"Currently, twenty-seven. With two more on order and a third that I'm on a waiting list for."

She snorted softly. "I guess you weren't kidding when you said you have all the wealth and possessions you need."

"No, I wasn't. And I don't kid."

She almost laughed at his bluntness. Instead, she hugged her bag to her chest. There wasn't much room for it elsewhere in the vehicle, but she was fine with that. It was good to feel the bottle safe against her. She tipped her head back and watched Lucien as slyly as she could. His handsomeness was becoming more apparent. "Thank you."

"For?"

"Letting me come to your house. I get the sense that's not an offer you make lightly."

"It's not an offer I've ever made." His eyes stayed on the road, but that did nothing to diminish the intensity of his gaze.

She stared at him outright. "You've never had company?"

"Company, yes. Overnight company, no."

"Is that an angel-of-death thing?"

"No."

He was a veritable fount of information. "You said we wouldn't be alone. Who else lives at your house, then?"

Silence spilled out between them until finally he spoke. "I have a…housemate."

That told her nothing. "I see." Except she didn't. And his unwillingness to share unnerved her. "Is this housemate someone I need to be concerned about?"

"Not unless you're afraid of ghosts."

She blinked at him, giving that some thought. The angel of death had a ghost for a roommate? That seemed odd even by Nocturne Falls' standards. "I've never met one, so I can't say. Is he one of those ghosts of Christmas Past with the chains and such?"

The corner of his mouth twitched. Was that an attempt at a smile? Or an attempt not to smile? "That was Marley in chains, not the ghost of Christmas Past. And no, she's nothing like that."

Imari wasn't sure what surprised her more: Lucien's knowledge of Dickens or that he lived with a female ghost. Maybe that was the only kind of woman an angel of death could be with. "She?"

He nodded, but said no more.

Imari sensed that was the end of the conversation. Of all conversation, really. She was fine with that. He was already putting himself out. She slipped down in the seat a little, getting comfortable. If he didn't want to talk, she wasn't going to force him.

Besides, she had plenty to think about. Lucien lived with a ghost. Questions filled her head. No doubt she'd learn more when they got to his house and she met this ghost. Why a female ghost? Was Lucien the reason this woman *was* a ghost? Why would a ghost want to live with the angel of death? Why would anyone? Were they in love?

The only reasons she could come up with were

either the ghost had no choice, or the ghost and Lucien had some kind of connection.

Which raised more questions.

But before she could organize her thoughts, the car turned into a parking lot she recognized. She sat up, little alarms going off in her head. They were back at Insomnia. "Why are you taking me here?"

"I live here."

"You live at a nightclub?"

"After a fashion, yes." He drove around to the back of the building, toward a decrepit loading dock. He pulled a little black remote from the side pocket of the door panel, pointed it straight ahead, and clicked it.

One of the cargo doors lifted, and the loading platform it sat on sank into the ground, revealing a down ramp.

He entered.

She glanced over her shoulder. The door and platform were already returning to their places. How very secret agent.

A thin band of lights illuminated the tunnel they were in. It went down for a good bit, then curved. A set of wide steel doors opened ahead of them. They drove through those as well, and as they did, new lights flickered on.

Her mouth fell open at what the lights revealed.

An underground garage with glossy black floors, like granite, and the walls and ceiling were luminous panels that glowed brighter where each car was parked. And the *cars*. Rare, priceless, and beautiful. All immaculate, too.

She'd never seen anything like it. And she'd seen some amazing things. "This is…" She shook her head. There was no right word.

He pulled into an empty slot, turned the car off, and looked at her. "I told you you'd like it."

She nodded.

His mouth curved in a genuine smile. "Nothing to say? No questions?"

She found her voice. "Just one. Are you actually Bruce Wayne?"

Despite the doubt and trepidation coursing through him, Lucien laughed. "No, I promise you, I am not Batman."

"No, of course not," she said, taking another look around. "He could never afford all this." She gaped at the vehicles, open-mouthed and shaking her head.

Impressing her pleased Lucien, for reasons he couldn't name. Perhaps it pleased him so because, outside of Hattie, impressing anyone wasn't something he'd accomplished in many, many years. Imari was a genie, after all, accustomed to great wealth and extravagant riches, and yet she found his collection interesting. That was quite a feat.

He also enjoyed the wonderment in her gaze. It was almost childlike. He was astonished that she could express that kind of emotion considering all she must have seen in her life. Even more astonished that he was the cause of such a response.

But it troubled him, too. Not her wonderment, but

how much he liked pleasing her. How much he liked evoking emotion in her. How easily he could see himself becoming addicted to the pleasure he was feeling in this moment.

Becoming addicted to her.

That couldn't lead to good things. Not for him, anyway. Or her, for that matter.

Everything in him tightened up, extinguishing the small joy he'd just experienced. An emotion like joy might be fine for her, but it was foolishness for him. He knew better than to let himself forget how untenable his life was. Doing so would only cause them both great pain later on.

He got out of the car and walked around to open her door. "We should go in."

She looked up at him, bag clutched against her. "Okay."

He stepped back to give her room as she swung her legs around, but the effort of getting out of the low Bugatti while holding on to her bag caused her to fall back into her seat on the first attempt.

He held out his hand. "Give me the bag."

She hesitated, and he remembered she'd put the bottle in there.

The muscles in his jaw tensed. "Give me your hand, then."

She took that offer, placing her fingers lightly into his gloved ones.

Color exploded back into his world, and he gasped at the sight of his beloved cars awash in all the brilliance of the rainbow. Slowly, he looked from one end of the garage to the other. Radiant sunny yellows, vivid marine blues, and fiery reds filled his vision.

Mixed in were gleaming silvers; a single emerald green; blacks so dark they seemed to absorb the light; a couple snowy, pristine whites; one garish, gorgeous citrus orange; and a royal purple that he had no recollection of agreeing to.

"You okay?"

He remembered himself and pulled his gaze back to her. "Yes." He helped her up, then let go of her hand, lingering for a second longer than he should have. The garage and everything in it returned to its normal shades of black and grays.

He stared at the ground. It was easier than looking at the cars and thinking about what he could no longer see. And it was far easier than looking at her and knowing what he could never have.

"You're not okay." She was right in front of him. Too close. The tips of her embroidered silk slippers were almost touching his Italian leather loafers. He could smell her perfume. Or her shampoo. Or whatever it was that caused her to smell like some exotic pastry and make his mouth water. "What just happened?"

"Nothing." He reached around her, closed the car door, then walked toward the entrance to his home.

Her footsteps echoed through the vast space as she hurried to catch up. Thankfully, she let the matter rest.

He reached the door ahead of her, opening it for her to go in first. She did, and he followed into the mudroom. It wasn't an impressive entrance. Spacious, but nothing special. He wasn't sure anyone besides him and Hattie had ever used it. Greyson always came in through the club entrance. "I'll show you to a guest room."

"If you don't have visitors, why do you have a guest room?"

That was a good question. The answer was Hattie, but he didn't want to explain all that to Imari. "My housemate prefers it that way."

Imari's expression said myriad things, but mainly that she had many questions. None of which he planned on answering. He was opening his home to her, not his life.

A voice rang out. "Lucy? Is that you?"

Imari's brows shot up, and her eyes filled with new questions, but she said nothing.

He closed his eyes and growled. That wasn't a nickname he'd wanted Imari to hear. "Hattie, we have a guest."

"Greyson?" She materialized in ghost form at the entrance to the mudroom.

"No." He gestured toward Imari. "This is—"

"Imari Zephara!" Hattie instantly became corporeal and clapped her hands. "What a nice surprise!" She sent a cross look Lucien's way. "Why didn't you tell me we were having company? I should have straightened up the house."

"The house is never un-straightened, Hattie."

"I could have made cookies."

"Didn't you do that this afternoon?"

She thought for a moment. "No, I made apple tartlets. Completely different."

"Are they?" Sweets were sweets.

"Yes. And you should have told me Imari was coming, regardless of what I baked."

Imari laughed softly.

Hattie threw her hands up. "I'm so sorry, we're going on like you're not even there. Come in, dear. I'm Hattie Dupree."

"Nice to meet you, Hattie. How do you know my name? Have we met?" Imari asked.

"We haven't met, but I have my hair done at the spa where you work. Shelley does it. You know, the little wood nymph with the cotton candy pink hair? She's so good." Hattie hooked her arm through Imari's. "Would you like a cup of tea? We have some excellent varieties."

"I bet you do." Imari glanced knowingly at Lucien before answering. "I'd love some."

Hattie and Imari headed down the hall toward the rest of the house, leaving Lucien behind.

He stared after them for a second, then shook his head and followed. "Hattie, perhaps our visitor might like to see her room first? Maybe put her bag away?"

Hattie sucked in a loud breath as she came to a stop in the living room. "Of course! I'm so sorry, Imari. We haven't had a guest in so long, I've completely forgotten how to behave. Come. I'll show you your room, and then we'll have tea."

"I'll show her the room." He flicked his gaze at his grandmother, hoping she understood he needed a moment with Imari. "That way you can start the kettle."

"Very good." She winked at Lucien, which Imari undoubtedly saw. "I'll be in the kitchen. But we should have tea here in the living room, don't you think?"

"Whatever you wish, *Mémé*." He almost cringed as the word left his mouth. He hadn't meant to call Hattie that in front of Imari.

But Imari didn't seem to notice. She smiled at him. "I would like to put my bag away, but the kitchen would be fine for tea. I'm not fancy."

Hattie smiled. "The kitchen it is, then. See you in a bit."

As his grandmother left, Lucien gestured toward the other side of the house. "This way."

Imari followed as he took them through the living room and to the right. He glanced at her. She was grinning wildly. "Does something about my home amuse you?"

"Not at all. And your home is beautiful. A little weird, being underground, but I like the way you've used the light panels to keep it from being dark. So yes, beautiful in its own way."

"Thank you. I think." He cleared his throat. "What's so amusing, then?"

"Your *housemate*."

"I apologize if Hattie came on too strong. I guess she's a bit starved for company."

"No, she was fine. It's just..." Her smile broadened, and she laughed. "I never would have guessed the angel of death lives with his *grandmother*."

He frowned. So she understood French. Or was just smart enough to know that the term of endearment he'd used meant grandmother. He sighed. "It's a long story."

"I'm sure."

"And she lives with me."

"Of course."

He stopped and opened one of the double doors that led into the guest suite. "Your room."

She didn't go in. "Listen, I think it's sweet that she lives with you. I'm not judging you. At all. I'd love to have my family around me." Her expression grew wistful. "Life for a jinn doesn't always work that way." She made a funny little noise, then stepped into the guest room. "This is lovely. And so big!"

"Hattie designed it." What colors she'd used, he couldn't recall. "I know it has its own bathroom."

"It's perfect." She set her bag on the bed and unzipped it. She took the bottle out and put it on the nightstand. "I don't think I've said a proper thank you for opening your home to me like this. I know it was a hard thing for you to do, and I want to be sure you know I'm very appreciative."

He stared at her. He wasn't used to conversations like this. "You're welcome." A few moments of awkward silence passed. "I'll leave you alone to get settled."

"There's really nothing for me to do." She walked toward him, narrowing the distance between them.

She was peering at him intently. "Do I make you nervous?"

He swallowed. "No. Not exactly." She was too close again.

"What, then?"

"I'm just not used to company."

She nodded, but her expression held a vast amount of skepticism. "Then why would you invite me to your home?"

He wanted to back up. "You needed help."

"And you were willing to put yourself out for me? When you don't really know me?"

"Greyson...I owed him."

She shook her head slowly. "You don't seem like the kind of man who cares about owing people."

He didn't know what to say to that. Mostly because she was befuddling him with her nearness and her scent and her impossible beauty. Genies must have the kind of pheromones that made men stupid. That was the only explanation he could think of.

She shrugged. "Whatever your reason, I'm glad you did."

Then she leaned up and kissed him. On the mouth. It was soft and sweet and the most unexpected thing she could have done.

He should have told her not to touch him. Instead, instinct took over, and he closed his eyes.

That didn't stop him from seeing color. It exploded in the darkness behind his lids, his own personal fireworks show. A million colors dancing and pulsing with the pressure of her mouth.

Then the kiss was over and the colors were gone. Far too soon. For both.

She turned toward the door. "We should go, or your grandmother's going to think we got lost."

"Uh-huh." Lucien's mouth was open, and he was unable to close it. A deep tingling filled his whole body, leaving him numb in some places and utterly, electrically alive in others.

Maybe he was dying. Maybe this was what death felt like for a broken grim reaper.

Or maybe, just maybe, he was getting a second chance at life.

What on earth was wrong with her? Who voluntarily kissed an angel of death? Was she mental? Maybe. She plastered a pleasant smile on her face to hide the fact that she was all sorts of mixed up on the inside.

That kiss had been impulsive and stupid. And five kinds of amazing. But also definitely impulsive and stupid. Especially because she didn't know Lucien well enough to know what he was capable of. He could have reacted badly. Thankfully, he hadn't, but still. Maybe her fear of the wish merchant was making her reckless.

Or maybe she'd seen a man before her so desperate for interaction, a man who had gone against everything he felt to offer her a safe space, that she'd been swept up in the emotion of the moment and lost to the desire to show him just how appreciative she was.

With her acute sense of intuition, it was impossible

to ignore the dark, haunted vibe that Lucien gave off. Feeling that, she couldn't help but want to thank him in a way that went beyond words. Especially after his kindness toward her.

Kindness he'd extended without the promise of anything in return. She'd never had that from anyone outside of her friends before. Everyone else in her life, human or supernatural, wanted something from her once they discovered what she was. Of course, her parents had always known what she was. That was exactly why they wanted so much from her.

But Lucien treated her as just another person. He seemed as interested in wishes as a housecat was in swimming. Which was to say, not at all. At least, he hadn't expressed any interest. And she believed him.

But who felt that way? Who wanted nothing? Sure, he had plenty of wealth. His underground acre of exotic cars proved that. But just looking at him she could see something was wrong in his life.

Angel of death or not, the man was unhappy. And didn't everyone want happiness? She did.

They made their way in silence back down the hall and toward the kitchen. She was okay with the silence, except she wasn't sure if she'd upset him with the kiss. Maybe she should apologize. Maybe she'd overstepped her bounds.

She couldn't afford for him to throw her out. Not with the wish merchant hot on her heels and aware of where she lived. She stopped in the living room, facing him abruptly. "I'm sorry. I shouldn't have kissed you. That was inappropriate, and I—"

He took hold of her arms, pulled her close, and shut her mouth with his.

She gasped, but didn't break the kiss. A split-second after her shock wore off, she leaned into him.

His kiss was hungry and insistent and demanding in a way that made her feel wanted in ways she'd never felt before. He tugged her closer, pressing her to him. She gave in, doing her best to meld her body to his. But just as she was about to start purring in delight, he let go of her and stepped back.

His gaze burned into her as hot and black as Hades. "*That* was inappropriate."

She just looked at him, slightly breathless and a lot bewildered. She finally remembered to close her mouth. The taste of him was still there. Dark and sweet and wicked. She cleared her throat to find her voice. Had it been this hot when they'd first gotten here? "Well. Good thing you showed me the difference."

How was she upright? How had her knees not buckled? They felt like warm butter. She had no idea what she was supposed to do next, just that she wasn't doing it.

Hattie saved the day, floating in. She was in her ghost form again. "Tea is ready if you two would like to come into the kitchen. I warmed up some apple tartlets too."

"Tea." Imari nodded, happy for the reminder. She followed Hattie into the kitchen. Lucien was right behind her. She knew because she could feel him there. His presence had become a palpable thing. She wanted to close her eyes and lean into him, to feel his strong, hard body against hers again.

Not exactly the kind of thoughts she should be having with his grandmother right next to her.

"Your kitchen is beautiful." Imari was happy to have something new to focus on. Frankly, it wasn't hard. It was unbelievable that such a room existed in an underground home.

The kitchen was bright and spacious and felt very much like a French farmhouse with its high, beamed ceiling, copper pots, and the brilliant blue island topped with marble. The rest of the cabinets were a soft buttermilk color, worn here and there to show the warm wood underneath. There was a large window over the apron sink that looked out onto an evening countryside scene. Stars twinkled in the blue-black sky, and light from a fat crescent moon shone down.

Imari stared at the view a moment before she realized it was a video screen.

"Thank you," Hattie said. "Lucien let me pick everything out in here."

"Well, you did an excellent job."

Hattie radiated pride.

Imari glanced over her shoulder at Lucien.

"I have work to do," he suddenly announced. Then he was gone.

Hattie frowned. "Excuse my grandson. His manners aren't the best. But he's had a rough go of things, so please, forgive him. He's a good boy, he really is."

"*Mémé*." Lucien's voice came from somewhere in

the house. It sounded like a command. Or a warning. Or a plea for mercy.

Hattie looked up. Apparently, it was a summons. "Let me just see what Lucien needs and I'll be right back, dear. The tea is ready. You help yourself to whatever you like. Our home is your home."

Imari seriously doubted that, but smiled anyway. "Thank you."

Hattie left.

Imari poured herself a cup of tea. The scent and color revealed it to be the same delicious Assam that Lucien had brought her in the club. She added a cube of sugar and stirred, thoughts of last night a temporary reprieve from thoughts of the kisses they'd just shared.

She glanced up. Were they under the club? They had to be. Insomnia was in this building. But it was also underground, so how far under were they now? The ramp into the garage had been a steep descent. Why would he choose to live here? Was an angel of death averse to sunlight the way most vampires were?

Hattie reappeared, corporeal this time. "How's your tea? Let me put one of those tartlets on your plate."

Imari sipped the tea. It was hot and sweet and delicious. Just like Lucien's kiss. She hoped Hattie thought the color in her cheeks was just from the steam rising off the beverage. "It's very good."

"Lucy—forgive me, I'm not supposed to call him that in front of you. Lucien likes that one best." She slid one of the tartlets on to Imari's plate, then put another on her own plate, poured herself some tea, and sat. She nudged a dish of whipped cream toward Imari and smiled. "It's so nice to have company. I don't have that many friends in town."

"Why not?"

She shrugged, her smile going a little sad. "It's hard for us. We need to keep a certain level of secrecy about us because of who we are."

Imari nodded, but she was sure it was only because of who Lucien was. Hattie's being a ghost wouldn't bother any of the supernatural residents in town. She wasn't even the only one. Pandora and Cole had the ghost of their home's previous owner living in their attic. "You go to the spa to get your hair done, though."

"I do. And once in a while, Birdie Caruthers and I do something. A movie, or lunch. Sometimes that nice Jayne Frost comes along. Do you know Birdie? Or Jayne?"

"Everyone knows Birdie. Or knows of her. I don't know Jayne, though."

Hattie smiled. "They're both very lovely women." Her smile dampened again. "But that's about as much interaction as I get beyond those outings. Just some casual conversations at the grocery store or post office."

"I'm sorry. That must be hard."

"It is. But I'm not complaining. Just wishing things were a little different. Still, this life is better than no life." She lifted her cup and sipped her tea.

Imari used her fork to cut a small piece off the tartlet. What did that mean? How had Hattie come to be a ghost? Would it be okay to ask, or would that be too personal a question? She decided to risk it. "I hope I'm not being forward, but how did you become a ghost?"

Hattie blinked a few times, smiling politely. She wavered, light filtering through her for a moment until she became fully solid again. "The usual way. I died."

That sounded very much like it wasn't a subject Hattie wanted to discuss further, and as Imari was a guest, she was happy to respect that.

Didn't mean she wasn't still curious. She was. Very much so. Maybe even more now after that response. But she let it be, choosing instead to eat the bite of tartlet on her fork. "This is excellent. Do you bake a lot?"

Hattie seemed relieved to have a change in the subject. "Oh yes, I love baking. I love all kinds of cooking, actually. Do you have any favorite dishes? I'd be happy to make one of them for you for dinner tomorrow."

"Don't go to any trouble on my account."

"Oh, it's no trouble. Actually, it's a pleasure. Lucien isn't a picky eater, but food isn't anything but fuel for him. He doesn't care much what he eats. So please, let me cook for you. What would you like?"

Imari pondered that. When was the last time someone had sincerely been interested in pleasing her? She smiled. When Lucien had procured tea for her at Insomnia. And now Hattie wanted to do the same. To see that Imari was happy. She leaned in. "You know what I would love?"

Hattie's face brightened. "What?"

"A good old-fashioned roast chicken dinner. With mashed potatoes and green beans and carrots and rolls with butter."

"And stuffing? And gravy?"

"Yes! With stuffing and gravy! How could I forget?"

"Don't worry, I won't." Hattie seemed on the verge of delirium. "That sounds perfect, by the way. I roast a mean chicken. What about for dessert?"

Imari thought back to her childhood. "My mother used to make this dish called Om Ali. It's like a bread pudding, but made with fresh bread, not stale, honey, chopped dates, and sprinkled with cinnamon and pistachios. She only made it on special occasions. Just thinking about it makes me smile."

Hattie was nodding furiously. "I can manage that. Om Ali. I'm all over it, you'll see."

They ate and talked about food, and by the time Imari had finished her tartlet, the nerves she'd felt earlier were long forgotten. She was looking forward to sleep and peaceful dreams.

She glanced at the clock on the microwave. "It's nearly midnight, Hattie. I don't know what your schedule is like, but I have to work tomorrow. I should really get to bed."

"Of course." Hattie stood and picked up the empty dessert plates. "I didn't mean to keep you up."

"No, no, I enjoyed chatting. Very much." Imari took the empty tea cups and saucers to the sink, joining Hattie there. "Thank you for your kindness."

Hattie smiled up at her. "Thank you for your company."

Imari's impulses took over again, but this time, she hesitated. "Can I hug you?"

Hattie laughed. "I would like that." She became corporeal.

Imari embraced the older woman. It had been a long time since she'd felt such caring and compassion. Hattie was warm and soft, just like a grandmother should be. The faint smell of rose water surrounded her, a very comforting smell to Imari. She released Hattie with reluctance and stood back. "Will I see you in the morning?"

"Absolutely. Who do you think makes breakfast?"

Imari smiled. "In the morning, then."

"Sleep well."

Imari headed back to the guest room. There was no sign of Lucien in the living room. Maybe he'd left. Maybe he was in the VIP section of Insomnia again. Making sure some other woman had exactly what she wanted to drink.

The green wash of jealousy stopped Imari in her tracks. Where on earth had that come from? That wasn't an emotion she had any business feeling. None whatsoever. If Lucien wanted to spend all his waking hours in that club talking to every woman in there, that was no concern of hers.

Still, she couldn't help but dwell on the image for

another second or two. Was that where he'd gone? Had his kiss been exactly what he'd said—a demonstration of what was inappropriate? She started walking again.

And ran into a wall. No, not a wall.

Lucien.

"Sorry, I didn't see you," she mumbled, embarrassed by her relief that he was still at home.

"Lost in thought?"

She nodded. "Something like that, yes."

"Going to bed?"

"That was my plan."

"Not yet," he said.

"No?"

"No. We need to talk."

First that kiss, now the genie smelled like delicious pastry and his favorite tea. It was as if the universe was using her to torment him. And doing a bang-up job of it.

But then, why wouldn't it? The universe excelled at tormenting him.

She stared up at him, hands on her hips, eyes round but slightly defiant. "About what?"

"I heard you tell my—Hattie, that you have to work tomorrow. That's not happening."

She snorted. "Um, yes, it is. I have a job because I have bills, and without that job, those bills don't get paid. You think it's free to live in the Excelsior? It's not. And you know what kind of car I drive? A five-year-old Toyota Camry. Which is a great car, don't get me wrong, but it's not a two-million-dollar limited edition Bugatti, so I need that job. Genies, at least this one, aren't independently wealthy."

He sighed. The urge to end this conversation by kissing her again was great, but he refrained because kissing her again was not going to be enough. "Can we discuss this in my study?"

Her mouth—that lush, full mouth that had felt like velvet against his—pursed with mild irritation. "I guess."

Was she mad that he'd kissed her? He wasn't. He'd known doing such a thing risked upsetting her, but he'd been powerless in the moment. Drugged by her beauty and charm. He still felt that way, but he'd had a large tumbler of cognac in the hopes of throttling some sense back into his head.

It hadn't worked.

He led her through the living room and to the other side of his home, then opened the study door for her and allowed her to enter first.

She did, stopping in the middle of the room. "This is definitely a man's space, isn't it?"

"What makes you say that?"

She turned in a slow circle. "Very masculine is all." She waved her hands around. "This much leather and dark wood."

"You don't like it?"

She faced him again, a slightly teasing gleam alight in her eyes. "No, I like it. It's very you."

He took that as a compliment.

She walked over to the Gustav Klimt painting, studying it for a moment, then peering closer before declaring, "That's a really good copy. I think I saw the original in a museum once. In Vienna."

"You're looking at the original now. The one in the Leopold Museum is a really good copy."

She turned, slightly astonished, but then she shook that off. "I shouldn't be surprised. Klimt, right?"

"Yes. *Death and Life*," he answered. The painting of a reaper and his myriad victims was really a composition showing the inevitable circle of life. It was a slightly morbid piece of art and had been a gift from his ex. Seemed fitting that she'd give him something so morose. He kept it as a reminder of how his attempt at a normal life hadn't worked. How he was never going to be anything but what he was. "You know Klimt."

"I like his work. I'm not crazy about this one, but the rest of his are very beautiful. I mean, this is beautiful in its own way, but it's also pretty...dark."

"I agree. It's a rather pessimistic view about the inevitability of things."

"Then why do you have it?"

"As a reminder." He didn't want to explain more than that. He pointed to the couch. "Sit, please."

She did, tucking her feet under her as she curled up against the arm of the big, leather sofa. She stood out in this room like a rose in a dung heap. So soft and feminine against all the stark, manly décor. He imagined if he could see color, the contrast would be staggering. She tipped her head at the bookcases. "Have you read all those?"

"No. But I will. Do you like to read?"

"I do. Maybe I'll borrow a book to take to bed with me. If that's okay?"

His throat tightened at the thought of her in bed. He'd much rather be the thing she borrowed. "Fine," was the best response he could get out.

She'd done something to him. Bewitched him in some way. Jinn magic. It was as complex and ancient as the reaper's. Perhaps more so, based on how he was feeling.

She was staring at him.

"What?" he asked.

"You wanted to talk to me about something? The job, perhaps, that you think I'm not going to?" The lilt in her voice made it clear how humorous she found that idea.

"You're not."

She kicked her feet out from under her to plant them on the floor. "Lucien, you can't forbid me to go to work. You can't forbid me to do anything. I am a free woman. I appreciate that you want to keep me safe, I do, but I need that job."

He studied her. The lines of her body were taut with indignation. It didn't make her any less attractive, unfortunately. "And how do you propose to keep the wish merchant from attempting to snatch you again?"

"Once I get to work, I'll be fine. Speaking of getting to work, my car is at the Excelsior. I'm going to need a ride over there in the morning to get it."

"You can take one of mine."

She barked out a laugh. "You're kidding, right?"

"No. They're cars. They're meant to be driven. And since you already have a car, you must know how to drive. Problem solved."

She was looking at him with her mouth open, eyes narrowed. "You're an odd one, you know that?"

"Why?"

"For a lot of reasons, but not caring that I might hurt one of your precious fancy machines is a big one."

His eyes narrowed. "My cars aren't precious. Life is precious. Things can be replaced. Very little else matters."

Her gaze went soft for a moment, then she looked down at her hands. "That's a nice sentiment."

"It's truth. Nice or not. Now, back to you going to work. I'm not forbidding it, but it would be a risky move on your part."

"Then come with me. Be my bodyguard."

He snorted. "I don't go out in public."

"You were in the club. And you came to my condo."

He didn't want to tell her that the trip to her home had been the first time he'd ventured beyond the boundaries of the Caldwell building in years. She would only pity him. Or think something was wrong with him, which she'd be very right about. "Those were both rare occasions. And both at night."

She sat back. "Does the sun affect you like it does a vampire?"

"Not exactly, but it's not my friend either." Being in daylight made it much easier to see his reaper form through his human one. The glimpses of skull and bones were enough to cause panic in those around him. It wasn't something he enjoyed.

"Okay. Maybe Hattie could go with me."

"And do what when the wish merchant approaches you?" He shook his head. "You must have some sick days that you could take. Or if you want, I'll speak to the owner of the spa on your behalf—"

"No." She stood abruptly. "Look, I appreciate your concern, but I don't need you to intervene for me. I can call my boss myself. I'm not going to, but I could."

Her refusal to let him help rankled. He banged his fist on the desk. "Why are you being so stubborn about this? You're the one who came to me for help, and now you're not letting me."

"I need that job."

"Taking a few sick days is not going to get you fired."

She sighed and sank back down to the couch. "I don't think the wish merchant will come after me during daylight hours when I'm surrounded by clients and co-workers."

"And if you're wrong?"

She frowned. Hard. "Fine. I'll call in sick."

"Good. Then we can work on a plan to keep you safe permanently."

She let out a sharp breath. "That's not going to be easy."

He lifted one shoulder. "Nothing worth having is."

"No, it isn't." She didn't make eye contact again, making him think she was more upset with him than she was letting on. "I'm going to bed. It's been a long day. Good night."

"Good night."

She got up and left. He watched until she was no longer in sight, then went back to the spreadsheets he'd been studying. His home was quiet again, the way he liked it, but there was a new level of energy in it.

Imari's presence. He had no other explanation. Hattie must be thrilled.

He pulled up the security footage of the wish merchant entering the club. The man was alone. Imari's guess that the man's genie had wished him to appear as a supernatural seemed spot-on.

He went back to his spreadsheets.

"Lucien!" Imari's tense exclamation shattered the stillness.

He heard the alarm in her voice and leaped to his feet, heading in the direction of the guest bedroom. He met her in the hall.

Anger blazed in her eyes. "Where is it?"

"What?"

"You know what. My bottle. It's not on the nightstand where I left it."

"I put it in the safe."

Her jaw clenched tighter. "You took my bottle."

"Yes." He spoke a little slower. "And put it in the safe. I thought you'd want that." Steam was practically coming out of her nostrils, so he guessed that wasn't the case at all. "I take it I was wrong."

"You *took* my bottle."

"You said that." He was utterly confused.

Tears welled up in her eyes, shocking him to his core. "Give it back."

"Absolutely." He returned to his study, unlocked the safe behind the Klimt painting, and retrieved the bottle. He rushed it back to her. "Here. Nothing happened to it, I assure you."

She snatched it from him. "Tell me you give this to me of your own free will. That it's a gift with no strings."

He didn't see the point in that, but also understood this was not the moment to argue. "I give you the bottle of my own free will as a gift with no strings attached."

The anger, the panic, the unshed tears, all of it disappeared, and she heaved out a breath. The bottle was in her arms, held tight to her body. "Thank you."

"Would you care to enlighten me about what just happened?"

She hesitated, then shook her head. "In the morning."

"Please. I obviously upset you in some way. That was not my intention. What did I do?"

Her body rose and fell with several deep inhales before she spoke again. "You *took* my bottle. And with it, control over me. For that span of time, until you put it back in my hands, I would have had to obey you. If you demanded me not to go to work, I couldn't have. I would have been powerless to do anything except what you commanded."

His breath caught in his throat. "I had no idea that's what I was doing. I am very sorry."

She nodded. "I know. And I also know I overreacted. I'm sorry about that."

"No, don't apologize. I can see why you would be so upset." He wanted to pull her into his arms and kiss her until her fears were gone, but he was wise enough to know she wouldn't welcome that. This was a woman who didn't want anyone to have power over her. "Would you care to put the bottle in the safe yourself?"

"I think for tonight, I'll just keep it with me." She hesitated, then stepped toward him, arms coming up.

He stepped back at the same time, the only thought in his head that she obviously needed space. Had she meant to hug him? That couldn't be. He was utterly confused. "I...would do the same in your shoes. Sleep well, Imari."

Her arms went back to her sides. "You too, Lucien."

He stood there a moment longer as she slipped back to the guest room. He thought about what she'd told him. How upset he'd made her without realizing what he'd done. How unsure he was of how to act around her.

His feelings didn't matter, though. She needed protecting. There was no way he would let the wish merchant ever endanger her again. Then the thought of what would happen to her if the wish merchant did get a hold of her bottle filled him with such anger that he decided to do something he hadn't done in a very long time.

He was going out.

To hunt.

Imari fell into bed. The mattress was plush, the sheets as soft as a kitten's belly, and she was tired enough that she ought to have conked out immediately, but sleep eluded her.

Lucien, however, did not. He was all she could think about. That and how bad she felt for yelling at him.

He hadn't known what he was doing, she knew that. He'd been trying to help. And she'd undoubtedly made him feel awful.

She huffed out a breath, angry with herself.

Maybe her past excused her behavior a little, but her temper was going to be her undoing someday if she wasn't careful. She hoped he didn't hold it against her. He was too good a man to lose as a friend. If that's what they were. They *were* that much, right? They'd kissed after all. Twice. But then, she wasn't so sure those kisses hadn't upset him either.

With a soft groan, she put one arm over her head. The pillows were the perfect firmness, but she was never going to sleep with all of this on her mind. She got up, tossed on her silk robe over her nightdress, and went to find him. She started with his study, but he wasn't there. Slowly, room by room, she went through the house.

Mansion was a better term. The place was *huge*. She never would have guessed just how large, even based on the parts she'd been through already.

It was easy to see where Hattie's touch had been the deciding factor on décor, and where Lucien's had been the final word. In most of the spaces, it was clear he had not been the winner. There were plenty more of the video screens masquerading as windows, too. Most of them showed nighttime views, making her wonder if they were programmed to reflect the actual passage of time. If so, it was a genius move for an underground dwelling.

There was a gym, a library that held more books than his study, and a craft room that was absolutely Hattie's space. In a small interior foyer that felt like it was about the middle of the dwelling, there were two sets of carved double doors opposite each other. She wondered if one went to Hattie's suite and one to Lucien's.

She wasn't going to investigate. First of all, those were private spaces. Secondly, if Lucien had gone to bed, she'd just wait until morning to apologize.

There was a hall on the left side, with a single steel door at the end. It looked industrial. Maybe it was another way out to the garage. She left it alone as well.

With a little more exploring, she found a rec room too, with a pool table, some video games, and a theater area complete with staggered seating for a dozen people and a popcorn machine. But who would come over to watch movies?

Past that room, she found stairs that led to a lower level, but she felt odd about going down there. Like that might be snooping. She caught a whiff of something familiar as she stood there, staring down the stairwell. She knew that smell from the lobby of the Excelsior. It was the faint scent of chlorine, and it occasionally drifted into the lobby where she lived since the entrance to the pool was near the elevators. Did Lucien have an indoor pool?

After seeing his garage, nothing would surprise her.

She circled back to the kitchen. And found Hattie at the table with a pot of tea. Her head was down, and she was poring over a Middle Eastern cookbook.

Imari cleared her throat softly to announce her presence.

Hattie jumped anyway, putting her hand to her heart. "Oh my, you startled me."

"I'm sorry, I didn't mean to."

"Are you all right, dear? I thought you'd gone to bed. It's late. I think." She peered up at the clock. "Oh yes, very late. Or semi-early. What's wrong? Can I help?"

Imari smiled. "I just needed to talk to Lucien. I owe him an apology. I sort of yelled at him earlier."

"I see. He has a tendency to bring that out in people." Hattie's mouth bunched to one side. "But I'm afraid he's not home."

"Oh." And yet he'd told her he rarely went out in public. Had he lied about that? She didn't want to think so. She wanted to trust him. She needed to. That need made her dig a little to see what else Hattie would reveal. "I guess he's in the club again."

"No, I don't think that's where he went."

So much for that. "Well, whatever the reason he left, I hope it wasn't because of what I said to him."

Hattie shook her head. "I don't know. He didn't tell me why he was leaving, just that he was."

"Never mind, then. It can wait." Imari turned to go back to the guest room.

"Don't hold it against him," Hattie said.

Imari looked at her again. "Hold what? His being out?"

"No. His...bad attitude. His grumpiness. Whatever you want to call it. I promise you, he's a good man. Fiercely loyal. Loving in his own way. He just has come up against a great deal of trouble in his life." She stared at the cookbook, her lined hand smoothing the page. "He's sacrificed a lot. Endured a lot. And he deserves to be loved."

Before Imari could respond, Hattie looked up, eyes rounded. "I didn't mean to imply that I think there's anything between you two. But if there was going to be, I think it would be a good thing. Even if it was just a friendship."

Imari wasn't sure what to say. That was a lot of information, and none of it precise enough to make any kind of judgment about. "I get the sense that he's a good man. He can be rather abrupt, though."

Hattie nodded. "I hate making excuses for him. I don't do it very often, though, seeing as how few people ever really get to know him. I think in time that gruff exterior would soften. For the right woman, anyway."

There was hope in her eyes. Hope that felt wasted on Imari. She didn't want to talk about her commitment to Khalid (that felt too much like accepting it), but she also couldn't bring herself to tell Lucien's grandmother that her grandson wasn't remotely interested in anything with the woman standing in her kitchen. Those kisses, she'd decided, hadn't been about anything but curiosity.

Especially not after the way he'd backed away from her when she'd gone to hug him in the hall.

Still, it seemed wrong to let Hattie pin her aspirations on a pipe dream. "Hattie, I'm sorry, but I'm not the right woman."

Hattie's optimistic smile thinned. "Oh. Well, you never know."

Imari put her hands on the back of the kitchen chair in front of her. "I do. I…kissed him. Just to say thank you. And he didn't respond well."

A glint sparked in Hattie's eyes. A glint that looked very much like fear. "You touched him?"

Imari nodded. "Should I not have?"

Hattie opened her mouth, then closed it. "No, I'm sure it was fine."

Well, that cleared things up. Imari pointed back toward her room. "I'm going back to bed. I'll see you in the morning."

"See you in the morning, dear."

Imari left, her head filled with all kinds of new thoughts and questions. Hattie was an expert in saying a lot without saying anything. What kind of sacrifices had Lucien made? What had he suffered? And why was touching him a bad thing? Was that because he was an angel of death? Maybe touching them was off-limits. Angel-of-death etiquette hadn't been covered in any of the schools Imari had attended.

She did know, however, that she should not be kissing him. She was promised to Khalid, and even if she had no intention of going through with that marriage, which she didn't, it wasn't right to carry on with another man until that situation was dealt with.

She returned to the guest suite and climbed back into bed. She pulled the covers to her chin and closed her eyes, hoping for a peaceful sleep. The rest would help, because she and Lucien were going to have to talk again in the morning.

About a lot of things.

Lucien had been out earlier tonight at Imari's, and he often went out at night for a drive, but tonight's venture was different. Tonight was more of a mission.

It felt like the old days. When he'd had purpose. When there'd been a soul in desperate need of relief, a soul in need of transport to the afterlife.

Tonight, however, he wasn't planning on reaping any souls. Unless the wish merchant did something stupid.

He'd taken Hattie's Range Rover. Not his typical choice, but the midnight blue SUV blended far better than any of his exotics, and the tinted windows gave him some added privacy. Looking around at the other cars in the Excelsior's lot, he could have gone a little more upscale, but there was a good mix and the Rover blended in well.

He was slouched in the driver's seat, parked in the far corner of the lot. From here, he could see the lot's entrance and the door into the lobby with ease. The lobby's front half was entirely glass, too, making it possible to keep an eye on anyone coming or going.

If the wish merchant showed up here again, which felt like a high probability, Lucien would watch him, then follow him back to wherever he was staying.

The downside of keeping a low profile in town was that, outside of his own club, he didn't know much else about where things were. That just wasn't something his lifestyle allowed him to learn.

On the rare occasions he'd traveled to Elenora Ellingham's, or her grandson Hugh's home, he'd gone at night. Or used the Basement access. The underground passageways that lay beneath the town were perfect for him, and they should be. He'd financed a good part of them in order to have access to them whenever he needed.

The night wound on with no sighting of the man. Which left Lucien with a lot of thinking time.

But only one person to think about. She was the reason he was here after all.

Beautiful, intelligent, intriguing Imari.

He scrubbed a hand over his face and gave in. Fighting was pointless. His head wanted to replay over and over the kisses they'd shared. His heart wished they'd gone on longer. Each time, warmth spilled through him. Each time, he could feel her mouth on his as if it was happening all over again. Smell her perfume. Taste her sweetness.

See color.

How did she do that?

Maybe genies had a way of making wishes come true without trying. Because while he'd never spoken the words out loud, being able to permanently see color again would absolutely be a wish come true.

But he wasn't the kind of man to spend energy on the impossible.

And yet, here he was, thinking about what life would be like with Imari at his side. He snorted in disgust at himself. Hades, he was pathetic. What would she want with him? What kind of life could he offer her? She was a bright, blooming flower.

He was a choking weed that lived underground.

Hattie would say he was being too hard on himself, but pretending helped no one. He preferred reality. All reapers did. It was part of the trade, part of their makeup. Life and death, black and white, wrong and right. There were no shades of gray in his life.

Just in his vision.

But he'd seen the way Imari had looked at his home. Her compliments had been sweet, but he wasn't an idiot. He knew they'd masked her distaste. At least, he thought they must. She couldn't be happy in a home like his.

Could she?

He rolled his eyes. He was really losing it. And over a woman. Considering how well that had turned out the last time, he knew better than to think a relationship was worth trying again.

An expanse of air wobbled beneath one of the parking lot lights. The sheen of glitter sparkled bright.

Lucien ducked lower in the seat as two people appeared in that very spot. The wish merchant and the genie under his command, Adira.

Lucien's pulse kicked up. The prey had arrived. The wish merchant glanced around the lot. Was he looking for Imari? Or for Lucien?

The man's gaze settled on something and he smiled. Lucien followed his line of sight. He was looking at a Toyota Camry.

The wish merchant thought Imari was here. He jerked his thumb at the car while looking at Adira. She nodded in response. She looked the same. Tired, worn down. Sad.

Lucien felt for her. If she was living the kind of life Imari had described, being the wish merchant's property, which it seemed pretty clear she was, then Lucien would do his best to free her as soon as he could. No one deserved that.

The pair made their way toward the lobby. Lucien got out, shut the car door quietly, and followed, keeping a safe distance. The lot was well lit, but he skirted the pools of light cast by the overheads and stuck to the shadows. If need be, he could disappear into the shadows altogether, but the wish merchant's attention wasn't on the parking lot.

He and the genie approached the doorman. The pair must not know which condo was Imari's. The wish merchant asked some questions, but the doorman shook his head. The wish merchant pressed him. The doorman looked upset. He reached for the phone. The wish merchant snapped his fingers, and the genie bobbed her head.

The doorman relaxed like he'd been put in a lucid coma. His hand left the phone to fall back to his side. Then he pointed to the elevators and said something. A number. Imari's condo number.

With a mocking smile, the wish merchant gave the man a salute, then put his hand on Adira's back and urged her forward.

Rage filled Lucien. He didn't want that man in Imari's condo, riffling through her things, touching what didn't belong to him.

But he couldn't justify reaping the man's soul, either. Not when there was no immediate threat to Lucien's well-being. There were strict rules for a reaper about when a soul could and couldn't be taken. Much like Imari's wish power, a reaper was never to take a soul in anger or for personal reasons. Reaping a soul before its time resulted in serious consequences.

Because of his unreliable powers, he'd been strongly advised by the sitting council to wear gloves to keep any further accidents from happening. He did his best to abide by that. Not only did he have no desire to inadvertently take another soul, but the inquisition after his grandmother's death was not something he wanted to repeat unless absolutely necessary.

But he had other tools at his disposal. He stuck his right arm out and pushed his sleeve back to reveal the scythe tattooed there. Then he opened his palm, commanding the weapon into being.

A second later, the ebony wood handle filled his grip and the deadly metal blade gleamed under the parking lot lights. He called up his reaper form and let it take over completely.

His suit became a loose, voluminous robe. His face and body took on the skeletal shape of his kind. And as he approached the lobby's glass walls, he could see in their reflection that the transformation was complete.

His eyes glowed like embers.

He was, once again, a War Angel. Not complete. He no longer had his horse. But for the sake of his mission tonight, he had everything he needed.

He glanced up at Imari's condo and used his reaper power of instant transportation to travel there.

Imari didn't know when she'd fallen asleep, just that she had and that she'd slept remarkably well. The luxurious bed had helped, but the biggest factor had been her peace of mind. Knowing the wish merchant couldn't find her or her bottle while she was here had done wonders.

Lucien, for all his peculiarities, had done her a solid.

She got up, showered, and dressed in her spa uniform, a tranquil sea glass green tunic and pants. They were sort of like fancy scrubs, and the outfit was very comfortable, which was important, considering her job was one of the more physical ones at the spa.

She headed out to the kitchen, happy to see Hattie already there. The window video showed a bright, sunny day. "Good morning."

Hattie turned from the stove, smiling. "Hello there. How did you sleep? Tea is made, so help yourself. Breakfast will be along shortly."

"I slept very well, thank you. And you?" Imari made a face. "Sorry, I don't know if you sleep or not."

"I rest. I can get tired, but it's not like what I used to feel. What wears me out now is being corporeal for too long. I mostly save that for when I go out. Getting groceries, seeing a movie, those sorts of things."

Imari walked over to the kettle to get herself some tea. "Don't feel like you have to be solid on my account. It doesn't bother me if you're see-through."

"Are you sure? I know it can be a little off-putting."

"Not an issue, I promise." Imari poured herself a cup and added a sugar cube. "I have a version of see-through myself."

Hattie remained corporeal, and Imari realized it must be easier to cook that way as the older woman added a big sprinkling of chopped herbs to the eggs in the pan. "Can you really? I didn't realize genies could do that."

"Sure. It's how we get in and out of our bottles. Sort of a cross between steam and smoke." Imari sipped her tea. It wasn't the Assam this morning. Instead, it tasted like Chinese black tea. "Is this Keemun? It's delicious."

"It is!" Hattie grinned. "You know your tea."

"I'm a thousand years old. I've had time to learn. Plus, the red color gives it away."

Hattie's mouth rounded. "A thousand? You don't look a day over thirty."

Imari laughed. "If I had any wishes to give, I'd give you one just for that. Do you need any help? I'm a fair hand in the kitchen."

"No, I'm just about to plate things up. Actually,

you can take the fruit to the table. It's in the bowl by the sink."

"Done." Imari set her tea at a place at the table, then retrieved the fruit. A blue stoneware bowl held chunks of peaches and plums, halved strawberries, whole blueberries, and red grapes. "This looks great."

"I hope so. And I hope you like eggs. Nothing too complicated this morning, just a scramble with some fresh herbs and goat cheese. Plus toast." She slid the eggs into a serving dish, then took another plate from the oven. It was piled with thick slices of toasted, grainy bread shiny with butter.

"Sounds perfect and looks even better. I can't tell you the last time anyone made me breakfast."

Hattie brought both dishes to the table. "I make breakfast every morning for Lucy. I think if I didn't, he wouldn't eat." She shook her head and frowned as she sat. "I don't know what he'd do if I wasn't here to take care of him sometimes."

Imari lifted her brows. "Should we wait for him to join us, then?"

Hattie's frown softened into something much more concerned, and she broke eye contact. "He's, uh, sleeping in this morning."

That seemed very unlike Lucien. It seemed more likely that he was avoiding her. "Are you sure I'm not the reason he's not at breakfast?"

Hattie's eyes widened a tiny bit as she looked up. "I...oh, I'm a terrible liar. Yes, you are the reason he's not here, but it's not a bad reason. He went to talk to the Ellinghams on your behalf this morning."

"What? He did? Why?"

"Because the wish merchant was at your home last night." Hattie's hands fluttered like dizzy birds. "Oh, dear, I'm not supposed to be telling you all this."

"Why not?"

"Because Lucien doesn't want you to worry."

"Wait. Why did Lucien go back to my place last night?"

Hattie rolled her lips in. "I shouldn't say anything else."

"No, you're right. I don't want you to get into trouble. I'll talk to him when he gets home. I'm sure he'll have plenty to tell me. Especially if he sees me dressed like this and thinks I'm going to work."

"You're not, are you?"

Imari sighed. "No. I'm wearing this because it's all I packed outside of pajamas. But I'd be lying if I said I wasn't worried about my job. I can't afford to lose it."

"You won't," came a deep voice behind her.

Lucien.

She turned in her seat to face him. He looked different this morning. At least, she thought he did. More handsome in some unfortunate (for her) way. She ignored that to ask, "And you know that because?"

"Because I just came from discussing things with Hugh Ellingham. Due to your special circumstances, you don't have to return to work until the wish merchant is no longer an issue, but you also don't have to worry about losing your job. Hugh is going to speak to the owners and explain what's going on."

"That was very kind of you. Thank you." Those words were harder for her to say than she'd expected. She wasn't used to being beholden to anyone. It was a strange feeling. But it was also very sweet that Lucien, the man who never left his home, had now left it three times because of her.

She smiled at him and pushed out the chair beside her. "Why don't you join us for breakfast? We were just about to eat."

He looked startled by her offer. "I…could do that."

Hattie jumped up and got a plate. "Good. Sit. The eggs are getting cold."

Lucien didn't move for a moment. When he finally did, he chose a different seat than the one Imari had pushed out. He settled into a chair that put him on the other side of the table from her and a little closer to his grandmother.

Imari helped herself to some fruit and tried not to overanalyze his seat selection. He was a grown man. He could sit where he wanted to. If that wasn't by her, well, then, that was her issue to get over.

She looked at him from under her lashes, trying to watch him without him noticing. He definitely looked different this morning. More handsome, yes, but brighter in some way. It was a strange way to think of him, but the only thing that seemed to fit. She offered him the bowl of fruit. "Did you sleep well? Or don't you sleep either?"

He took the bowl. "I sleep. Not much last night."

"Lack of sleep looks good on you." She speared a peach chunk with her fork. "Makes me look like a hag."

He scooped a helping of fruit onto his plate. "I doubt that very much. You are easily the most beautiful woman I've ever met."

Imari stared at him. She hadn't expected such a compliment from him. Or at all, really. "Thank you. I doubt that's true, but it's still a very kind thing to say."

Hattie grinned and slathered her bread with butter. "He's right. You are the loveliest thing that's ever walked through these doors. Even Kora isn't as pretty, and she is quite beautiful. Of course, she's usually rotten on the in—"

Lucien's sharp hiss interrupted her.

Hattie's mouth closed as her nose wrinkled. A second later, she took a big bite of her toast, chewing robustly while she stared at her grandson.

Imari watched the tense exchange with interest. "Who's Kora?"

Lucien grimaced. "No one important at the moment. I was at your apartment last night."

That was an abrupt change of subject, but Imari let it be. She was more interested in hearing about Lucien's second run-in with the wish merchant than one of his old girlfriends. "And?"

"The wish merchant and Adira were there again."

Imari shrugged. "The doormen there are pretty strict. They aren't going to just let people up. They always call first to announce a visitor."

"Except the doorman let me up a second time without calling. I told him I'd left something and he just nodded as I went by." Lucien let out a breath.

"And the wish merchant made Adira use her magic on the doorman. Didn't take long at all and he let them go up to your condo."

Imari's grip on her fork tightened. "What?"

"That's terrible," Hattie muttered.

"I watched them," Lucien continued. "He ran the show, telling Adira what to do. She cast some kind of spell over the doorman that made him complacent. He gave them your condo number and off they went to the elevators."

Imari's heart thudded. "But they didn't get into my condo, did they?"

He held her gaze. "They did. I was able to scare them off before they touched anything."

"Thank you—how did you get in? Did you follow them up?"

"I can appear anywhere I need to. It's one of my skills."

"Oh. Right. I guess it would be." Walls couldn't keep an angel of death out. "Well, I'm glad you were there. I hate that they were in my condo. I feel violated. Even if they didn't touch anything."

He added eggs and toast to his plate. "You have every right to feel that way. It's shown me something too. You won't be free of this man until he gets what he wants."

"That's very reassuring." She punctuated her sarcastic answer with a sigh. "I'm sorry. You don't deserve that tone. I'm just so upset and I feel helpless."

"I understand." He glanced at her hand. Like he wanted to touch her. To comfort her. He didn't, though. "I'd hoped to follow them when they left, to see where they were staying, but Adira poofed them away again."

Imari sighed. "Of course she did. That's the easiest way for him to travel."

"I have an idea."

A tiny spark of hope flamed to life inside Imari. "You do? What is it?"

"Let's give him your bottle."

Judging by Imari's shocked expression, Lucien needed to talk faster. "I don't mean *your* bottle exactly. Just a very close replica of it."

That calmed her considerably. "Oh."

"Does he know what your bottle looks like?"

"I don't really know the answer to that. It's possible. All genie bottles have a similar look. Fancy glass, lots of jewels and metal work. But they're also unique to each genie. Like a snowflake. Or a fingerprint."

"Then we need the replica to be as close as it can be."

She pushed the eggs on her plate around with her fork. "What you're suggesting might have some merit, but re-creating a bottle like that isn't going to be easy. And if you really want to re-create it, it's also going to be very expensive. And I don't have the kind of funds that allow for a craft project made of diamonds and sapphires and gold."

"I do and—"

"I don't want to be in your debt. More than I already am, that is. So I'm very appreciative of this offer, but I'm sorry, I can't."

"Imari, please," Hattie said. "Lucien can afford this. And—"

"But how is it really going to help?" Imari asked. "Once the wish merchant figures out the bottle isn't mine because he can't command me just by owning it, he'll be back on my trail. It's just an obstacle the wish merchant will easily overcome, not a solution to getting him out of my life. If anything, it will most likely just anger him."

Lucien cleared his throat and held fast to his patience. Imari was upset, and understandably so. "I was going to say that we'd use the bottle as a decoy in a sting operation. Attempted kidnapping might fly in other parts of the supernatural world, but absolutely not in Nocturne Falls. The man will be apprehended and punished."

Imari seemed to think that over. "But he's human. Supernatural law doesn't apply to humans."

"He's trafficking in supernaturals. He's made himself a special case. And the Ellinghams not only agree, but they're willing to prosecute accordingly. We've already discussed it. Not to mention there's the added bonus that the genie he's already holding hostage will be set free. Don't you think she'd testify against him?"

"I'm sure she would." Imari stared at her breakfast plate. "But this still means I'd be in debt to you."

He lifted one shoulder. The money was nothing to him, but clearly, she didn't share that feeling. "Then we'll have the bottle dismantled and the materials resold. Would that make you feel better?"

"Yes. You won't get all your money back, though."

He stared at her. "But you'll be safe. So will countless others of your kind. That seems a very good reason for me to absorb a small monetary loss."

She smiled a little, lightening his mood. "Yes, it does. You are so kind. But how do I thank you for this?"

"You don't need to thank me with anything more than words. It hasn't been often in my life that I've been able to help. Please. Let me."

"That's all you want from me? A thank you?"

Her friendship would be nice, but he was not so pathetic as to ask her for that. "Yes. That's all."

"Okay." She breathed out, like she was releasing a great burden. "I will. Thank you. Although that is not enough by half."

"Excellent," Hattie said.

They all went back to eating, but Lucien almost laughed as he dug into his eggs. Hattie was buoyant with happiness over this, he could tell. From her smile to the sparkle in her eyes, she was beyond delighted. That alone made whatever expense he might incur in this undertaking equally as worthwhile as freeing Imari. Today was a good day. Better, certainly, than it had started out when he'd faced down the Ellinghams to ask for a favor.

Before this, the only favor he'd asked for was to be

left alone. To be allowed to live as anonymously as possible.

Now he'd been on their doorstep, asking for help for a woman. Astonishing how things had changed in such a short period of time.

"How is this going to work?" Imari asked. "I assume you'll have Willa create the bottle?"

"Willa?" Lucien cursed his solitary life. No doubt Willa was someone he should know if she was capable of reproducing a bottle like Imari's.

"She's the best jeweler in town. And she's fae, so her work isn't just beautiful, but magical as well. When the piece demands it. She's a friend of mine and a wonderful person." Imari looked at Hattie. "You must know her."

"I know of her," Hattie answered. "I bought Birdie a pair of earrings at Willa's shop for her birthday. Her designs are beautiful. I have no doubt she could re-create your bottle. Although I haven't seen your bottle."

"It's elaborate," Imari offered. She looked at Lucien. "I hope pictures will be enough. I don't want to take the bottle out in public."

"Nor should you." Lucien thought about it. Perhaps photos wouldn't be enough to convey the beauty of the bottle.

"I know," Hattie said. "Let's invite Willa over here."

"No," he snapped. Then it was his turn to take a breath. He lowered his voice and softened his tone. "Hattie, I don't think that's a good idea."

"Well, Imari can't exactly make a big appearance

at Willa's. The wish merchant knows what she looks like."

"But he doesn't know she's here. Or that she'd be going to see Willa." He hesitated. "Where is her shop?"

"On Main Street," Hattie answered.

"Illusions," Imari elaborated.

He thought a moment about the part of the town he did know. Then he spoke again, mostly to Imari. "If I can arrange safe passage to this shop, will you go? With your bottle?"

"Safe passage?" She looked skeptical.

"I assure you, it's possible."

The doubt in her eyes didn't fade. "I'll consider it."

"Good." He pushed his chair back. "If you'll excuse me, I have more work to do."

Imari spent part of the day with Hattie. They watched a movie in the rec room's theater, then had lunch, after which Hattie had to go out grocery shopping for the ingredients for dinner, so Imari found herself in the library.

Not being at work gave her a sense of playing hooky, and what a room the library was to play hooky in. It was a gorgeous space with tall ceilings and two rolling ladders to access the books higher up. The windows were video screens, just like they were in the rest of the house, but the art mixed in among the books was what really drew Imari's gaze.

Several standing glass cases around the room held

first editions: Shakespeare's *Othello*, Tolkien's *The Lord of the Rings*, and two of Dickens', *Bleak House* and *Great Expectations*.

Another display case hung on the wall and showed off three small Egyptian faience figurines and an enormous scarab made of the same blue-green glazed pottery. There was a Rembrandt in a niche. And the chandelier overhead looked like it had been made by Chihuly, the famous glass artist, which, undoubtedly, it had been.

Lucien's taste in the finer things was as impressive as it was eclectic. It made her curious to know more about him, but she got the sense it wasn't going to be easy to get him to reveal himself to her.

In the back corner of the library, there was a particularly comfortable-looking chair. Beside it was a wooden magazine rack. Much to Imari's surprise and delight, the rack's bars hung heavy with gossip rags and entertainment magazines. They were the last sort of reading material she expected to find in this room, but then she realized she was once again seeing Hattie's influence.

She smiled as she settled into the chair and began to devour them, feeling like a child let loose in a sweet shop.

"Enjoying yourself?"

She looked up. Lucien was in the doorway. At some point during the day, he'd changed from his suit to a simple black sweater and gray twill pants. It was the most dressed down she'd seen him. It was a very good look.

So good she forgot what he'd asked her. "What?"

"I asked if you were enjoying yourself."

She unhooked her legs from over the arm of the chair and straightened up. "Yes. I have to confess, Hattie and I share the same taste in trashy magazines." She closed the one on her lap, smiling a little self-consciously.

He smiled back. "Those are mine. Hattie reads them, but she prefers cooking and decorating magazines."

"Now you're teasing me."

"I'm not, I promise."

Well, that was a revelation. If it was true. "So who's your favorite Kardashian?"

He grimaced. "None of them."

"Good answer." She laughed. He'd passed the test. "Your library is amazing, by the way."

"Thank you. It's one of my favorite places."

"I can see why."

He stuck his hands in his pockets. "I hate to cut short your time here, but can you be ready to meet Willa in half an hour?"

"Sure." She got up, tucking the magazine back onto its spot on the rack. "Are you positive it's going to be safe?"

"Yes."

She bit her lip.

"You don't believe me."

"It's not that, it's just...I'm scared." There. She'd said it.

A warmth filled his gaze. "I will not let harm come to you, Imari."

It sounded like an oath. And she believed him. She nodded. "Okay. I guess I'm ready now. I don't really have anything to change into. I didn't pack very well. And I only thought I'd be here overnight."

"Not to worry. Hattie picked some things up for you while she was out. They're in your room. But you don't have to change if you don't want to."

"I'll go have a look."

"Very good. Meet me in the living room when you're ready."

She twisted her hands together. "Bring the bottle, right?"

"Yes. I promise, it will also be safe." With a nod, he turned and walked away.

She followed after him, turning the lights off behind her, but when she walked into the hall, he was already gone.

In the guest room, laid out on the bed, she found stacks of new clothing. Jeans, dress pants, yoga pants, and leggings. In another pile were sweaters, T-shirts, casual tops, and blouses. In the third were underthings, a nightgown, some workout wear, and several swimsuits.

There were five shoe boxes as well. Sneakers, sandals, short boots, and two pairs of flats.

All designer brands. All very high end. And all her size. How was that possible?

She chose jeans, a light sweater in a beautiful cobalt blue, and the short boots. The outfit was chic and gorgeous. Hattie was an incredible personal shopper.

Imari wrapped the bottle in a towel and secured it in her weekend bag, then went out to meet Lucien.

He nodded when he saw her. "I take it the clothes are to your liking?"

"It's an impressive bunch of stuff. All of it lovely and all of it things I would wear."

"That should hold you for a few days, then. Are you ready to go?"

"Ready."

"Follow me."

He led her toward his study, but they passed that, and based on her investigations last night, she realized they were going toward the small foyer that she'd assumed held the doors into his and Hattie's bedroom suites.

She was right about the direction, but when they reached the foyer, they turned toward the hall that ended with the industrial metal door.

They went through it into another small foyer, this one painted black with black carpet underfoot. The faint, thumping bass of music vibrated through the space. When he shut the door behind them, total darkness took over for a split second.

"I apologize for the lack of light, but your eyes should adjust in a moment."

"They already have."

A set of steps led up. They ascended and entered another hallway. One side held shiny black panels.

She moved toward the first panel. It was a window. But the longer she looked through, the more she understood exactly what she was seeing. And why the thump of music made sense.

Insomnia.

And the window was actually one of the many mirrors lining the walls of the nightclub.

Lucien hadn't wanted to bring Imari through here, but it was the only way to get to the elevator that would take them to the Basement without going out through the garage or the main entrance, which led out through what appeared to be an ordinary side door of the warehouse. "We should go. Willa is waiting."

Imari's eyes stayed on the scene inside the club.

Lucien looked in. There wasn't as much going on as there would be later tonight, but there was a small crowd dancing and a decent handful at the bar.

"What is this?" she asked. "I mean, I know that's Insomnia. But what is this room we're in? Why are these two-way mirrors here?"

He went with the first thing that wasn't a lie. "Security purposes."

She glanced over her shoulder, and her expression implied she might not be buying that.

"We should go," he repeated. He wasn't going to

delve deeper and explain that sometimes, watching the crowd through these windows was the only connection to humanity he had.

Thankfully, she let it be. "Lead on."

With long strides, he got them to the elevator, swiped his keycard through the reader, then tucked it away and waited for the lift to arrive. The doors opened a few seconds later.

He held his hand toward the car's interior. "After you."

He followed her in and pressed the button for the Basement. The doors slid shut, then opened again seconds later when they arrived. "Here we are."

She approached the doors and looked out. "Where?"

"The Basement."

"Of Insomnia?"

"No, the Basement of Nocturne Falls."

She stepped out, allowing him to do the same. "The town has a basement?"

"It's an operational area. And Basement is capitalized." He tried to see the wide, bright halls through her eyes. This wasn't a place most in town knew about, but as one of the Basements' financiers, he didn't need permission to introduce anyone to it. Anyone supernatural, that was. "Remember when the town lost power a few months back due to that incredible winter storm?"

"Yes, that wasn't fun, but at least the power wasn't out for too long. The Excelsior only went about eight hours before it was restored."

"No doubt Julian's residence there had some pull, but the banks of generators needed to run the rest of the town are down here. Among other things."

"That's really interesting. I had no idea."

"Most people don't."

She studied him for a moment. "Why do you live under Insomnia? Your sound-proofing is great, by the way. You can't hear the music at all in the house. But it's an interesting choice, to say the least."

He ran through a hundred different answers, finally settling on the truth. "It's close to the heart of town, but not too close, so it's convenient for Hattie. And the club also creates enough traffic that any of our comings and goings don't stand out."

"Do you own the building?"

"Yes." He wasn't sure where all the questions were going, but he felt oddly indulgent.

"I guess the rent from Insomnia pays for gas, huh?"

"There is no rent from Insomnia. I own that as well."

"Really?" She glanced back at the elevator. "I don't know why that didn't occur to me, but it makes sense considering the kind of businessman you seem to be. No wonder you got treated the way you did that first night in the VIP section." She squinted at him. "I have to say, you don't seem like a nightclub kind of guy, though."

"I'm not. Not really. But it serves my purposes." He checked his watch.

"I know, we need to go. I take it we're using the Basement to get there?"

"Yes. It's the safest way for us to travel. There's an access right behind Illusions, so we can be in and out the back door without being seen."

"Kind of a long walk from here." She glanced down at her short boots. "I should have chosen flats."

"No need." He walked over to a rollup door, pushed a button to lift it, and revealed his sleek black club car. "We're taking this."

"A golf cart? Cool."

"Club car. Golf carts are a little more...delicate."

She was smirking. "Right. This one has knobby tires. Much more manly."

He ignored her sarcasm as he climbed in. He unhooked the charging cable, tossing it aside.

She got in next to him, still smirking. Maybe she was laughing at him, but he didn't care. He enjoyed amusing her. It meant she wasn't thinking so much about the wish merchant. She hooked one hand through the grip near the roof while the other held fast to the bag with the bottle in it. "Ready when you are."

He pushed the start button, pulled out of the small garage, and off they went.

She was quiet for a moment, mostly looking around and reading the directional signs as they went past. "Is this Basement under the whole town?"

"Not all of it, but a good deal."

She didn't ask for specifics, seemingly content to ride and take it all in. Or maybe she was temporarily out of questions.

When they got closer to Main Street, the central

passageway branched off into a few smaller corridors. They passed one of the gargoyle shifters coming out of the fountain room, and Lucien expected more questions then, but Imari just waved back.

Another block in, he pulled the car over and parked. "We're here."

"That was fast."

"Having no traffic or lights to contend with helps." He turned the vehicle off and applied the brake before getting out. He gestured toward the stairwell behind him. "We're going that way."

"Right behind you." She got out of the car and followed him up the steps to the street level and the small landing there.

"Wait." He opened the door and checked around outside. Twilight had fallen, but Main Street was a fairly well-lit area. Not this back alley so much, but he didn't want to take any chances. "All clear."

They slipped out and stood in the alley. Lucien knocked on the first back door they came to. It was tucked under the stairs that led to Willa's apartment over the shop. At least, that was how Willa had described the door when he'd emailed with her earlier.

"You sure this is the right one?" Imari looked at him. "It doesn't say Illusions. Or anything."

"Wouldn't be prudent to mark a jewelry shop's door. Even in a town as safe as this one."

"No, I suppose not."

The door opened, and a woman Lucien assumed to be Willa Iscove, the owner, appeared. She smiled at them. "If you're with Imari, you must be Lucien. Hi, Imari. Come in."

"Hi, Willa. Thanks for helping us out."

"It's my pleasure." Willa got out of the way so they could enter.

The door led them into the shop's backroom. It was small and mostly taken up by a workbench and desk. A huge, whiskered beast sprawled on the desk, blocking access to the laptop. The door to the shop was closed, but a large window over the desk looked out onto the storefront. The tint of the glass made Lucien think it was another two-way mirror. Customers milled about in the shop, and two other employees stood at the ready to help them.

Lucien frowned at the window, not sure if his guess was right. "Do you have a shade you can pull?"

Willa shook her head. "That's a two-way mirror. No one can see in."

"Very good."

Imari scratched the cat's head. "What a pretty baby. I love orange cats. I didn't know you had a cat, Willa. Must be a boy, right?"

"Right," Willa answered with a smile. "Jasper. And he is my baby. He's almost always in the office here, but if you don't come back here, you'd never know it. Now, let me get the bottles I was able to collect." She turned to a sturdy cardboard box on the workbench.

Imari glanced at Lucien. "Most orange cats are male. Did you know that?"

"I wasn't even sure that was a cat."

She blinked at him in astonishment. "Did you just make a joke?"

"I…yes?"

She laughed. "Good for you."

Willa opened the flaps of the box. "I scoured a few of the local antique and junk shops in town, and these five bottles are the closest I could come up with as a base for yours."

"That was so kind of you," Imari said.

"It was fun. I found some nice ones." Willa pulled the bottles out and set them one by one on the workbench, then looked at Imari. "Do you think any of these will work?"

Imari studied them, her mouth screwed up on one side. "Maybe. Will you be able to manufacture a stopper? None of those have one."

"I'm sure I can. Which one of those looks the closest?"

Imari pointed. "Probably that pale blue one. The shape is right."

Lucien tipped his head at the bag in Imari's hand. "Why don't you show her the real thing?"

Imari stopped petting the cat to grip the bag with both hands.

Willa smiled gently. "This is a safe place, I assure you."

"I know. You're right. It's just…you know." Imari set the bag on the desk in the little space beside the cat and took the bottle out. "Here it is."

Willa sucked in a breath. "That is unbelievable. I've never seen anything like it, and I assure you,

125

some of the crown jewels from my kingdom are breathtaking. I need to take some notes and, if you don't mind, some pictures. Especially of that stopper. I have the one photo that Lucien sent me—"

"You sent her a picture?" Imari looked at him.

"I did. So she could find a suitable bottle to use as the base for the replica." He held his hands up. "It was on your nightstand. I didn't touch it."

Imari shook her head. "No, that's fine. Thank you." Then she smiled tentatively at Willa. "You can take pictures. It's all for a good reason. And obviously I trust you."

Willa set the second bottle aside and returned the rest to the box. "The pictures won't be shared with anyone else, I promise."

"Thank you, I know that, too. I'm sorry to be so protective about this, but—"

"Don't apologize," Willa said. "And you don't have to explain. I've done a little research on the jinn. I know how important your bottle is to you."

Imari visibly relaxed. "That's kind of you. And I'm being silly." She held the bottle out. "Here. If you're going to re-create it, you need to examine it close up."

The move surprised Lucien, but he said nothing. Maybe Imari trusted Willa more because they were friends. Or because she was a woman. Maybe Imari's past included her bottle being owned by some unscrupulous men. The idea of what that might mean, of what might have happened to her, stirred new anger.

He stood with his back to the wall, his hands

126

clasped in front of him, and tried not to let the anger out. Strong emotion could cause his reaper form to become visible. It was a reaction, pure and simple, and he didn't wish to alarm Imari or Willa.

He drifted into his own thoughts for a moment. He hadn't told Willa what he was. She might already know. But if she didn't, he wanted to keep it that way.

He shifted his attention to the cat. The animal was on his side, head upside down, eyes closed, and he looked very much like he didn't have a care in the world. What a lucky beast.

Lucien moved closer and reached a hand out. His instinct was to stroke his fingers lightly down the animal's side. He hesitated. His gloves were on, but the old fear was there.

He pulled his hand back to his side.

Willa was saying something about the bottle's stopper again, then stopped to speak to him. "You can pet him." She nodded at the cat. "He won't bite. Jasper loves attention."

"I shouldn't. I...might be allergic." It was the best he could do and considerably better than *I might accidentally take his life*.

Willa shrugged and went back to inspecting the bottle while discussing the finer points of design with Imari.

Lucien found himself drawn to the cat again. He picked up a pen and used the end to scratch Jasper's back. The cat rolled over a little more and stuck his paws in the air and started to knead them back and forth. It was kind of charming, really.

With a little smile, Lucien put the pen down. Hattie had been trying to get him to let her have a pet for years. Maybe it wasn't such a bad idea. If he could be certain his ruined powers wouldn't hurt the animal.

Hattie didn't need any more loss in her life.

"Twelve, thirteen, fourteen…" Willa was counting softly as she inspected the bottle. Every so often, she stopped to jot something down.

At last, she looked at the list she'd created, did a quick tally, then faced Lucien. "The good news is, I can re-create this almost exactly in about two days. Maybe two and a half, depending on how hard it is to source that emerald for the top. I'll have to order the stones, but I can do most of the metal work tomorrow so that when the gems arrive, I'm ready to set them. That will take another day."

"That sounds more than reasonable." He'd expected her to say a week. "What's the bad news?"

She glanced at the bottle before answering him. "It's going to be very, *very* expensive."

Imari cringed at those words, even though they confirmed what she'd told Lucien earlier. Her bottle was covered in gold and gems. There was no way around it. Replicating it wasn't going to be cheap. Especially not with that uncut hunk of emerald that adorned the stopper.

And she didn't expect any kind of discount just because she and Willa were friends. The woman had bills to pay just like anyone else.

Lucien didn't react like it was any big deal. "When we're done with the bottle, will you be able to recover any of the materials?"

Willa made a curious face. Half-smile, half sly smirk. "I was thinking, if neither of you mind, I have a few collectors who might be willing to buy a piece like this from me."

Imari nodded quickly. That was a perfect solution. "It's not a real genie bottle, so I'm all right with it. So long as you don't say it's a replica. I don't want anyone else knowing what my bottle looks like."

Willa held her hands up. "No, of course not." She glanced at Lucien. "What do you think? There might even be a profit in it if I can get a little bidding going. Which I think I can."

He looked at Imari before answering. "If Imari is fine with it, I am too."

Imari nodded. "Totally fine."

Willa stuck her hand out to him. "Then it's a deal. Thank you."

Lucien didn't move to return her handshake, and the moment spread toward awkwardness as Imari realized what was happening. Or rather, what *wasn't* going to happen.

She sidestepped toward him, putting herself in front of him, and filled Willa's palm with her own. "That's perfect, Willa. You're so dear to do this. I owe you a lunch when this is all over."

Willa's perplexed gaze shifted from Lucien to Imari. "I'm happy to help a friend, but happy to take you up on that lunch, too. I'll call you if I need anything more, but I should be fine with the pictures and notes I've taken. And I'll keep it *all* safe. You have my word. Hopefully, the next call I make will be to let you know it's done."

"Thank you so much." Imari turned to shoot Lucien a what's-wrong-with-you look, then packed up the bottle in the overnight bag. "We should go and let you get to work."

He nodded. "Yes. Thank you."

She put her hand on his elbow, the bag's strap over her shoulder, and moved him toward the back door.

He stiffened at her touch, but walked forward, stopping only when they reached the door, which almost caused her to run into him. "Let me check outside."

"Okay."

He did the same as he had when they'd left the stairwell, looking in both directions twice. "All clear."

Imari gave Willa a little wave. "Thanks again."

Then she and Lucien left, closing the door behind them. He had his keycard in his hand already and slid it through the reader as soon as they reached the entrance to the Basement. He opened that, let her through first, and down they went.

The golf cart was right where they left it. She climbed in, clutching the bag in her lap. "That went pretty well."

"It did."

She turned to face him, no longer concerned with politeness as much as she was figuring him out. "Except for that weirdness at the end. Why didn't you want to shake Willa's hand? Or pet Jasper?"

"I did pet the cat."

"With a *pen*. That's not really petting."

He looked at her for a long moment, then started the car and drove back toward Insomnia.

She let a minute pass, and when he still hadn't responded, she asked again. "Lucien, what aren't you telling me? What's the big secret? Do you not like to be touched? We've touched." But he'd never taken his gloves off at Illusions, either.

"No, I don't like to be touched."

She sat back, feeling a little like she'd been slapped. She was a massage therapist after all. Touching people was kind of a big thing. And she'd been thinking about offering him a massage as a way of saying thanks.

He was such an odd man. On one hand, he was about to spend a sultan's ransom re-creating her bottle just as a decoy in the hopes of snaring the wish merchant so she could be safe, and on the other, he'd answered her so sharply that it seemed like he'd suddenly become someone else.

How could he be so kind and generous, but so prickly and hard at the same time?

More than that, she sensed he was lying. Maybe not lying, but skirting the truth at least. When they'd kissed, he hadn't seemed to mind being touched despite his sudden declaration to the contrary.

She snuck a look at him. Thunderclouds of unhappiness darkened his face. Whatever was going on inside him must be a torment.

And then something occurred to her. The truth, maybe. He probably loved to be touched. Most people did. That's why they came to her for massage therapy. Touch was healing. It gave comfort. It restored the body and soul. Maybe this wasn't about him being touched, but about him touching others. After all, she'd touched him and she was fine.

But was he? Did contact, in his case, come with a price? If so, what was it?

What power did an angel of death's touch possess? It couldn't actually be death, could it? As far as she knew, angels of death were only message bearers. Unless he'd done something to change that. Was he being punished for something?

That might explain the dark cloud he seemed to live under.

She sat back and stared straight ahead. What could it be? Who could she ask? Not Hattie. Imari didn't want to put her in that kind of situation. There was only one other name that came to mind. The same man who'd helped her find Lucien.

Greyson.

Neither Imari nor Lucien said anything else until they returned to his home. They went in the way they'd left after parking the golf cart in the Basement's garage. Up the elevator, through the hall that skirted Insomnia, down the steps, and back into the odd, beautiful underground mansion.

Hattie called out to them as they got closer to the living room. "Lucy? Imari? Is that you? How did everything go?"

The succulent smell of roasting chicken and all the accompaniments made Imari's mouth water. She'd forgotten about the dinner Hattie had wanted to prepare for her.

With a smile, she called back, "It's us. It went well."

"Good. Dinner is just about ready. Get washed up and come on in."

Imari laughed softly. It had been a long time since anyone had told her to get washed up for dinner.

Lucien didn't seem to notice. Instead, he appeared to still be trapped in a prison of his own making.

Seeing him like that cut Imari to the quick. "Hey," she said, trying to get his attention. "Lucien."

He glanced at her. "What was that?"

"Nothing. I just want you to know that whatever it is that's bothering you, whatever's going on in your head, I hope you can get past it. You're a good man. One of the best I've met. And I've met a lot. You deserve to be happy."

He stared at her, storms rolling through his eyes. "No, I don't."

Her heart broke a little at that answer. "Everyone deserves happiness."

He shook his head and looked away.

"Why don't you?" she pressed. "What have you done that's so awful? Why do you think you deserve misery instead?"

"Because I…" He raised his head. "I just do."

"Dinner's on the table." Hattie's voice sang out, reminding them they were not alone.

Imari wished she knew how to comfort him, but even if she did, she doubted he'd welcome it. She smiled gently. "I disagree with you. Strongly. But I respect your right to feel however you want to feel. Now, we should get to dinner before Hattie comes looking for us."

He nodded and swallowed like he was trying to keep himself from arguing further. "Right. Dinner." He gestured toward the kitchen.

"I'm going to my room first." She lifted the bag in her hand. "Need to put this away."

"Of course."

When she'd done that, she headed for the kitchen. He wasn't there, making her wonder if he'd had enough of her. But he showed up a few minutes later while she was at the sink washing her hands.

He joined her there to do the same.

Hattie was puttering around behind them, setting rolls out and whatever else was necessary.

Imari hadn't been part of a family dinner like this, such as it was, in ages. It felt almost surreal, and yet, it was a very happy feeling. She realized that, for the first time in a long while, she felt truly safe. More than that, she felt like she wasn't alone anymore. It was incredibly comforting. "Everything smells so good, Hattie."

"Thank you. I hope it tastes the same."

"I'm sure it will." Imari reached for a towel. As she turned, she caught a glimpse of a tattoo peeking out from the ribbed cuff of Lucien's sweater. The part of the tattoo she could see looked like the end of a handle. Of what, she had no idea. The ink started a few inches above his wrist.

She looked away before he saw her staring. All the man did was raise more questions in her head. She finished drying her hands, folded the towel, and left it by the sink for him. "What can I do to help, Hattie?"

"Just sit down and eat until you're stuffed."

Imari laughed. "I can do that."

"Red or white wine?"

"Water is fine for me. I don't drink. A lack of inhibitions is a dangerous thing when you have the power of life-changing wishes."

Hattie giggled. "I guess it would be!"

Lucien came to the table and pulled out her chair for her. "But you don't have any wishes left to be dangerous with."

"True," Imari said, feeling very exposed for her lie. Had he said that because he knew? How could he, though? No, it was only because she'd told him she was out of wishes. She was just being paranoid. Although, she was suddenly aware of how close he was. Inches away. Wasn't he afraid of them touching? She made herself smile in a light, casual way. "But old habits die hard."

She took her seat, then he helped Hattie with hers.

As he walked back to his own chair, Hattie spoke. "Carve the chicken, would you, Lucy?"

He frowned at her, probably for the use of his nickname, but picked up the knife and serving fork and did as she asked. He piled their plates with slices of the steaming bird, while Imari and Hattie took turns with the rest of the dishes.

"I can't believe you made all this." Imari shook her head at the feast laid out before her. "What a lot of work you went to."

"I loved every minute of it." Hattie smiled.

"She's an excellent cook," Lucien added, lifting his glass to her. "The best food I've ever eaten. Thank you for this, *Mémé*."

"Yes," Imari said, raising her glass as well. "This is outstanding."

Hattie blushed. "You two are being silly and letting the food get cold. You're welcome. Now eat."

They dug in. Each bite was more delicious than the last, and with the good food came good conversation. Hattie told stories about Lucien as a boy, which Imari found endlessly fascinating. It was hard to picture him as a child, but Hattie's stories were endearing. Especially the one about him wanting to be an archaeologist and how she'd buried pieces of broken pottery in the backyard for him to find.

But Imari noticed that when a story got too personal, Lucien would interrupt with a memory about Hattie. How she'd lived in Paris and served as the muse for two different artists. How she'd had three marriage proposals at once. The time her *coq au vin* had won a local cooking award. He told the stories with a rare smile and loving pride in his eyes.

Imari's heart ached with happiness at how much joy his grandmother brought to his life, but there was another emotion mixed in. Not jealousy exactly, but longing. That someday she might have the same kind of loving, easy relationship with a man that Hattie had with Lucien.

Of course, they were family, but the way they teased each other and laughed and clearly loved each other was so sweet and endearing. Would Imari ever have that? Anything was possible, she supposed.

Unless she was forced to marry Khalid.

They'd been at the table for nearly three hours, but the time had flown. Lucien put his cloth napkin beside his empty plate and sat back. He couldn't remember when he'd had such an enjoyable evening. It made him keenly aware of just how much his isolation had cost him and his grandmother. He regretted that to his core, even if it couldn't be helped. "I am beyond full. This was quite the meal, Mémé. You outdid yourself. Everything was perfect, right down to the dessert."

"Yes," Imari said. "The dessert was spot-on. What a treat that was. Just like my mother used to make. Maybe even a tiny bit better."

"What a nice compliment." Hattie sat back as well, looking pleased with herself. "I'm so glad you both enjoyed it." She sighed rather elaborately and got up from the table. "I guess I should tackle these dishes."

Lucien got to his feet instantly. "You did plenty. I will clean up."

Imari stood, too. "I'll help. It's only fair after all the effort you put in, Hattie."

"Well, now, isn't this a nice surprise?" Her smile was a little coy, telling Lucien that her sigh had been dramatic for this purpose. "I might just go put my feet up and watch one of my stories. But only if you two come in and join me when you're done. I'm not ready for the evening to be over."

Neither was Lucien, but he snorted anyway. "I'm not sure Imari will want to watch *Sword and Scepter* with you."

Imari sucked in a breath. "I love *Sword and Scepter*!"

His brows lifted. "Not you too."

"See?" Hattie said. "I told you it's a popular show."

He took a few plates to the sink. "I don't get the appeal. It's basically a soap opera featuring a made-up royal family in a made-up country, and all they do is cause one drama after another while wearing a lot of fancy clothes and expensive jewelry."

Imari laughed. "For someone who supposedly doesn't *get* the appeal, you just *nailed* the appeal."

Hattie chuckled. "That is pretty much exactly why I watch it." She waved at them as she left. "Well, you kids have fun cleaning up."

"We will," Imari called back. She joined Lucien at the sink with more dishes. "How about I load the dishwasher and clean the table while you pack up the leftovers, since you know where the containers are?"

"Deal."

They went to work without saying anything else. The sound of the television filtered in a moment later, filling the silence. The cleanup became a choreographed dance of sorts, each of them moving through the kitchen with purpose, side-stepping each other so that they passed within inches, never touching, but almost.

For Lucien, the tension seemed palpable. He watched Imari when he could without being obvious. When she'd taken him by the elbow in Willa's shop, she'd been behind him and he'd been unable to enjoy seeing her beautiful face in color.

Now, he wished he could see it again. He moved to the dishwasher where she was putting silverware into the rack, then bent to add the spoon he'd been using to ladle mashed potatoes into a storage container. He deliberately ran his hand into hers. He kept it there a second longer than anyone else would have, just to see her face as she looked at him.

So beautiful. He tried to imprint the moment in his mind, like a photograph he could call up later. Then he moved his hand. "Sorry."

But he wasn't, of course.

Her eyes lit up, something he didn't need color to see. She straightened. "You got mashed potatoes on my knuckles."

He pressed the tip of his tongue into his teeth to keep from laughing as he stood up. "Did I?"

"Mm-hmm." She held his gaze while lifting her hand to her mouth. Then she flicked her eyes down and licked the mashed potatoes off.

His throat closed at the sight of her tongue. He put his hand on the counter to make sure he stayed upright. There was one thought in his head. One single, stupid, impossible thought. He *wanted* Imari.

He wanted her here. With him. In his life. At his dinner table. He wanted her to pester him with questions. He wanted to smell her perfume in this house all the time. To hear her laugh. And sigh. And gasp.

He wanted to tell her everything.

But most of all, he wanted the impossible. He wanted her to love him.

Because he had no doubt that with a woman like her by his side, the wretchedness of his life would lose its impact. After all, he could touch her without reaping her soul. For whatever reason, it was true. They'd touched enough times for it not to be a fluke.

And Hattie already loved her. Thankfully, Imari seemed to genuinely like Hattie as well.

Imari tipped her head. "You're giving me an odd look. Is licking mashed potatoes off one's hand a breach of angel-of-death etiquette?"

"No," he whispered. He turned to the counter and stared at the food container. "I was just lost in thought is all." Foolish thoughts. The kinds of thoughts that could get him into a trouble there was no returning from.

"You do that a lot."

He shoved those thoughts down. "Do I?"

"Yes. What were you thinking about?"

The urge to unburden himself was overwhelming,

141

but the desire to keep her safe won. "Nothing." He took the container to the refrigerator.

She snorted softly. "You're a terrible liar."

He put the mashed potatoes away, shut the fridge, and turned to look at her. She was bent, putting a lid into the dishwasher. The overwhelming urge returned. He fought it once again. "You shouldn't like me."

She closed the dishwasher and looked at him, frowning. "What?"

"Do you like me?"

"Is this third grade?"

"Do. You. Like. Me?"

"Yes, I do." She leaned against the kitchen counter. "Very much. You're a conundrum for sure, but you've been so kind and generous to me. You opened your home to me. You saved my life. And you're helping me eliminate my wish merchant problem. How could anyone not like a person who did all that for them?"

He wanted to grab her and kiss her, then shake some sense into her. He took a step toward her, but it was only so he was closer to the exit. "When this is over, you should forget about me."

She moved into his path. "That's not going to happen."

"Then you're not as smart as you look." He tried to go by her, but she moved again, blocking him.

She crossed her arms, dark sparks flashing in her eyes. He'd made her angry. Good. Angry would keep her safe. From him. "That's not a very nice thing to say."

Two, maybe three inches was all that separated them. "I'm not a very nice man."

"You're lying again." She looked up at him, tilting her head inquisitively. "Do you like me?"

He ground his teeth together. It was so much harder not to kiss her when all it would require is a slight bend forward. "No."

"Then you don't want to kiss me?"

He reared back slightly, swallowing hard. "N-no."

She leaned in. "I think you do."

He glared at her, hands fisted, head and heart at war. What was wrong with this woman?

Her hands went to her hips. "Well?"

"Fine." He bent forward and captured her mouth with his. Fireworks went off behind his closed lids, fireworks that mimicked all the colors in her apartment. He threaded his fingers into the silk of her curls and took hold of her head so he could tip her face toward him even more.

A soft little half-moan left her throat, and she moved closer to him.

Every inch of him turned into starlight and atmosphere. He was lost in the galaxy of Imari, blinded by her brilliance, and running out of air. He could die this way and find peace. But there was life in her, warm, pulsing, undeniable life.

His want for her grew. Except, as the kiss deepened, and she pressed into him, with those soft mews of pleasure filling his ears, he realized it wasn't a want so much as a need. This woman made him feel alive again.

Him. Death's merchant. The reaper of souls. A War Angel.

She was a miracle.

And she would run from him as soon as she realized what he was.

He broke the kiss, pulling away sharply, but not before he caught one last glimpse of her in all her colorful glory. Her cheeks were flushed and her lids heavy. She was panting a little. And her lips were red and ripe and he wanted to kiss her again.

And again.

"What are you doing to me?" she whispered. She put her hand to her throat as if feeling the thrum of her pulse. "You tell me to forget about you? That you're not a very nice man and that you don't want to kiss me? Then you do and I can't remember my name."

"I…" But he had no reason, no excuse.

She took a step back. "Lucien, if you don't tell me what in the name of Hades is going on with you right now, I am leaving."

"You don't mean that."

She lifted her chin and looked him square in the eyes. "I have never meant anything more in my life."

"I can't."

"Why?"

"You'll leave." Or worse.

"I'm already going to leave, so you have nothing to lose."

But she did. He closed his eyes briefly. He didn't consider himself a weak man. Except around her. He exhaled slowly. "I am…*not* the angel of death."

He couldn't look at her, but he could feel her eyes on him. "Then who are you?"

"Perhaps we should discuss this in my—"

"Who are you, Lucien?" Her voice was soft and reassuring.

Not the tone he'd been expecting. He raised his gaze to her. There was no going back. "I am a grim reaper."

For a moment, fear glinted in her eyes. Then she laughed. "Come on."

He shook his head. "No, that's what I am. Who I am."

She hesitated. No doubt thinking that through. "So you're not just death's messenger…"

"No. I am a reaper of souls."

She took a breath, setting her shoulders back like she was making herself come to terms with that information a little faster than she might have under different circumstances. "Okay, then that's what you are. No big deal."

"Except…" He sighed. He had to tell her the whole truth. "My powers haven't been reliable in many, many years."

She shrugged. "So you're retired. Who cares? You have a pretty great life. You've got all those snazzy cars, this great house, your nightclub is super popular, and you have your grandmother with you. I don't know why you're so glum."

"I am *dangerous*."

More hesitation. "In what way? How unreliable are your powers?"

"Very." He glanced toward the living room where the sound of the television suddenly seemed louder.

Imari's lips parted as she watched his eyes. "Are you saying…Hattie?"

He nodded. "Yes." It was good to tell her the truth, to have it out there. But that was all that was good about this.

Imari swallowed hard. "You killed your grandmother."

It wasn't a question. "I reaped her soul. Accidentally. I was able to get it back, but her life was forfeit. She can only exist in her current state."

"How did you accidentally reap her soul?" Imari's tone wasn't quite so soft and reassuring now.

He braced himself. "By touching her."

Imari's eyes widened. "*That's* what's wrong with you? That's why you didn't want to touch me? Or be touched? Wait, why have we touched at all?" She rubbed the spot between her eyes. "Okay, I need to calm down. Nothing's happened to me. I'm fine."

She was talking to herself, it seemed, but he had to say something. "Yes. Thankfully."

She glared at him. "Thankfully? Don't you think you should have mentioned this earlier?"

"Yes."

Her mouth thinned to a hard, firm line. "I should punch you. But violence is not the answer. Although I think it would make me feel better. But that *would be touching you*."

She was angry, but she wasn't leaving. That gave him hope he had no right to. It also lightened his mood considerably. "If you think it would help, I'm willing to endure it. Especially if it would make you feel better."

Her glare sharpened. "Don't be cute."

He almost laughed. "I'm not capable of that."

She shook her head slowly. "Still lying, I see."

Could he have killed her? Imari wasn't sure. She was immortal, after all, but this wasn't some standard mortal way of dying, like having a fatal illness or being in a car accident or falling over a cliff.

This was a real, live grim reaper she was dealing with. His job was collecting souls. And she had one of those.

But they'd touched now more times than she could count, and she hadn't felt the slightest hint of her final destination looming in front of her. Not a single day of her very long life had flashed before her eyes.

That didn't mean she wasn't angry. She was. And she did *kind* of want to punch him. But kissing him was much more enjoyable. And it was easy to see by the conflict on his face that confessing this truth to her had cost him dearly.

What kind of response he'd expected, she wasn't sure, but it hadn't been a good one. That alone explained so much about him. The pain in his eyes.

The torment that seemed to rock him constantly. The seeming need to isolate himself.

But then he'd accidentally taken his grandmother's soul. Imari couldn't imagine how she'd go on if she'd been the cause of a loved one's demise.

Even more painful, Hattie lived with him. No doubt having her close was a comfort, but it was also a constant reminder of what he'd done to her.

Imari's heart broke for Lucien. For this burden he carried. The weight of it must be crushing him, she thought. No wonder he was afraid to touch and be touched. That he never left the house. And yet somehow, he'd found the courage to not only do all he'd done for her, but to share this burden with her.

She could very easily love a man like this. She might already, just a little.

Instinct drove her forward. She embraced him, pulling him against her. "I'm so sorry for all you've been through."

He sucked in a breath and stiffened, his voice thick and cracking when he spoke. "You still want to touch me?"

She pulled back enough to see his face. "I'm still alive, aren't I?"

"But—"

"But nothing. I'm immortal. All jinn are." The mood needed lightening. And he needed to know all was not doomed. She lifted one shoulder and gave him a mischievous look. "Your powers clearly aren't broken enough to do me in."

But his expression shifted to one of dismay. "This

isn't something to make light of. If I were to harm you, I could never forgive myself."

"You can't hurt me."

"You don't know that."

She stepped back, then took his hands and placed them on her face. "Look. You're touching me and I'm not dying."

"This isn't a joke." He tried to pull away, but she held his hands there.

"No, it's not."

He shook his head, the odd look in his eyes unreadable. "You don't know what this does to me."

"Then tell me."

He swallowed. "When we touch, I can see color again."

A new wash of shocked revelation swept through her. "What do you mean *again*?"

Another sigh left him before he spoke. "My color vision was taken from me when I became a reaper."

She grimaced. "Are you serious? No color? None?"

"Just black, white, and shades of gray."

"That's awful. That's unlivable. How could they do that to you? Color is everything. Color is the world around us. It's emotion. It's beauty and joy and happiness. It's life."

"That's how. Because it's life. And life was not my job." His hands relaxed to cup her face. "I was assigned to a division known as the War Angels. Our job was to patrol the battlefields of the world, reaping the souls of the soldier and civilian casualties. Being unable to see color, specifically the color red, was supposed to make our job easier to bear."

She layered her hands over his. "I cannot imagine how hard that was."

"I'm glad you don't have to." He leaned in ever so slowly and put his forehead to hers. "I can't believe I can touch you. It's been so long…"

Since he'd touched anyone. She understood that's what he was saying, but it didn't detract from the specialness of the moment.

Then he pressed his lips to the same spot. "I'm so glad it's you."

She smiled. All was forgiven in that instant. How could she not after all he'd done for her? "Hey," she said softly. "As reluctant as I am to end this moment, we should go out and sit with Hattie or she's going to come in here looking for us."

He chuckled. "That she will."

They went out to the living room. Hattie was hovering in her chair, engrossed in her show, but she materialized to tap the pause button. "Bigger job than I thought, apparently. You missed the whole opening."

"We'll catch up," Imari said. She waited to see where Lucien would sit. He took a spot at the end of the couch. Good. She sat in the middle.

Hattie pressed play, and as the show started up again, Imari coasted her hand across the space separating her and Lucien and curled her pinky over his.

He glanced at her, a little surprise in his gaze.

"It's a very colorful show," she whispered. "You'll see."

Understanding filled his eyes, and he smiled.

That smile melted parts of her. It was dazzling and warm and made her breath catch in her throat. She smiled back without trying.

Had he always been so handsome? Maybe it was knowing what he'd been through and understanding the weight of what he was carrying that made her see him in this new light. Whatever the reason, she was content to be at his side, fingers interlaced, doing nothing more than watching television with his grandmother. The grim reaper, the genie, and the ghost. What a trio they were.

It wasn't anything she'd ever thought she'd be doing, this kind of domesticated scene, but it was peaceful and comfortable and gave her a happiness inside unlike anything she'd ever felt before.

Was this what married life could be like?

She'd balked at marriage since her arranged betrothal, but then, that future had always included Khalid. It still did, and she still didn't want it. But this? This was different.

This was good.

So were the next day and a half.

While they waited for Willa to complete the bottle, she and Lucien (and often Hattie) enjoyed life. They watched movies in the theater room, played billiards and cards, lounged and read in the library, cooked, ate, and laughed.

On the second day after breakfast, Lucien and

Imari swam in the pool that was indeed on the lower level. And what a pool it was. There was a slide, a grotto, fountains, and a video screen system that covered the walls and ceiling, making it seem like they were outdoors on a sunny day beneath a brilliant blue sky. The space was as large as the garage and filled with a variety of palms and exotic flowers that were thriving under sunlamps. The ambient sounds of a gentle breeze and tropical birds completed the feeling of being somewhere far away.

And just for fun, an enormous inflatable swan bobbed in the center of the pool.

Hattie had waved them off, claiming she had errands to run, so Imari and Lucien were left to lounge and swim on their own.

And get a really good look at each other in their bathing suits.

Lucien's trunks, no surprise, were charcoal gray with a few black stripes down one side. The trunks hung low on his hips, showing off his trim, muscled body. He was, in a word, mouthwatering. The tattoo she'd spied peeking out from his sleeve turned out to be a scythe. Which made sense, given what she knew about him now.

One of the suits that had shown up in Imari's pile of things was a bright blue floral. The other was a softer turquoise with splashes of hot pink. She chose the bright blue bikini, and as she dropped her robe onto one of the chaises set around the pool's edge, a rare emotion swept through her.

Shyness.

How odd.

Lucien's eyes were on her. Just like hers were on him. The muscles in his stomach tightened, and he shoved a hand through his hair. "That suit looks good on you."

His voice was low and gravelly and drew a finger of pleasure down her spine. She shivered from it. "Thanks."

"Cold? I can adjust the temperature."

"No, just…feeling a little exposed." She laughed softly. Nervously. How odd to be this old and this experienced and yet suddenly feel like an unchaperoned teenager.

He turned away, a little smile on his face. "Get in when you're ready." Then he took three long steps and dove into the pool, cleanly slicing through the water with one easy, graceful motion.

He surfaced several yards away and turned. "The water is fantastic, in case you were wondering."

"Good to know." She had no reason to be shy. The suit looked good on her. Lucien had said so. Or he was just being kind, but seeing as how he couldn't stop staring, she believed him. He wasn't so hard to look at either.

She was being silly. She put her shoulders back, walked to the edge, and dove in after him. She had to swim a little to meet him since he was halfway to the swan now. "The water feels amazing. I can't believe you have a pool like this."

"I don't use it as much as I should." He glanced toward the giant inflatable. "Race you to the swan."

"Okay." She took off without waiting for him to say go. It was the only chance she had, but he beat her handily. She liked that he hadn't let her win.

He hoisted himself onto the inflatable, making it wobble, then offered her a hand as she approached. She took it, letting him pull her aboard. He held on to her hand and looked around. "Wow, the colors are really something."

"Have you ever seen this room in color?"

"Never. None of my house. Except for what I've seen when you've been touching me." He lay back to stare up at the projected blue sky, tugging her back with him.

She glanced at him. Their fingers were still entwined, but they were touching at the shoulders and hips too. It was nice. Very nice. She went back to looking at the ceiling sky. The moment was so surreal she had to say something. "You realize you're a grim reaper, I'm a genie, and we're lying on a giant inflatable swan that's floating on a pool two stories underground and yet we're staring up at a sunny, blue sky."

"Three stories. Insomnia, then the house." He snorted. "I guess it is kind of odd, though. But it's one of the best mornings I've had in a long time." He turned to look at her. "Thank you."

"You're welcome." She smiled at him. "And thank you. You've done so much for me. You know, you should let me give you a massage. I'm really good at it, and I think it would do you a world of good."

He propped himself up on one elbow. "How about now?"

"We'd have to get off the swan. I need to work on a stable surface."

He lay back down. "Later, then. I'm too happy to move at the moment."

That suited her just fine.

A few moments of quiet passed, the sounds of the lapping water and the feel of the manufactured sun sending Imari into a blissful state. Holding hands with Lucien didn't hurt either.

"The sting is all set, by the way."

It took her a second to realize he meant the plan to catch the wish merchant. "Is that what you were working on yesterday morning?"

"Yes."

She was almost afraid to ask the next question. "What's my role in it?"

"Nothing. You don't need to be there, nor should you. It's too dangerous anyway. I'm not even going to be there."

She leaned up on one elbow to look at him. "You're not?"

He shook his head. "No. The wish merchant knows me. Too much chance he'd figure out it's a setup and ruin the whole thing. And after our last *meeting* in your apartment, he knows his genie can't control me."

She hadn't asked him for the details of that evening, but that conversation was coming. "Who's doing it, then?"

"Greyson."

"You're going to end up owing him another favor."

Lucien frowned. "Don't remind me."

She poked him in the chest. "Hey, the first one didn't turn out too bad."

He caught her hand and kissed her fingers. "No, it didn't."

Hattie suddenly appeared above them. "Lucien!"

Imari jerked back, so startled by seeing a woman hovering over her that she fell off the side of the inflatable. Lucien's now unbalanced weight caused the swan to tip over and pitch him into the water as well.

He bobbed to the surface, spitting out water. "Hattie, what on earth is going on?"

Imari grabbed hold of the swan, which had righted itself. "Are you okay?"

Hattie nodded. "I'm fine, but there's trouble. Big trouble. Willa just called. Her shop was broken into and the bottle's gone."

Lucien stormed into the kitchen, dressed in a suit, but still buttoning the cuffs of his shirt. He hadn't taken the time to dry his hair, either. He barely managed to get dressed with all the anger that was coursing through him. "I'm going down there."

Imari and Hattie looked up at him from the table. Imari was in her robe and swimsuit, her wet hair piled on top of her head. Worry bracketed her eyes.

Hattie shook her head and spoke first. "Do you think that's wise?"

"Yes, I do. I need to know for sure whether or not the wish merchant was involved in this."

"What if he was, and he's watching the scene? He might see you," Imari said. She was clenching a cloth napkin in her hands so tightly that her knuckles were lighter than the rest of her. An untouched cup of tea sat before her. Her deep anxiety over this was clear.

They were all upset by it, but this had definitely

unsettled her to a much greater degree. Of course, she had a lot more at stake.

"I'm okay with him seeing me," Lucien answered. "If he was involved in this, and I have no doubt he was, then he needs to know I'm *still* involved in this. That should give him some pause."

Imari made a face. "But he might follow you back here."

"I won't let that happen. I'll come home through the Basement if need be."

She nodded, but there was no confidence in her posture. She slumped like she was defeated. She let go of the napkin to rub her hand over her mouth.

Lucien narrowed his eyes. She was far too worried about a replica. "Why are you so concerned about a bottle that isn't even the real one?"

She squeezed her eyes shut and sighed before answering him. "Because it wasn't just a replica."

"What are you talking about? The real bottle is in your room. Isn't it?"

"The bottle is. But not the stopper."

That set off a small alarm. "Explain."

"Willa wasn't sure about matching the stopper. It's a very unique emerald crystal. So I offered to let her keep it to make comparisons easier. Just until the bottle was ready, of course."

"I don't remember any of this. When did this happen?"

"When you were playing with the cat."

Hattie's brows shot up. "You were playing with a cat?"

He groaned. "No, not really, but I was distracted by one. Imari, what does it mean if the stopper has been taken?"

She swallowed. "It means the wish merchant might be able to use it to track me. Or rather, his genie will be able to. And it won't really be tracking me, but my bottle."

"Then I need to leave now and find out what his involvement in this was." He searched for reassuring words, but comfort wasn't his currency. "I'll be back as soon as I can."

Imari nodded. "Okay."

"I'm sure it'll all be fine." That was the best he could do at the moment, except he wasn't sure at all. "You're very safe here."

Imari gave him a tentative smile. "Good. Because I feel safe here."

He sent Hattie a look, cutting his eyes from her to Imari and hoping she understood that he wanted her to distract the genie while he was out.

Hattie gave him a subtle nod. "Imari, do you think you could help me with one of my projects in the craft room? You have such an eye for color."

Lucien headed for the garage. He took Hattie's Range Rover again for its ability to be incognito. He'd considered going the Basement route, but he wasn't sure if he'd be coming straight home. If any possibility existed that he might have an opportunity to confront the wish merchant, he was going to act upon it.

When he arrived at Willa's, the only indication

that anything had happened was the sheriff's car parked out front.

Lucien knew Sheriff Merrow somewhat. Insomnia did its own policing, but the sheriff was kind enough to send a patrol car through the lot every night anyway. For that, Lucien made a generous contribution to the First Responders Benevolence Fund each year.

He parked, got out, and headed into the shop.

Willa and the sheriff were in the back office, the open door the only way he spotted them. One of her employees greeted him. "Can I help you find something, sir?"

"I'm here to see Willa."

At the sound of her name, she leaned forward and waved him back.

As he came around the counter and entered the office, she frowned. "I'm so sorry about this."

"It's not your fault." He gave the sheriff a nod of greeting. "Sheriff."

The sheriff nodded back. "Dupree."

Lucien spoke to Willa again. "What happened?"

"I don't really know." She glanced around. "Nothing was broken. Nothing was damaged. I opened up like normal this morning, no idea anything was wrong, went to get the bottle out of the safe to work on it, and it was gone."

Lucien looked at the sheriff. "No signs of forced entry?"

"None," he grunted.

"The alarm wasn't bothered either," Willa added.

"It wasn't tripped or turned off. I checked the log. I was the first one to punch the code in since last night."

He caught her gaze. "What about the *other* part of the bottle?"

Her brows pulled together in a sympathetic expression. "Also gone. I'm so sorry."

Lucien let out a curse. "If that's all that was taken, then this had to be the wish merchant."

"Who's that?" the sheriff asked.

Lucien filled him in.

He took notes, nodding. "He has to be staying in town."

Lucien snorted. "Good luck finding a man with no name."

The sheriff almost smiled. "You'd be surprised what my aunt can do. We'll check for prints here, too."

"There won't be any. Not if the wish merchant is behind this."

The sheriff made a face. "How do you know?"

"Because he uses magic." Lucien turned back to Willa. "Do you mind if I have a look at the safe?"

"Sure." She took him over to it, the sheriff following. The door was still ajar.

Lucien looked over his shoulder at the sheriff. "I need to touch this."

"You keeping the gloves on?" the sheriff asked.

"Yes."

"Fine."

"Willa, where was the bottle and the stopper?"

She pointed to an empty space on the top shelf. "Right there."

Lucien reached in and drew his finger along the shelf, then held it up to the light. Fine black particles sparkled back at him. "Glitter. This was the wish merchant all right."

Willa let out an amused sound. "The wish merchant leaves behind a glitter trail?"

"No," Lucien said. "The genie he's enslaved does."

Imari appreciated Hattie's attempt to occupy her, and working on the shadow boxes had been fun, but she couldn't stop thinking about the wish merchant. If he had the stopper, he could get his genie to track her. It wouldn't be easy. Jinn magic was slow and unreliable when used against other jinn, but with enough patience and determination, it would work.

He would find her. And he would enslave her too.

Unless… She shook her head.

"What is it, dear?" Hattie asked.

"Nothing." She picked up a glue stick. "Just thinking."

Hattie's smile was warm and understanding. "It'll be okay."

"I hope so."

A door slammed deeper in the house. They both jumped off their stools and turned to look.

"Lucien?" Hattie called out.

He appeared seconds later at the door to the craft room, his eyes on Imari.

She almost didn't want to ask, but she had to know. "The stopper?"

"Gone."

She closed her eyes and sat down, the sinking feeling in her belly nearly undoing her. "He'll find me. It's just a matter of time now."

"There has to be another way," Lucien said. "Give me the bottle. I know you don't want anyone else to have possession of it, but you know I won't use it against you."

"It won't work." She looked up at him. Her world was crumbling. This would be how it ended. She couldn't even go back into the bottle and return home. Not without the stopper. "The bottle is incomplete. I'm such a fool. I never should have given Willa that piece."

Hattie clucked her tongue. "Now, now. You had no way of knowing what was going to happen."

"Doesn't matter. I'm still a fool. I just…I felt so safe here. I got complacent."

Lucien came into the room and took her by the shoulders. "Is there any other way you can think of that would make you safe from him?"

She stared at him, the grim reaper, the best man she'd ever known, and wanted to laugh. The only way he could save her would destroy the life she'd known up to this point. It would ruin whatever this was that had begun between them. It would turn her family against her. Make her an outcast among her own kind.

She couldn't bring herself to say the words.

"Tell me," Lucien said softly. "Whatever it is, we'll do it. I'll do it. I will not let that man touch you."

She shook her head and tried not to weep. "There is one way."

His eyes brightened, and he gave her shoulders a little squeeze of encouragement. "What is it?"

She swallowed and tried to form the words. "You have to marry me."

Lucien wasn't sure how much time passed as he stood without moving or speaking, but it was long enough that Hattie became corporeal and swatted him on the arm, causing him to let go of Imari.

"Answer the woman, child."

He blinked and frowned at his grandmother. "Mémé, you know how I feel about marriage. How things went the last time."

Imari leaned back. "You were married once already? Not that it matters, this would be in name only, obviously."

"Yes, I was married before," he muttered. "And it didn't work out. She and I were...not compatible."

"Is that the Kora I've heard you speak of?"

"No," Hattie answered, giving him a sharp look. "Kora is his daughter."

Imari's mouth fell open in shock. "You have a child?"

"She's an adult, but yes. Now back to you." They

could talk about Kora later. Imari needed help. "This marriage, how long would it have to last?"

"Just until the wish merchant is dealt with."

He thought about that. Without the bottle to lure the man in, Lucien wasn't sure how they'd catch him. It could take some time until they devised a new plan. "Do you think he'd eventually get bored and leave?"

She nodded. "It could happen. That doesn't solve the problem of the genie he's already snared, though."

"No, it doesn't. She needs to be rescued. And he needs to be stopped." But that didn't give Lucien an end date for this marriage of convenience either. "You would have to live here, I suppose."

Hattie rolled her eyes. "Like she's already doing?"

He started pacing. "Yes, true."

Imari exhaled softly. "If you don't want to do it, that's okay, I understand. It's not like marrying you is side-effect free for me either."

He twisted to look at her, the words cutting deep as they sank in. No wonder she'd been so reluctant to tell him about this option. She didn't want to marry him. And why would she? Why would any woman? "I am aware that I am not the most desirable man, but I promise you, I would not expect you to fulfill any *traditional* marriage requirements."

She gave him an odd, blank look for a second, then her eyes widened. "Are you talking about sex?"

Hattie let out a little squeal, then slapped her hand over her mouth to stop the giggling. Lucien and Imari frowned at her. She held up her hands and floated a few feet higher. "I'm an adult. I've had sex, you know, so you can carry on."

Imari shook her head. "Lucien, I'm not talking about that at all. I'm not talking about your desirability, which I find pretty off the charts, frankly. I'm talking about...what being married means to me. The effect it will have on me."

He wanted to hear more about his desirability, but that could come after she was done explaining. "What effect is that?"

"My family won't approve."

"Because I'm not jinn?"

"Because you aren't the man I've been promised to." She let out a soft groan. "Marrying you, even if it's to protect me, will be seen as me breaking my betrothal. Which will make me a pariah. I'll most likely be cast out of my family, and probably won't be able to return home again."

"That's not good at all." He crossed his arms, suddenly seeing things in a new light. "But if we could put a pin in all that for a moment, if you're already betrothed, why have you been kissing me?"

Hattie clapped her hands, which didn't sound like much, as she was in ghost form. "You two have been kissing?"

"Later," they both said in unison.

Imari sighed. "I was promised to Khalid before I was born. Before I was named. It was a contract between his family and mine, and I just happened to be the firstborn female child. And the only one, as it happens. I have no desire to marry him. And I certainly don't love him. I've only met him once. And while I'm sure he's not the worst jinn to walk the Chaos Realm, we've never even spoken to each other, outside of the traditional greeting. You and I have had more meaningful interaction this week than he and I have had in the thousand-plus years we've been promised."

Lucien understood having your life designed for you. Being a reaper was that exact kind of life. But for the most part, he had derived a certain satisfaction from his job. Imari, on the other hand, would have no satisfaction from marrying a man she did not love. "Can't you just tell him you don't want to marry him?"

She barked out a laugh. "It doesn't work like that in jinn culture. This marriage contract is a serious thing. Trying to get out of it means Khalid would be gravely dishonored. As would my parents. Then they would be forced to disown me. I would no longer be welcome in my childhood home or my land of birth." She looked down at her hands. "And I would lose my ability to regenerate my wishes."

"I thought you were retired because you were out of wishes."

She stared at her hands a while longer. "That isn't the complete truth." She was silent for a moment. Like she was gathering her courage. "I have one wish left."

"Like a safety net," Hattie said.

"Yes," Imari answered. "But it's more than that. It's my security. To replenish my wishes, I either have

169

to go back into my bottle, which will return me home. Or use my last wish, which will return me home by sunrise of the next day." She opened her mouth as if to say more, then shut it again.

Lucien had an idea where this was headed, but had to know for sure. "Why don't you want to do that?"

She ran her hands through her hair. "Because when I go home, out of wishes, I will be forced to marry Khalid."

"So if the wish merchant catches you…"

"He will either demand I go into my bottle, or demand me to grant him a wish, which will be my last. Either way, I will then return home and be forced to marry Khalid."

"But the wish merchant will still have your bottle. Won't he still be able to command your magic?"

"Not when I'm married. Jinn magic is old and archaic and bound by the kind of rules few follow anymore."

Lucien nodded. "Then you either end up belonging to the wish merchant, or a man you do not love."

"Yes."

Hattie made sad noises. "You poor dear."

Lucien agreed. Imari was trapped between the proverbial rock and a hard place. "Is there no way to go home and avoid Khalid? To just get more wishes and leave?"

She stared at Lucien, her gaze filled with anger that obviously wasn't directed at him. "Not when

Khalid is the captain of the guards who patrol the Well of Wishes."

"I see."

She threw her hands up. "It doesn't matter anyway now. I can't use the bottle for anything without the stopper. It has to be complete."

"It will be. We'll get the stopper back. But before that happens, we have a very quick wedding to plan."

Hattie let out another squeal as Imari met his eyes. "So you'll do it?"

He held out his hand to her while at the same time finding it impossible to believe what he was about to do. "Imari Zephara, will you temporarily marry me?"

For all his desire to be left alone, Lucien was either very well-connected, or very well-respected. Or perhaps, Imari thought, her groom to be was a little of both. Because in less than two hours, they were assembled in the Basement with a justice of the peace in front of them.

Hattie and Birdie were witnesses. Hattie had graciously offered her own wedding ring for the ceremony, and Birdie had somehow come up with a simple white bridal gown for Imari to wear.

There was even a small bouquet of lavender roses that had shown up, no doubt from Marigold Williams, owner of the Enchanted Garden flower shop in town, and a friend of Imari's. How many people had Birdie told, she wondered? Hopefully not too many since this was temporary.

Lucien was still in his suit, hair dried now, and looking…willing, but a little uncomfortable.

Imari understood. He'd already had a bad experience with marriage, now he was doing it again for reasons that had nothing to do with his future and everything to do with hers. He had every right to feel some apprehension, but she hoped that he didn't think she was using him.

Even if she kind of was.

But what choice did she have? And he *had* offered. She vowed right then and there to be the best temporary wife she could be. Although, if she let herself be honest, she wasn't fond of the word *temporary*.

At least not with Lucien. She would very much like to have him as part of her life for always.

He didn't seem to want that. She understood. He liked his privacy and being alone. His living situation was proof of that. She wasn't going to argue. He'd done so much for her already that he deserved to have whatever ending to this that he wanted, which was probably going to be a quick annulment.

She smiled, despite the feelings inside her, because this was supposed to be a happy occasion. Even if it was a short-term arrangement.

Hattie was beaming. She didn't seem to care that it wasn't the real till-death-do-us-part event.

The justice of the peace spoke his lines, Lucien and Imari answered, and before she knew it, Lucien had kissed her—a fleeting press of his mouth to hers—and they were husband and wife.

Just like that.

Birdie hugged her. "Congratulations. I know it's not really the real thing, but still seems like congratulations is in order. Now if you'll excuse me, I best get back to the station and back to tracking that wish merchant down. No luck yet, but I'm bound to turn up something."

"I hope you do," Imari said. Even so, she knew he was probably using the genie's magic to cover his tracks. "Thank you for being our witness."

"Of course." She looked at Hattie. "Let's do lunch next week."

Hattie nodded, still smiling like she'd won something. "That would be lovely, Birdie. Call me and we'll set it up."

Birdie left with a wave and Hattie came to hover beside Imari. "You really are a lovely bride."

"Thank you."

The justice of the peace collected his fee from Lucien and left, and then the three of them were alone again.

Imari clutched her bouquet. "That was fast."

"It did the job." Lucien gestured toward the elevator that would take them back to the house.

Hattie rolled her eyes. "You're so romantic, Lucy. I don't know how your first marriage failed."

"Mémé." His sharp tone matched his look. "I had nothing to do with my marriage failing, and you know it."

She pursed her lips. "Yes, I do know it, and I'm sorry. But don't be so gruff. You just got married. It's not like you were forced to walk over glass or something."

She floated by him and into the waiting elevator.

He caught Imari's gaze. "I'm sorry if I was gruff. I'm just eager to get back to figuring out how to solve the wish merchant problem."

She smiled indulgently. "I know. Don't worry about it. I'm very aware that this is just a marriage in name only."

"Yes, well..." He seemed at a loss for words. "We should—"

"I know, get back to work." The sooner he could get her out of his house. She headed for the elevator.

He caught her hand. "No, I was going to say we should still celebrate."

She blinked at him. "You were?"

"It's not every day a person gets married, for whatever reason. So yes, we should do something to mark the day."

"Okay." There was no need to force a smile this time. "What would you like to do?"

"I'm going to leave that up to you, Mrs. Dupree."

At the sound of her married name, an unexpected laugh bubbled up out of her. "All right, then. I'd like to go on a date. It doesn't have to be anything fancy. Do you think we can do that safely?"

"In public?"

"That is where most dates happen."

"I don't think that's wise."

He was right. "No, of course not. I guess I just got caught up in the moment. It wouldn't do to be out and about with the wish merchant trying to find me. Not when he probably already has his genie using her magic to home in on me."

"I'm sorry."

She nodded, but the sinking feeling in her stomach made it impossible to smile. "What I wouldn't give to just sit in a park for a while."

"I doubt he'll be looking for you in a park, but I still don't think it would be safe right now."

Hattie whistled at them. "Are you two getting on this thing or what? I have dough in the proofer."

They both laughed. Lucien answered. "Coming, Mémé."

He took Imari's hand as they walked onto the elevator. "Say, do you have any theories about how the wish merchant found out about the bottle Willa was making?"

"Yes. He most likely had the genie under his control cast a fortune-hunter spell. It's pretty common. Genies use it to locate the kinds of raw valuables a lot of humans wish for. A spell like that alerts the genie whenever quantities of the item they're seeking shows up in one spot."

He frowned. "Then how have they not already used that spell to find you?"

"They probably did. Adira probably searched for glass, precious metals, and gems, and ended up honing in on your home, but since the wish merchant had been to Insomnia he had to have dismissed it."

"Because a nightclub has a lot of glass in the form of mirrors." Lucien tapped the button to close the doors.

"Right. And when it's full, which Insomnia often is, the patrons have a lot of precious metals and gems on them."

"I see. Interesting. I'm glad to hear my home is such a safe haven for you."

She was too. "There are a lot of false positives with a fortune-hunter spell. I'm sure they're checking all the places that come up, but in a town like this, that's going to take some doing. In fact, I bet they'd already been to Willa's once before."

"What would it take to really get the attention of a spell like that? Like make a blip that would outshine all other possibilities."

"Large, and I'm talking *large*, quantities of the thing being searched for. It's easier to find a bar of gold than it is a nugget. Make sense?"

"Absolutely."

Hattie chimed in. "The biggest collection of gems and precious metals is probably at Elenora's house."

Imari looked at her. "Elenora Ellingham?"

Hattie nodded as the elevator started to move. "The woman loves her sparkly bits. Just ask Birdie. She always tells me when Elenora gets a new piece."

Imari smirked. "How does Birdie know?"

Hattie grinned. "Birdie knows everything."

Lucien rubbed his hands together. "This gives me an idea."

Imari glanced at him. "The wish merchant isn't likely to be fooled by a replica anymore."

The elevator doors opened, and they all stepped out.

"I wasn't thinking about a replica," Lucien answered. "But rather, a pile of jewels so over the top that his genie won't be able to ignore it."

"It would have to be really something. In fact, I'm not sure anything outside of my actual bottle would do the trick."

"What if it was your bottle *and* a pile of jewels?"

Imari bit her lip. "I don't love the idea of including my bottle, but it might be the only way to draw him out."

"We can work it so that your bottle is never at risk."

Hattie hmphed. "You'd better. I don't want any trouble coming to my granddaughter-in-law."

"Yes, Mémé." He met Imari's eyes again. "Give me a little time to put this together, but I promise the kernel of a plan is taking shape."

"I'm willing to do just about anything at this point. I have to have that stopper back."

He nodded. "We'll get it." He squeezed her hand. "Whatever it takes, you're going to be free. You deserve to live the kind of life you wanted. One of us should, and it might as well be you."

Lucien didn't like owing anyone anything, but these favors were for Imari's safety. Her life. Her freedom. And really, it wasn't just for her, but also for the genie the wish merchant had already captured. Adira deserved her freedom just as much. Those two reasons were more than enough for him to change his ways.

Besides, Imari was no longer just a woman he was helping. She was his wife.

Wife. Not a word he'd ever thought he'd use again.

Granted, it was a temporary arrangement that would soon be nullified—very soon, if this plan worked—but there was something reassuring about that. How badly could he mess up a marriage that already had an expiration date?

It was freeing.

And yet, at the same time, the thought of losing Imari was equally upsetting. No, not equally. It was *much* worse. But he held on to the hope that they would remain friends. That would be enough.

Another lie. It wouldn't. Not by half. But it would be far better than losing her completely.

With that in mind, he went to work arranging a meeting with the Ellinghams. All it took was a quick back and forth of emails, and the meeting was set. The Ellinghams could always be counted on to act when it came to the protection of Nocturne Falls' citizens.

He wasn't as sure about Elenora, which was why he hadn't broached the subject of her involvement yet. He figured he'd talk to Hugh and Sebastian and get them on his side first. Then they could help persuade their grandmother to lend her support.

He turned his computer off and headed to find Imari. She was, not surprisingly, in the kitchen with Hattie. They were making bread of some kind. Imari's hands were sticky with dough, and there was flour on her cheek.

It was utterly captivating to see her getting on so well with Hattie, but he tried not to dwell on what was only temporarily his. Then it occurred to him how utterly heartbroken Hattie was going to be when Imari left.

She would stay in touch with Hattie, wouldn't she? He believed she would. She was too good and too kind.

He would make a point to ask her about that as soon as the time was right. He cleared his throat to get their attention. "I'm going to the Ellinghams. I'll be back as soon as I can."

Imari smiled. "I really appreciate this."

"I know you do." He turned to go.

"Aren't you going to kiss your wife goodbye?" Hattie asked.

Imari chuckled softly and rolled her lips in like she was trying not to laugh too much.

Lucien cut his eyes at his grandmother. "Imari might not want me to—"

But Imari suddenly puckered up and closed her eyes while leaning in his direction.

"See?" Hattie said.

Bemused but very willing to play along, Lucien sighed with great exaggeration. "Yes, Mémé."

He walked over to Imari and kissed her. Not as properly as he would have liked, but a good kiss nonetheless. "There, wife. Are you happy?"

Imari's eyes danced with amusement. "Oh yes, husband, that was perfect."

"Are you happy, Mémé?"

She frowned at both of them. "You're a rotten pair, you know that? But mostly you, Lucy."

He leaned over and kissed her on the cheek as well. "But I love you, so you have to forgive me."

"I guess," she grumped.

Laughing, he headed off to the garage. How odd that was, to be laughing. It wasn't something he'd done much of in his life. Even odder still that there was a woman who was his wife in the house. A woman he liked so much he hoped she would stay. That was too much to ask, he knew.

She'd had a life before him. This new arrangement between them didn't mean any of that had changed.

He'd told her when they first met that he had nothing to wish for.

That was no longer true. But he couldn't tell her. It wouldn't be fair. She might feel indebted to stay because of what he'd done for her, and he didn't want that. If she wanted something more between them, it had to be because she wanted it. Not because she felt some sense of obligation.

Or worse, pity.

No, if anything was to come of this relationship, Imari would have to make that decision. He'd chased Pavlina, and look how that had ended.

When he arrived at Sebastian Ellingham's home, Sebastian's rook, Greaves, led Lucien to the library. Hugh and Sebastian were waiting for him there.

He would have liked to ogle the library and the array of books in it, but the matter of the wish merchant was much more pressing. "Thank you for meeting me."

Sebastian and Hugh were both standing, but Sebastian gestured to a grouping of club chairs and a large, leather sofa. "You're welcome. Have a seat and tell us what's going on."

All three got comfortable, although Lucien was anything but. It prickled him to ask for help like this, but he reminded himself it was all for Imari. For her, he would do anything. "I need help. Or rather, another citizen does, and I am trying to facilitate things for her."

"I see," Sebastian said. "Why you? Why doesn't she come to us herself?"

"Is this about Imari Zephara?" Hugh asked.

"Yes."

Hugh turned to his brother. "She's the genie I was telling you about. A wish merchant is hunting her here in town. Abominable." He nodded at Lucien. "We'll help."

Sebastian frowned. "You don't know what he's asking yet."

"Seb, this is Lucien. And a woman is in danger."

"Two, actually." Lucien explained about the other genie in the wish merchant's clutches. "This man needs to stop being a problem. Permanently."

Sebastian nodded. "Agreed. I wasn't aware of the full extent of his crimes. Explain how you need us to help."

Lucien took a breath. His next ask was a big one, and he knew it. "It's really more what I need your grandmother to do."

Both vampires raised their brows, but Hugh spoke first. "And that is?"

Here went nothing. "I need to use her extensive jewelry collection as bait for the wish merchant."

Somewhat stunned expressions met his words.

"The wish merchant is trying to locate Imari's bottle through the use of a treasure-hunting spell. There's no way a good cluster of your grandmother's finer pieces could be ignored by such a spell. We could lure him in and deal with him once and for all that way."

182

THE REAPER RESCUES THE GENIE

Sebastian shook his head. "Elenora isn't going to like that. She's going to want extensive reassurances that her jewels will remain safe. Especially after what happened with her pink diamond."

Lucien had heard about that piece being stolen, but he also knew it had been recovered. Still, he understood that Elenora might be a little hesitant after such an experience. He laid out his plan. Both men listened intently, and in the end, they were nodding in agreement.

"Sounds solid," Hugh said. "Are you sure Imari will go for it?"

"Yes." Except Lucien wasn't. He just didn't see any other way. "But I need to get Elenora's assistance in place before we move further. I wish I could come up with a plan that didn't require her jewels, but we tried replicating the bottle and his genie homed in on it before it could be finished. She stole the replica right out of Willa's safe."

"I'm sorry to hear that," Sebastian said.

"Us too." Lucien grimaced. "That attempt cost Imari the stopper on her bottle because Willa was using it for reference."

"I'd say it cost you a hefty sum, too," Sebastian added.

Lucien hadn't really thought about that. "The money isn't important. But that stopper is. Imari has to have it back, or the bottle is useless to her."

"Then it's settled." Hugh looked at his brother. "We'll convince Elenora that there is no other way. Her jewels won't be in danger, they're just to lure the wish merchant in. The rest will be up to Imari."

Sebastian's response came slower. "Elenora will want Alice involved. As backup."

"Alice?" Lucien seemed to recall the woman was Elenora's secretary.

"Alice Bishop. She's a powerful witch who works for our grandmother." Hugh's face didn't express a lot of love for the woman. "If Elenora wants her there, we won't be able to keep her from the scene."

"That's all right," Lucien said. "I don't know if witch magic will have any power against a genie's, but it couldn't hurt to have them there." Then an idea came to him. "Although a witch can use her magic against a human, can't she?"

"Yes." Hugh nodded. "It's not necessarily what they prefer to do, nor do they openly approve of it in the coven, but the witches in town have been helpful in certain cases like this before."

"Could we get a second?" Lucien's thoughts were spinning faster than he could control them. "Another strong witch?"

"We could," Hugh said.

"Are you thinking of Corette?" Sebastian asked his brother.

"Yes. And I know she'll help." Hugh answered Sebastian before glancing at Lucien. "Corette is my rook's fiancée. The mother of Marigold, Charisma, and Pandora. All of whom are friends with Imari, I believe, so I'm sure Corette will assist us in whatever way we need. What are you thinking?"

"Very much like before, but with a little added

insurance." Lucien explained what he was thinking, and with each word, his confidence grew.

This plan was going to work. And it was going to be foolproof.

Imari stared at Lucien as he finished explaining his plan. She felt like she'd been gut-punched. "You're asking a lot of me."

"I know, but I don't see another way."

"I don't either." She sat back, still reeling from what he was asking her to do. He didn't understand it, not fully. So she had no choice but to explain. "The thing is, it won't go down exactly like you've plotted."

"Why not?"

"Because when I use that last wish, with the stopper already in place on the bottle, I'm going straight home."

"I know, but—"

"Straight home means straight to Khalid. And I am now a married woman. Do you understand what I'm saying?"

Lucien nodded and looked quite pleased with himself. "That you're not going to have to deal with him?"

"Lucien, that's not at all—"

Then, as if he'd suddenly remembered everything else she'd told him, he frowned. "I know, you're going to have to deal with the breaking of the betrothal, but I'll go with you and help you explain to your parents.

And to Khalid if need be. Surely they'll all understand you had no other choice."

She wished that was true. He was so good-hearted to think his presence would make a difference. "Dear, sweet Lucien. It's not going to matter. I broke my betrothal. That's all they will understand."

He narrowed his eyes. "Then I will talk to them myself. I will make Khalid understand. I'll tell him that the marriage was in name only. That it was just to save you. If he truly cares for you, he'll thank me."

She snorted. "You live in a different world, reaper. Khalid would as soon run you through with his bladed staff than thank you for marrying me."

Lucien pushed to his feet, shadows of his reaper form flickering across his face as his eyes went dark with anger. "He can try. And if he is truly that much of a fool, he doesn't deserve you."

"Sit. Getting angry on my behalf is flattering, but it isn't going to solve anything. I need to think about this." She didn't. Not really. This was the defining moment she'd known all her life was coming. The moment in which she was going to have to stand up to her parents and Khalid and tell them the truth about what she wanted for her future. And then deal with those consequences.

Because there would be consequences. Khalid would still expect the betrothal to be honored. At least, she thought he would. Lucien wasn't jinn, so there was a good chance neither Khalid nor her parents would consider the marriage valid.

What a mess this was going to be.

"We could keep the stopper separated from the bottle," Lucien said.

"That will only delay the inevitable." She put her head in her hands and sighed loudly.

"Are you crying?"

She looked up into Lucien's concerned face. "No." Not yet anyway.

"We'll figure this out. I promise. I won't leave you to face this alone."

She tried to breathe out all the stress clogging up her body and shook her head. "It's okay. I'll deal with it. This moment has been coming all my life. You'd think I'd be ready to finally face it head on, but avoiding it has been so much easier."

"Maybe we should avoid it a little longer and get out of the house." He snorted with amusement. "Get out of the house. I've never said those words before."

That made her laugh. "Then you really should take a break from this place, because you clearly haven't done it enough. But I thought you said going out was a bad idea? What's changed that?"

"You need a break. And if the wish merchant shows up, I'll protect you. We won't go anywhere too populated. But some new scenery would be good for you."

"I'm not going to argue. Let me go change, and we'll head out. But I don't think I could take being around people all that much right now. How about we just go for a drive? Is that all right?"

"That's perfect. I'll go wait in the kitchen with Hattie."

"Okay." She went to her room and put on jeans and a dressy T-shirt with flats. She brushed her hair back and wound it into a bun, which she secured with a couple of hair ties. She would have liked some sunglasses. Maybe Hattie had some.

She turned to go ask, and Hattie was already at her door.

"Oh! You startled me." She let out a little laugh as she put her hand to her heart. "I was just coming to see if you have any sunglasses I can borrow."

"I'm sure I can rustle up a pair." She smiled. "I didn't mean to frighten you. I forget how quiet I am when I'm in ghost form. Sorry about that."

"It's okay. I'm actually getting used to it."

Hattie hovered by the door, hesitating. She seemed pensive.

"What is it?" Imari asked.

"I don't know how to find a way to ask this question, so I'm just going to ask it. Do you...have feelings for my grandson?"

Imari opened her mouth to answer, but she paused to search her heart. Lying to Hattie just wouldn't do. "I like him very much." She might go as far as to say she loved him, but that was a dangerous thing to put into words for a woman betrothed to another. "But I am still technically betrothed to Khalid. I don't think he's going to accept my marriage to Lucien as a reason I can't uphold my part of the contract."

"What?"

Imari let out a slow breath. "Most jinn tend to

think they're at the top of the food chain, if you know what I mean."

"I do." Hattie pursed her lips. "Terrible business, the whole thing. You should get to pick who you want to be with."

"Agreed." She hesitated. "Unfortunately, I don't think Lucien's interested in being involved with anyone again."

Hattie nodded, sadness in her eyes. "I think that too. But you've already been so good for him. If you were just to tell him how you feel—"

"I can't do that. Not now. Not with so much still unsettled. Not with another man fully intent on claiming me as his bride, Hattie. And I can't risk pushing Lucien away when I need him at my side." She would have taken the woman's hands in hers, but there was nothing corporeal to grab on to. "I've never had anyone fight for me before. And I've had almost no one in my life, outside of my friends here in Nocturne Falls, that didn't want me for what I could give them. Lucien doesn't care that I could bring him wealth or riches or anything, really. He doesn't want a thing from me. And that's amazing. I value his friendship more than I can say."

"I understand." Hattie looked utterly dejected.

"No, Hattie, I don't think you do. I could see myself with him. I could. But I just don't think he feels the same way. Not in a long-term romantic sort of relationship, anyway."

"But you've kissed."

"I know. But kissing doesn't make a future. He's a

solitary creature. As much as I wish he felt otherwise…" She shrugged.

Hattie seemed smaller suddenly. Deflated. "He didn't mean to do what he did to me. To take my soul. It was an accident."

"I know that, too. I absolutely do." It broke Imari's heart to think that Hattie felt the need to defend Lucien to her. "Just like I know he would give anything to change that moment. And I know he's a good man. A great man. And even if he has changed a bit these last few days, you know him better than anyone. What's between us is a temporary thing. It has to be."

Hattie frowned. "But why?"

She took a deep, shuddering breath to keep herself from crying. "Because I have a feeling I'm going to end up someone else's wife very soon. And there's nothing Lucien or I can do to stop that."

Hattie looked on the verge of tears herself. "It isn't fair."

Imari blinked hard and made herself smile. "Not much of life is."

Hattie drifted toward the door. "I'll go get you those sunglasses."

Lucien let Imari pick the car she wanted to go for a drive in. He wanted her to be happy in it, but he was also curious as to what she'd choose.

She didn't disappoint when she walked to the Lamborghini Aventador. It was black, if memory served. "This one," she said as she tapped a fingertip on the hood. "Top down."

"Excellent choice." He smiled. "But it's not really top down so much as it is top off."

She smiled back. "Right. Targa top versus convertible, different and yet the same. At least the panels store in the front compartment."

He put his hand to his heart. Her knowledge of cars alone was enough to make him fall for her. "That's correct. Would you like to help me take them off?"

"Yes, but you'll have to show me how."

"It's easy, just a latch to undo." He walked to the driver's side. "What made you pick this car?"

"It's a beast of a machine." She walked around the car toward him, her fingers coasting over the carbon fiber body. "I've never ridden in one. It's one of the few in your garage that lets you feel the wind in your hair." She came to a stop in front of him. "And, if I'm being honest here, it looks like the Batmobile, making me once again wonder if you aren't really Bruce Wayne."

He laughed out loud, hard. "I told you I'm not."

She narrowed her eyes and gave him a smug little look. "Which is exactly what Bruce Wayne would say."

He wanted to kiss that smugness right off her face. She was his wife after all. But in name only, he reminded himself. Not really his to kiss. Not until she was here because she wanted to be, not because he was the lesser of other evils. Although he hoped she didn't consider him an evil.

He opened the driver's door, putting a barrier between them. "I have to put the windows down before the tops can come off." He pointed at the passenger's side. "But you can help from that side if you want."

She nodded. "I'm all over it."

He got in the car, powered the windows down, then climbed out again. "Seats have to come forward, then you pull the lever right behind it."

They got the targa tops off and stored. She was about to get in.

"Hey, wait. Catch." He tossed her the keys.

She caught them and gave him a funny look. "What are these for?"

"If you don't know what the keys do, maybe I shouldn't let you drive after all."

Her eyes went wide. "You want me to drive."

"If you want to."

"I—what—yes!"

He laughed as they switched places. She climbed in behind the wheel and started the car.

"Wow, that's a nice sound," she said as the pleasing deep rumble of the powerful engine spilled through the garage.

"It is." He showed her how to open the big exit door, and the heavy purr vibrated into them as she slowly pulled out of the garage and rolled through Insomnia's parking lot.

She stopped before turning onto the road. "Which way?"

He shrugged. "Whichever way you want."

She looked in both directions, then at him. "You go for a lot of late-night drives, don't you?"

"Yes."

"Then take me on your favorite one."

"I can do that." He pointed. "Go that way."

She checked for traffic one more time, then pressed down on the accelerator, snapping them both back into their seats.

"Whoa," Imari said. She gripped the steering wheel harder, and her breathing picked up.

"Too fast?"

"Nope. Too fast for you?"

"No such thing."

She was smiling, grinning really, from ear to ear, and that made him smile. "Push it harder, then."

"For real?"

"Sure. Take it through its paces. I'll tell you where to turn." He did just that, calling out rights and lefts and following a familiar route that wound into the hills of Nocturne Falls. He'd driven it many times, mostly because it was a course with lots of twists and turns that really showed off the car's agility.

Twenty minutes later, he slowed her down as they approached the largest property in Nocturne Falls. The road in front of it was one of his favorite stretches for laying on some speed, but not today. He didn't want to do anything to anger the home's owner.

Imari glanced out the window at the sprawling estate. "That's Elenora Ellingham's mansion."

"Yes, it is."

"Have you ever been inside?"

"Once." He thought back. "When I first decided to move to Nocturne Falls. Have you been in?"

"Yes. I won tickets to one of the Black & Orange Balls through the spa a couple years ago. It was a lot of fun. And the house is pretty nice."

He snorted. "Pretty nice?"

She shrugged and gave him a quick, coy look. "No indoor pool."

He shook his head.

Imari went back to watching the road. "What if she doesn't agree to help us?"

"She will. Her grandsons will persuade her."

"I hope you're right."

Lucien did too.

She seemed so at ease behind the wheel. It was pretty sexy watching her drive. She caught him looking and smiled. "Where to now?"

"Home, I guess. Unless you want to keep driving?"

"I'm good. It's been a *very* fun ride, but I have a lot of thinking to do."

"Okay." He'd hoped to take her mind off all that, but there was only so much distraction he could provide.

When they got back, she helped him replace the targa tops, then they walked into the house together.

"Thank you for letting me drive. That was incredible." She paused at the living room. "I'm going to my room to think. I need to sort this all out in my head."

"Sure. Take all the time you need. I'll let Hattie know too."

"Thanks." With a smile that didn't reach her eyes, she went off toward the guest room.

Lucien found Hattie in the library, reading through a cookbook. She looked up when he came in. "You're back sooner than expected."

"Imari needs to do some thinking. She's in her room and would probably like to be left alone for a bit."

Hattie nodded. "I won't bother her until dinner."

He tugged a chair toward hers to sit closer. "I would like you to be at this meeting with the wish merchant. I wouldn't ask if I thought there was a chance you could be harmed. Your presence would mean a lot to Imari, I think. She likes you very much."

"Of course I'll be there. I like her very much, too." She smiled at him, a little sadly.

"Don't worry, it's going to be fine. A little tense maybe, but he's going to figure out pretty quickly that he's been caught and the game is up."

"That's not...I was just thinking about you and Imari."

"What about us?"

"What a nice couple you make. How she makes you laugh and smile and how I haven't seen that in so long I thought I'd forgotten the sound of your laugh. Or that you'd forgotten how." She reached out to touch his cheek even though she was in ghost form. "You deserve happiness, Lucien."

He didn't want to argue with her, and while he loved the new light Imari had brought to his life, he couldn't bring himself to agree that he deserved it. Not while looking into the eyes of the woman he'd turned into a ghost. "I don't know about that, Mémé."

"You do. Your powers being on the fritz aren't a measure of what you deserve. Stop punishing yourself for something that happened accidentally. Imari likes you. In fact, I think she loves you. Or she would if there wasn't that bothersome issue of her already being promised to that Khalid person." Hattie shook her finger at him. "You need to fix that."

He choked out a laugh. Khalid was more than a bothersome issue, but Hattie had her own views on most everything. "I've already married her, and I'm not sure that's going to make a difference. What else can I do?"

She swatted his arm. "I'm serious, Lucy."

He sighed. "I know you are. So am I. And I plan to do everything I can. I've already told her I'm going to go with her to explain everything to her parents and Khalid. But she says I don't understand her world. That nothing will stop her parents from disowning her. And that Khalid will just want to fight me. And still marry her."

Her hands clenched into fists. "So fight him back. Stop him from marrying her. You're one of the deadliest creatures on the planet. You're a grim reaper, for crying out loud. You carry a scythe capable of taking men's souls."

He held his hands up. "First of all, I already told her I would fight him if that's what it comes to. And secondly, it's not like you to be so bloodthirsty, Mémé."

She smoothed the front of her silk blouse. "I just think your happiness, and Imari's, matters more than some stupid old tradition."

"So noted." He doubted Imari's parents or betrothed would think their traditions were stupid.

The phone rang, distracting them. He got up. "I'll take that in my study."

He answered the phone on the fourth ring. "Hello?"

"Lucien? It's Sebastian Ellingham. Elenora's in."

Relief coursed through him. It was like he could breathe again. "Excellent news. When will she be ready?"

"Tonight soon enough?"

"I'm not sure."

"Well, I'd advise you to become sure as quickly as you can. When Elenora wants something done, she wants it done immediately."

"And Alice, her witch?"

"Also in. Corette too. All we need is you and Imari."

Imari sat on the guest room bed and ran her hands over the gems embedded in the filigree on her bottle. They were beautiful. Everything in the jinn world was. Precise and beautiful and all according to tradition. Everything had to be just so. It was the main tenet of jinn life. Order kept order.

Which was why she'd undoubtedly end up marrying Khalid. Sure, her life would be ruined, but at least the ceremony would be spectacular.

She picked the bottle up by the neck and jerked her arm behind her, about to throw it across the room. Then she stopped and set the bottle down.

There was no point in that. It wouldn't break. Genie bottles were indestructible. All she'd end up doing is damaging something in Lucien's home, and he didn't deserve that.

A knock on the door made her jump. "Sorry to bother you, but I have some news."

Lucien. She got up to let him in, happy for the distraction despite all she still needed to sort out. "It's okay. What's the news?"

He leaned against the door frame. "Elenora is going to let us use her jewelry. And she wants to do it now."

"Now? You mean tonight?"

"No, I mean immediately."

Imari glanced back at the bottle on her bed. "I'm not sure I'm ready for this. But I guess I have to be."

"You can pick out the car we take, if that makes you feel any better."

It didn't, but it was sweet of Lucien to offer, so she pretended like it did. "Okay. The Lamborghini again."

"Perfect, since you already know how it handles."

"Why would I—are you going to let me drive again?"

"Yes."

Her smile became absolutely real. Now *that* was how to distract someone.

21

After being introduced to Corette, then her fiancé, Stanhill, who was Hugh's rook (a new term for Imari and one that was explained as a human who'd been half-turned into a vampire), and Hugh's brother Sebastian, Imari stood next to Lucien and just sort of watched. She'd never been around so many vampires before, and it was fascinating.

Not as fascinating as Elenora's opulent mansion, however. But what struck Imari, despite all the richness of the place, was that as extraordinary as Elenora's house was, her library didn't impress Imari like Lucien's did. As soon as she'd stepped inside his, she'd known he was a man who loved books and valued the experience they could give a reader.

Elenora's library looked as if the books had been mostly chosen to complement the color scheme and impress visitors.

Which wasn't Imari disrespecting the woman who was about to help her. It was merely an observation about how truly wonderful a man Lucien was. She wasn't just saying that because driving the Lamborghini (for a second time!) had been absolutely thrilling, either.

The pain of having him stripped from her life was going to hurt more than she could imagine.

Because, while all of this had come together with great speed, leaving her a bit whiplashed by it, she didn't need more time to know that explaining to her parents why she'd married him wouldn't change anything. No amount of days or thinking would stop them from disowning her. The only thing that could stop that is her marrying Khalid and that was the last thing she wanted to happen.

In fact, it was Khalid she worried most about. Namely, his reaction to her marriage. Lucien might be a grim reaper, but he seemed like a peace-loving man. Reluctant to use the deadly skills he had. She liked that about him.

Khalid, on the other hand, was in charge of the well guards. He was as serious about his job as he was about everything. His honor included. She might not know him well, but she knew enough. And she'd known enough well guards to know his type. Their whole lives were spent keeping order.

Order was everything in the Chaos Realm. Order and honor were practically interchangeable. Order was life. Order kept order.

And Khalid was in charge of the men who kept order. He lived in a state of combat readiness. The only thing that matter to him more than his guards was that order. He would do anything to keep it intact.

How was Lucien going to go up against a man like that? She feared the outcome. For both her and Lucien's sakes. She didn't want him hurt. Or worse. Lucien might not be ready for a real commitment, but that didn't stop her from realizing she loved him.

Maybe if she agreed to marry Khalid peacefully, he would let Lucien go unharmed.

Life as Khalid's wife would be an exercise in misery, but she hoped her time with Lucien would carry her through. That it would help her remember that true happiness, however brief, had existed in her life once upon a time.

The library doors swung wide, and Elenora strode in, dressed in a navy blue and cream suit. Pearls and diamonds adorned her ears, neck, wrists, and fingers. She was elegant and handsome in a way that was both aspirational and intimidating. An older woman, dressed very practically, followed behind with a large leather case in her hands. The woman seemed more stern governess than ancient witch, but she had the rare air of great power about her. Was this Alice?

Elenora answered that question without meaning to. She gestured to the small round table in front of her, which appeared to Imari to have been cleared off for this purpose. "Alice, if you would."

Alice set the case on the table, then went to stand in the corner of the room. Her gaze stayed on Imari in a rather unsettling way. Imari chalked it up to the woman's protectiveness of her boss.

Elenora put her hands on the box and looked at Imari. "How do you want this done?"

Imari wasn't immediately sure how to answer. "You mean...the jewels?"

"Yes." Her perfect eyebrows lifted a centimeter. "I'm certainly not *dumping* them onto the table."

"No, of course not. They should be displayed around my bottle. Touching it. That will create a pull on the treasure-hunting spell that's impossible to ignore."

Elenora nodded, then looked around the room. "And everyone knows their parts? Because if any of my jewelry goes missing, you won't like my response."

Hugh stepped forward. "It will be perfectly safe, Didi. Nothing leaves this room."

Didi? How did that nickname come about for Elenora? There was a story there. Especially because of the slightly sour pucker the moniker seemed to cause.

"Except," Sebastian interjected, "the wish merchant. He'll leave in cuffs."

Elenora narrowed her eyes briefly, then lifted her chin. "Let's get this started, then."

Imari understood that to be her cue. She pulled the bottle from its bag and set it on the table in front of the leather case.

"That's a beautiful piece," Elenora said.

"Thank you."

Elenora opened the case and started carefully removing some of her own baubles. First out was a heart-shaped pink diamond the size of a baby's fist.

Imari blinked at it. "That is stunning. And it's probably all you'll need to add."

An indulgent smile bent Elenora's mouth. "Thank you. I'm happy to add a few more."

And she did. A chunky emerald and diamond ring. A strand of fat pink South Sea pearls that matched the white strand she was wearing. A starburst brooch comprised of white and yellow diamonds. A wide ruby and diamond bracelet that might have been from the art deco era. Then the surprise of diamond and sapphire tiara.

Each was arranged carefully around the bottle so they all touched.

Elenora closed the case and stepped back. "How long before this awful little man appears?"

"Shouldn't take long," Imari said. "The genie he's controlling will transport them here. Most likely right into the room."

Lucien stepped forward. "Everyone on their guard."

Hugh nodded at Stanhill, who'd positioned himself by the door. "Lights."

Stanhill hit the switch, pitching the room into darkness, but it didn't take long for their supernatural vision to adjust to the moonlight filtering through the windows.

Then the sizzle of approaching magic zipped through Imari. Jinn magic. "They're coming," she whispered.

"I feel it too," Corette added.

Seconds later, blue-green sparks snapped through

the air, and the wish merchant and Adira appeared in the center of the room.

Imari's heart pounded in her chest. She'd known clustering the gems would work, she just hadn't anticipated how fast. The end was near. For the wish merchant and for her. It was both exhilarating and terrifying.

The wish merchant spoke. "I wish for lights, Adira."

"Yes, master."

But before Adira could magically turn them on, Stanhill did the job for her. "Don't move, mate. The gig is up."

Panic filled the wish merchant's face. "Adira, get us out of—"

Corette and Alice both thrust their hands out at him and in unison proclaimed, "*Stagnacio!*"

The wish merchant went utterly still. Not even a blink.

Lucien stepped forward, and Imari followed. He held his hand out toward the genie. "You know me, Adira. You've seen me before."

She looked terrified, managing only a shaky nod.

Imari understood how scared and confused the girl must be. "We're here to help you. I'm a genie just like you. And this is my…" She couldn't introduce Lucien as her husband. Adira was jinn. She'd know how unlikely that was. "Very good friend. He's not going to hurt you in any way. None of us are. We just want to free you from the wish merchant's clutches. Where is your bottle?"

"I-in the cabin where we're staying. Up on Goblin Drive. Number seventeen."

"That's maybe eight or nine minutes from here," Sebastian said.

Stanhill snorted. "Not if I drive."

But Imari hadn't gotten all the information she needed yet. "Is the stopper to my bottle there too?"

"Yes," Adira said. "Both are locked in a case in his bedroom."

Imari let out a breath of relief.

Hugh nodded at Stanhill. "Let's go."

The two men left to retrieve the bottle and stopper.

Adira glanced at the wish merchant before speaking to Imari again. "What are you going to do with him?"

Sebastian joined Imari and Lucien. "We're going to detain him and charge him with theft, breaking and entering, kidnapping, false imprisonment, and attempted kidnapping. He's never going to enslave another genie ever again."

Adira went pale. "I-I did the breaking and entering. He made me. He has my bottle. I had no choice."

Sebastian, for all his sternness, managed an expression of kindness. "We understand that."

"You're going to be freed," Imari said. "But it would be good if you could testify against him."

Adira nodded vigorously. "Yes, of course."

A question popped into Imari's head. "How long has he had your bottle?"

"Almost eight years."

"Wow. How awful for you." Imari shuddered at the poor woman's fate.

"Thank you." Adira stared at her hands.

"Do you have any idea why he's been tracking me? Does he have a buyer already?" Because if that was the case, the buyer might need to be dealt with too.

Adira took a seat on one of the couches. "I only have about a hundred wishes left. And he's said repeatedly he's tired of me and ready for someone new." She frowned apologetically. "That was supposed to be you."

Imari barked out a laugh and crossed her arms. "That fool would have soon discovered what a mistake he'd made. I only have one wish left."

Adira's eyes rounded. "Then why not just let him take you and be done with him? You could figure out a way to escape when you're home? That's what I'd hoped to do."

"You know how hard escape is when your bottle is not your own. Besides, I have my reasons." Like not wanting to be transported home to face her betrothed, something she was about to do anyway. She glanced at Lucien. At least she wasn't going back alone.

"Well, then," Elenora said. "This all seems to be under control. I'll just return these jewels to a safe place. Sebastian, see that this is all tidied up when you're done."

"Yes, Grandmother."

She packed her baubles into the leather case and headed for the door.

"Thank you," Imari called out. "Thank you so much."

Elenora looked back and smiled, showing off her fangs. "You're welcome." She glanced at Alice. "Tea in the solarium when this is all done."

Alice gave a stiff nod in return. "Yes, Elenora."

Then the grand dame was gone.

Lucien sent a concerned look toward Alice and Corette. "You two doing all right?"

Alice's perturbed expression was her only response, but Corette, who seemed very much like a genteel Southern woman, gave him a lovely smile. "Quite well, thank you. This is not a difficult spell to maintain."

She extended her smile to Alice. "In fact, I'm sure I can manage it on my own if you'd rather go, Alice. Seeing as how Elenora's jewels are no longer in any immediate danger."

With a loud sniff, Alice dropped her hands and brushed them off on her skirt. "I should get tea." She shuffled out of the room without a backward glance.

Imari leaned toward Lucien and whispered, "She's an odd one."

Sebastian answered her. "Yes, she is, but she's responsible for the magic that keeps this town functioning, so we abide."

Imari felt her cheeks heat with color. "I didn't mean—"

He chuckled. "Don't worry about it. I only meant to confirm your statement. Say, how long will you need with the wish merchant before we can transport him to a holding cell?"

"Not long at all. As soon as I have my stopper back, a minute. Maybe less."

He walked over to stand in front of the wish merchant. "I suppose I should call the sheriff, then. That way we can wrap this up as soon as possible. Pardon me a moment." He took his cell phone from his pocket as he stepped into the hall.

Imari smiled at Corette. "It's so nice of you to help."

"I'm happy to do it. You gave me the loveliest massage once."

"Did I? I'm sorry I don't remember, but people look different lying down."

"Don't worry about that." Corette gaze took on the warmth of memory. "My daughters gave me a gift certificate to the spa for my birthday some years back, and that's one of the things I did with it." Then her smile broadened. "Did you like the wedding dress Birdie brought you? I tried to find something that would suit you."

Imari's mouth fell open. "That was from you? But of course it was. Who else in this town owns a bridal salon? Thank you so much."

Corette's eyes sparkled with pleasure. "I love love."

Sebastian stepped back in. "Sheriff's on his way, and judging by the squeal of tires, Stanhill and Hugh just returned."

Imari swallowed and looked at Lucien. She was thrilled to be getting the stopper to her bottle back, but terrified of the confrontation that lay ahead.

He seemed to understand her fears and whispered the word, "Together."

She nodded, too overcome to tell him that while that might be the way they returned to her homeland, it certainly wouldn't be the way they left.

Lucien instantly recognized the fear in Imari's eyes. As a reaper, he knew that look all too well, because when he'd been active and working, he'd seen it regularly. People feared death. They feared *him*. And while Imari's physical life wasn't at stake, her freedom and happiness were.

But he'd come to realize something in the last few moments. His life, without her, was pointless. He loved his grandmother, and he knew she loved him, but he also knew that she could live without him. Especially in a town like Nocturne Falls. And at least then she wouldn't be reminded of what he'd done to her every time she saw his face.

He needed Imari. Needed the spirit and color and joy she was capable of infusing into his life. When she was around, he remembered what living felt like. With her by his side, he *was* living. And he wanted to do more of it. So while he wasn't certain about her feelings for him, he was crystal clear on his feelings for her.

He loved her.

He would do anything and everything in his power to ensure that whatever happened when they returned to her home was in her favor.

And if, in the end, she decided she didn't want a relationship with him, he could at least go on without the regret of never having at least tried. It wouldn't be much of a life without her, but it hadn't been much of a life before her, either.

Hugh and Stanhill strolled in. The rook held a small trunk by its handle. He set it on the couch next to Adira. "I believe you'll find your bottle in there, miss."

She looked up at him and shook her head. "I don't have a key, and he wished that I would never be able to open it with magic."

"No worries. Magic isn't everything." Hugh grabbed the lock and twisted it off. Lucien almost laughed. Brute vampire strength for the win. "There you go."

"Thank you." Adira opened the case and drew in a happy breath. "That's it. My bottle." She looked at Imari. "And your stopper."

"At last." Imari went over and took it from the case, then placed it into Lucien's hand. He did as planned and tucked it into his pocket for safe keeping. Her face was a combination of relief mixed with what looked like disappointment. Or anxiety. Perhaps because of the impending confrontation. If so, Lucien completely understood.

Adira smiled weakly. "Even though he made me do it, I'm still sorry about stealing that."

"It wasn't your fault," Imari said. "We must do as we are commanded by those who hold our bottles."

Adira glared at the wish merchant. "I wish he didn't hold mine."

Imari glared at him too. "That's about to change."

"But how?" Adira asked. "Our magic doesn't work against humans."

Imari smiled. "There's a loophole for that."

She picked up her bottle from the small table where it still sat and turned to Lucien, holding it out to him. "For you."

He hoped she knew how much he valued her trust in him. He gave her a wink as he took the bottle. "Thank you."

He slipped the stopper from his pocket and seated it in the bottle's opening, making it whole again. Then he tucked the bottle under his arm and held his other hand out toward Adira's bottle. "Genie, bring me that bottle."

Imari craned her head at him. "The one that belongs to the wish merchant?"

"Yes. I wish to own that bottle."

Her smile was strong, but her eyes still held a hint of that fear he'd seen earlier. "As you command, master."

She gave a sharp nod toward the bottle in the case.

Glitter spilled through the air, and instantly, Adira's bottle appeared in his hand. Without a moment's hesitation, he repeated the words Imari had taught him. "Adira, I return this bottle to you. And I give you the bottle of my own free will as a gift with no strings attached."

With tears in her eyes, Adira leaped from the couch to take her bottle. She hugged it to her chest, weeping softly. "Thank you. Thank you. I'm free. I can't believe it."

Imari turned to Lucien, her voice soft and a little strained, despite the smile on her face. "That was my last wish."

"Are you ready? Or do you want to wait until sunrise?"

She took a deep breath. "No. I want to go now. On my own terms."

He handed her the bottle that had started everything. "I return this bottle to you. And I give you the bottle of my own free will as a gift with no strings attached."

She took it. "Thank you."

"This is your show now."

She stared at the bottle. "I don't know if I can get through this."

"You can. I'm right here with you."

She took the bottle, then held out her hand to him, sighing out a trembling breath.

He laced his fingers with hers. Her grip was firm but a little shaky. He had the briefest thought about how restrained the colors of Elenora's library were and how that seemed perfectly suited to the austere woman, but the task ahead pulled him back. "Ready when you are."

She nodded, then tucked the bottle under her arm and pulled out the stopper.

In a flash, everything changed.

For a second, they were surrounded by brightly colored swirls of smoke. Or maybe they *were* brightly colored swirls of smoke.

When it cleared, they were no longer in Elenora's library. They were...he wasn't sure where. But they were whole again.

Three arches of pale, polished stone intersected over a pool of sparkling blue water. From each arch, wide stretches of bright blue cloth reached out to poles anchored in the sand, providing shade. More of the same pale stone ringed the pool three rows high.

Three beautiful women in gauzy jewel-toned dresses sat on the stone edge. One held a silver flute in her hands, another had a scarlet bird with long tail feathers perched on her shoulder, and the third played with a small, crystal ball, rolling it through her fingers. They offered Imari and Lucien lazy smiles, but said nothing.

Two guards stood at either side of the pool, but they didn't seem the least bit interested in Imari or him.

Colorful woven rugs covered the shaded ground surrounding the pool. Here and there were piles of fat pillows. It reminded him of an outdoor version of Imari's apartment.

Beyond the pool and arches, in the distance, sat an immense palace of the same pale stone, but it was decorated with elaborate colorful mosaics. It seemed like something out of a dream with its curved lines and delicate arches.

In all other directions, the landscape was palm

trees, exotic flowering plants, and farther on, sand dunes that stretched as far as the eye could follow.

His instincts told him this was a mirage, but mirages weren't real. And if this was a desert of some kind, did that make this…an oasis? But whose oasis? Who lived in that palace?

He glanced over at Imari, who was still, thankfully, gripping his hand. "Is that where you live?"

She was staring at something in the distance. She shook her head. "No. This is the Well of Wishes, and that palace is—"

"Beloved," a voice boomed. "You have finally returned."

Lucien followed the sound.

And found its owner coming through a stand of palms. The voice belonged to a mountain of a man. A dark, towering creature with long, black hair braided back from his face, a full complement of leather body armor, and a glittering blade-tipped staff in one hand. He was walking toward them with steps that seemed to shake the earth.

Lucien blinked to make sure this wasn't another mirage. It wasn't. He let out a soft curse.

"Indeed." Imari's face went ashen. "That is the captain of the guard. And my betrothed. Khalid."

Khalid.

For a few seconds, Imari was unable to move or respond or think. Then she snapped out of it and the

216

reality of everything returned, sending an icy shiver down her spine. She lifted her chin and faced the man who stood before her. There was no putting off the inevitable. "We need to talk."

He nodded. "Yes, I agree. You have been gone a very long time."

"I have been gone as long as it took to use up my wishes."

"I grew tired of waiting. We are to be married."

She didn't need the reminder. She also didn't want to tell him out here in front of his soldiers and the maidens of the well that she was already married. Such a public announcement would only worsen the situation. "Khalid, we should find a place to talk."

"We can talk here."

"I'd rather not."

For the first time, he seemed to notice Lucien. Imari had to hand it to the reaper. He showed no fear in the face of her betrothed. He hadn't let go of her hand, either, something she'd expected. Then she realized that was selling him short. Lucien wasn't the kind to back down, was he?

That could prove his undoing with a man like Khalid in front of him.

Khalid's gaze narrowed in on Lucien. "Who are you?"

Imari hoped against hope that he did not introduce himself as her husband. That would not go over well.

Lucien straightened, somehow growing taller and broader and darker in the blink of an eye. Not quite his reaper form, but not altogether human either. "I am Lucien Dupree, reaper of men's souls, War Angel, Rider of the Pale Horse, and death's own chosen emissary. Who are you?"

Now was not the moment to smile proudly, but Imari had never heard Lucien introduce himself in such a manner before and it was rather impressive.

Khalid seemed to feel similarly as he pondered Lucien's words for a few seconds longer than Imari expected. "I am Khalid Sherazahn, Captain of the Well Guard, son of Khan Memnat, Prince of the Chaos Realm, and betrothed to the one at your side."

Imari decided that was the perfect time to change the subject. "How is your father, the king?"

Lucien very quickly cut his eyes at her as if to say, *You might have mentioned your fiancé is the son of the king.*

True. She might have. But she'd only feared that would make things worse.

Khalid frowned. "He is tired of awaiting grandchildren."

Imari couldn't contain herself anymore. She rolled her eyes. "He's going to have to wait awhile longer."

"Yes. Nine months from our wedding night."

"That's not what I meant," Imari said. "At all."

Confusion filled Khalid's dark gaze. "What did you mean?"

"We should really find somewhere else to talk."

He tamped the end of his staff into the sand. "Tell me here. Now."

She stamped her foot, just to match his arrogance.

"Fine. You want to know why he's going to have to wait for grandchildren? Because you and I are not getting married." She sighed. "I hope not anyway."

A collective gasp went up from the well maidens, and the bird squawked.

The guards might have flicked their eyes at Khalid, but otherwise remained unmoved. Their training was exceptional. Whatever faults Khalid might have, he was a good leader. Or they were afraid of him. She wasn't sure which.

A storm rolled through his eyes, then he leaned in. "*Why* are we not getting married?"

Something crunched in Imari's hand, and she realized the sound came from her grip on Lucien. She eased her hold on his hand and looked at him apologetically.

His face was a mask of steel. He took a half step forward and in front of her, putting himself nearly into Khalid's personal space.

She realized too late that he'd taken her glance of apology as a plea for help.

Lucien stared into Khalid's eyes. "You are not getting married because Imari is already my wife."

The low rumble that came out of Khalid was, Lucien realized, actually a word. Upon further reflection, it was the word, "What?"

Lucien understood the man's consternation. Losing one's promised fiancée must be a very troubling thing, especially without any kind of prior notice. He felt for the man, but what had been done was not as easily undone. All Lucien could offer now was an explanation. "We are already married. As Imari said, this is a conversation better had else—"

The razor tip of Khalid's staff was suddenly in Lucien's face. "How dare you?"

Lucien wasn't prepared to go full reaper just yet. That felt like too much of an escalation. And he was hoping that with a full explanation, this could all be worked out. "It was the only way to protect her. We'd be happy to give you the whole story once you get that weapon out of my face."

Khalid stayed exactly where he was.

With a loud, exasperated sigh, Imari pushed the staff away. "Khalid, enough. What Lucien said is correct. It was the only way to protect me. Now, please, do the right thing and let me go."

"Break our betrothal? Never," he snarled.

She grimaced. "You act as if we were madly in love and inseparable when the truth is we've been promised since birth but don't know the first thing about each other. We don't love each other. We don't even know each other."

"This isn't about love," he growled. "This is about—"

"Honor and order," she finished. "Yes, I know. That's also why I didn't want to have this conversation here." She crossed her arms. "And since I still have to break the news to my parents, why don't we go there and have this all out?"

He lowered his staff, planting the end on the ground. "They will disown you. You will never be allowed to return home."

"Sadly, I'm prepared for that. Now, do you want to hear the whole story, or would you rather be mad and pouty?"

Khalid's dark brows pulled together in consternation. "I am not pouty."

"Happens to the best of us," Lucien muttered.

Khalid arrowed in on him. "What was that?"

"Nothing." He returned to Imari's side, certain she was no longer in any immediate danger, and put his hand on her back. "Lead the way."

She looked at Khalid. "Are you coming or not?"

"Of course I am coming."

She uncrossed her arms. "Then we're going to need a bigger carpet."

Khalid cut his eyes at Lucien. "I am not sharing with this *jinabi*."

"What did you call me?"

Imari snorted. "It just means foreigner."

"Well. I am that." Then he thought about what Imari had said. A bigger carpet? For what? And as for Khalid not wanting to share... Lucien kept all emotion from his face and held his tongue, even though his immediate response was to smirk and say, "Too late."

Imari ignored them both and headed for the rugs surrounding the pool. In a couple spots, there were piles of rugs still rolled up. She grabbed one of those, hoisted it over her shoulder, and brought it back.

"I could have helped you with that," Lucien said.

She shrugged as she dropped the rug to the ground. "I'm stronger than I look."

"I have no doubt of that."

Khalid had also picked out a carpet.

Imari unrolled the one she'd chosen, then stepped on and took a seat cross-legged before patting the spot next to her.

Lucien sat, sudden realization lighting upon him. "Is this what I think it is?"

She smiled. "Depends. What do you think it is?"

He wasn't sure he wanted to say. Sure, he was a grim reaper, and he'd seen more types of supernaturals come through Insomnia than he could count, but this was something different. This wasn't the kind of magic he'd come across before. "It's...a magic carpet?"

"Winner, winner, chicken tagine dinner." She laughed. "You're not afraid of heights, are you?"

He snorted. "No. Many types of reapers, War Angels included, actually do ride horses, and just so you know, those horses fly."

Her eyes widened a little. "Now that would be a fun ride."

"It was." He turned to look out toward the horizon. "But Phantom was reassigned when I retired."

"Sorry about that." She touched his arm. "I didn't mean to bring up a bad memory."

He smiled at her. "You didn't. I miss him a little, but I have a garage full of horsepower now."

She laughed. "That you do."

"Speaking of, show me what this thing can do."

"You got it." She gave a command in jinn, and the carpet went taut, then lifted into the air and off they went.

The ride was far smoother than Lucien had expected. It was a little like sitting on a firm water bed, fluid in that kind of way, but he felt secure.

The ground beneath them fell away, and he could see the extent of the oasis they'd been in. "Where are we exactly?"

"The Chaos Realm. It's the world of the jinn."

He peered over the side. "Doesn't look very chaotic."

"It's well controlled."

"It must be."

"It has to be. Or things would go bad very quickly."

They followed a swath of palms to the east. A road had been carved through the center. It all seemed very well planned. The palms were all perfectly aligned, the road was surfaced with shell-shaped pavers, and tall brass lighting fixtures curled up from the ground at regular intervals. Well controlled was beginning to make a lot of sense.

If he'd leaned over and trailed his hand below the carpet, he swore he could have touched the palms. Every now and then, a bird darted past and into the foliage.

The palms below fanned out on the other side of the road, then smaller roads forked off the main one, all at even intervals. At the end of each road were more beautiful homes. Not the size and grandeur of the palace he'd seen, but stunning nonetheless. And they seemed to get larger the deeper in they flew. Again, all in a very symmetrical, planned way.

He glanced over his shoulder. Khalid wasn't far behind on his own carpet. And he was glaring daggers at Lucien.

Lucien rolled his eyes and went back to sightseeing. Khalid was entitled to his feelings, but this wasn't a place anyone outside of the jinn could access, so Lucien might as well take it in. He would be dealing with Khalid, and Imari's parents, soon enough.

Imari gave another command, and the carpet

descended and veered right to follow one of the side roads.

The home at the end of that road was a sprawling fortress of blue-tile-capped turrets, polished sandstone, and undulating curves.

The carpet slowed, and they sailed past intricate gardens laden with fruit trees and more types of palms than he'd known existed.

Guards patrolled the grounds, and it suddenly occurred to Lucien that if Khalid was a prince, he wouldn't be betrothed to just *any* woman.

Who was Imari, exactly? Or perhaps the question was, who were her parents?

The carpet came to rest in the courtyard outside the main doors, which were a pair of intricately carved, arched wood panels at least ten feet tall and just as wide.

He got to his feet, offering Imari a hand, as the doors opened.

An older man in a long embroidered robe came out to greet them. "Welcome home, Imari."

She gave him a little bow of her head in greeting. "Thank you, Ravi." She glanced at Lucien. "Ravi manages my parents' home."

A butler of sorts, then. Lucien nodded at the man.

Khalid had landed behind them. He now strode forward. Ravi bowed deeply. "Prince Khalid."

"Ravi. We need an audience with Imari's parents immediately."

"Yes, Your Highness. Right this way."

Khalid followed, forcing Imari and Lucien to fall in step behind him.

"How chivalrous," Lucien said.

"Chivalry is not a jinn concept," Imari answered.

"I see that."

Ravi led them through another, more ornate courtyard, this one with large cushioned seating pallets, brass stands holding brightly colored birds, and a beautiful tiered fountain. More palms and some stretches of fabric like he'd seen before offered shade.

Suddenly, he realized he and Imari were no longer holding hands, but he could still see color. How odd that the Chaos Realm had that effect. But then, Imari was born here. So it made sense in some way he hadn't yet fully figured out.

Once inside the house, it was much like he'd imagined. Gleaming tile everywhere in intricate patterns and colors, sumptuous rugs underfoot, delicate filigree lanterns covered in cut crystal that sent sparks of brilliance over everything. Polished wood shutters kept out the strongest of the sun's rays while still allowing light through. The house was cool and calm, with the faint burble of water from the fountain drifting in and the occasional tinkling of chimes.

Every inch of the residence spoke of restrained wealth. And sometimes, like in the case of the mother-of-pearl mosaic stairway that led to an upper level, not so restrained. But it was always precisely laid out and balanced. Symmetry reigned. Elaborate, expensive symmetry.

He leaned over to whisper to Imari. "Who are your parents exactly?"

She whispered back, "My father is the Vice-Minister of Oasis Management, a position held by the men in his family for the last twelve hundred years. And my mother is the king's Vizara of Strategy."

"What is that?"

"She is basically his Secretary of Defense."

"I see." And he did, very clearly. Imari's family was interlaced in the politics of the Chaos Realm as thoroughly as if they were royalty themselves.

This was not going to be a fun conversation.

Ravi stopped at a new set of doors. "If you will wait here, I will bring your parents."

"Thank you, Ravi."

He opened the doors, bowed, then left them.

Khalid didn't wait for Imari and Lucien, just went in and stood by one of the windows.

Lucien held his hand out. "After you."

Imari's smile was tight. No doubt her nerves were as well.

They went in. The room was as beautiful as the rest of the home, with tall ceilings and tall windows that overlooked another spacious garden space, but the main feature of this colorful garden was a cobalt blue pool.

Lucien walked to a window to see it better. It was the size of a small lake and built to look natural among the palms and flowers. Waterfalls cascaded down an outcropping of stone on either side. There appeared to be a grotto underneath each one.

"Beautiful," Lucien said. "Like everything else."

Imari stood at his side looking out the window. "It is."

"You grew up here?"

"I did."

"Happy memories?"

She hesitated, and he wondered if he'd asked something he shouldn't have, but then she answered. "Yes. Mostly. It's just odd to be here after so many years and see that nothing has changed. But that's how the jinn keep a handle on things. No change means no chaos. And so the old rules are the same rules we follow. No deviations, no adjustments, no questions. Order keeps order."

It made sense to him. If something was working, and holding the chaos at bay, why on earth would anyone want to tempt fate and do something different? But in Imari's case, upholding tradition would mean losing herself.

Even in the face of chaos, he couldn't justify that.

"Imari, you're home."

They turned to see two people walking in who must be Imari's parents. It was no surprise to Lucien that her mother was beautiful or her father handsome. There seemed to be no one on this realm who wasn't perfect. How much of that was controlled by magic, he wasn't sure.

They were dressed much like Ravi had been, in embroidered robes. More elaborate, but very similar styles. Imari's mother complemented her outfit with gem-studded gold jewelry, and her father wore a gem-studded sash around his robe. Their slippers were also decorated with gems.

He felt the sudden urge to bow, but restrained himself.

"Mama, Papa." She bent her head as she dipped into a slight curtsey. When she rose, she put her hand on Lucien's arm. "Lucien, these are my parents, Zakir and Farozza Zephara. Mama and Papa, this is my—"

"Husband," Khalid spat.

Lucien sighed. So much for easing into things.

Imari watched the joy drain from her parents' faces. Their reaction caused a tremor of fear to zip through her, but it was exactly what she'd been expecting from them.

"What is the meaning of this?" But her father wasn't looking at her. "Prince Khalid, it is a great honor to have you in our home, but I do not understand."

Khalid answered him. "Vice-Minister Zephara, what is there to understand?" He jabbed a finger at Lucien. "*That* is her husband. She has married another in an attempt to break our vow. And with a *jinabi*, nonetheless. What else do you need to know?"

Imari's mother clenched her hands tightly at her sides and looked at her daughter. There was steel in her gaze and a warning in her voice. "Is this true?"

"Yes, Mama, but—"

"Why would you do this?" Angry lines bracketed her father's eyes. "Why would you bring such shame upon us?"

With a sharp, quick movement, Lucien stepped forward. "Is there shame in protecting one's self? Imari had no choice. A wish merchant tried to kidnap her."

Her father came a few steps toward them, the smallest hint of compassion in his eyes. "A wish merchant? Why didn't you just come home?"

Lucien tipped his head to look at her, and Imari understood.

This was her question to answer. Her chance to tell her parents the truth. She had to do it. She took a breath. "Why do you think it's been so long since I've been home?"

Her mother, Farozza, shook her head. "You have been busy. Genies cannot always just leave unless the owner of their bottle grants them such liberty. We understand that."

Imari rubbed a spot on her temple that was beginning to ache. "No one has owned my bottle in years, Mama. I didn't come home because..." She glanced at Khalid. "I knew I'd be forced to uphold the marriage contract you bound me to. And I didn't want to marry Khalid. I didn't want to marry anyone."

Although she felt differently about that now. With a man like Lucien, who treated her as an equal, that kind of marriage held promise. It was one she could consider. A partnership. Not a dictatorship.

Her father snorted. The compassion in his eyes was gone. "And yet, you married this, this...whatever this man is." He threw his hands up. "You make no sense, Imari. Have you forgotten all the values you were raised with? Have you forgotten the importance of tradition? Or honor?"

Beside her, Lucien went stiff with anger. She could tell he was nearing a point of no return. She put her hand on his arm before addressing her parents. "As Lucien said, I had no choice. The wish merchant had made several attempts to capture me and my bottle, and he'd succeeded in stealing the stopper. If he'd gotten the bottle, I would have been his."

"Only until you ran out of wishes," her mother said. "Then you would have been able to return here."

Imari rolled her eyes. It was like her parents heard only what they wanted to. "Yes, to be married off to Khalid and enter a different kind of servitude. And even if I hadn't been betrothed, my other option would have been to bathe in the Well of Wishes and then return to my captor. There was no good choice. So I married Lucien to protect myself. It was my choice."

"I don't care what my daughter says." Her father thrust his finger at Lucien again, coming closer. Almost like he wanted to poke him in the chest. "You will also be held accountable in this."

"If saving her life makes me guilty, then so be it. I will accept that." The hollows of Lucien's cheeks sank in, and the shadows on his face shifted, revealing hints of his reaper form. "But I would advise you not to touch me. My powers have a mind of their own. I would hate to add to my guilt."

Her father jerked back. "Are you threatening me? Who do you think you are to come into my house and speak such words to me?"

"Papa," Imari cried out in frustration. This was all going exactly as she'd feared. Horribly. "Lucien isn't threatening you. He cannot control his gifts. He's simply telling you the truth. And as to who he is, he's a good man. A man willing to sacrifice a great deal for me. But you don't seem to want to hear that."

Khalid tossed his head with great impatience. "This conversation grows wearisome. Banish her. Agree that she has shamed your family and mine and let us be done."

Fear filled Farozza's eyes. "We would lose our jobs. Our positions. And we would be opening the door to chaos. Prince Khalid, I beg you, please reconsider. This man is not jinn. The marriage means nothing. You can still marry her."

Skepticism bent Khalid's mouth. "The prince's bride must be untouched by any other man."

Farozza sighed in defeat. "I understand. Perhaps you find it within yourself to just…move on? Surely her father and I are not to blame for her decisions."

His hand tightened on his staff. "And invite chaos into my own life? How do you suggest I just move on? You know I cannot. You know honor demands that I continue upholding our betrothal, regardless of your daughter's infidelity."

Lucien growled softly. "She has not been unfaithful."

Khalid sneered. "You're telling me you haven't touched her?"

Imari rolled her eyes hard. "I can technically get married in white, yes. But I still wish you would let this go."

He snorted. "So I should remain unmarried and heirless and spend the rest of my life awaiting the return of a bride who has no intention of ever honoring our marriage contract?" He jabbed a finger at her parents. "You cannot put this on me. She is your daughter. You must be the ones to bear the burden of her transgression."

Zakir stared at Lucien for a long moment, then looked at Khalid again. "You could challenge him. It's been done before. Tradition allows it. And when you win, the only one who will bear the shame of this betrayal will be Imari."

Imari snorted. "I'm the one doing the betraying, am I?"

Khalid shifted his gaze to her, raking her up and down like he was appraising her worth, but when he spoke, it was to her parents. Like Imari wasn't even there. "You would still have to pay me the bride price owed."

"Of course," her mother said, nodding. "We would double it for your inconvenience."

Lucien let out a soft growl, but Imari put her feelings into words. "Is that what I am to you? An inconvenience?"

Her father snapped his fingers. "Quiet, girl. There is far more at stake here than your delicate feelings."

234

The understanding of how little her parents cared for her ripped through Imari like a hot blade. "Is that what matters most to you? Your jobs? Your titles? Your place in this stunted society? I am your flesh and blood. Your only daughter."

"Your brothers would not dishonor us this way." Her father's eyes flashed with an anger she couldn't understand. She couldn't imagine treating a child of her own with such rage. "You made your choice when you broke your vows."

She swallowed to keep from crying as she looked at Lucien. "You see? I told you this would happen."

He shook his head. "You did, and I still can't believe it." He cupped her cheek. "I am so sorry."

She put her hand over his, her voice ragged with emotion. "I'll be okay." She didn't know how, but time would heal. Especially time with the man in front of her.

"I know you will be." There was kindness in his eyes and such tenderness in his voice that she wanted to fall into his arms and let him hold her until all of this was over. "You're incredibly strong and brave, and you deserve better."

She laughed through the tears fighting to break loose. That this man still wanted to be her champion after seeing how little her family cared just floored her. The pain in her heart wasn't nearly as bad as it had just been. She could survive anything with a man like this at her side. "You're something else, you know that, reaper?"

"Enough," Khalid bellowed at Lucien. "I challenge

you, destroyer of vows, violator of the innocent, breaker of oaths, to fight me for the hand of Imari. Death will decide which one of us gets her."

"My innocence has *not* been violated," Imari snapped back.

Lucien started to turn, but Imari pressed her hand harder over his, keeping his eyes on her. "You can't fight Khalid. He will win."

Lucien smiled, then pressed his mouth to hers in a soft kiss. "He can't win. Not if death is going to decide which one of us gets you. Death already knows he's taking you home."

Then Lucien dropped his hand from Imari's cheek and faced Khalid, placing himself so that Imari was slightly behind him. "Whatever the outcome, I will only fight you if Imari is allowed to choose her own future. She isn't property to be bartered or promised. Do you understand?"

Khalid sneered. "You have no understanding of our customs."

"I understand that they are rigid and stiff, and things without flexibility always end up broken." He took a few strides toward Khalid. "I also understand that you have no idea who you're up against, or how badly I want to win, or what I am capable of, so consider this your one and only warning."

Khalid's face twisted in confusion, then after a second of thought, he laughed long and hard. "You are the one who doesn't know who he is up against." He planted his hands on his hips and shook his head. "You talk like you love her."

"You talk like you don't." Lucien faced Khalid squarely. "And the mouth speaks what the heart is full of. Challenge accepted."

There were no flying carpets this time, just a caravan of camels and donkeys and silk-curtained wagons to take them to the arena where the challenge would take place. A flying carpet might make for too easy an escape, although Lucien had no intention of attempting that. Neither did Imari, as far as he knew.

He and Imari rode in one of the wagons. It wasn't as comfortable as the carpet had been. The curtains had been pulled back, so that they were visible on all sides. Perhaps Imari's parents thought their daughter needed to be watched?

Lucien wondered about that, especially because her parents rode behind them on donkeys. The beasts were saddled with fancy gold and leather tack and had designs painted on their hides.

Khalid rode up front on a camel, also adorned with paintings on its hide. Maybe Khalid's position at the head of the caravan was because he was a prince and therefore the highest ranking. Lucien didn't know and didn't care. He had other things on his mind.

Like how he had never considered himself a fighter, nor was it something he did much of. Reapers, for all their appearance and reputation, rarely had to fight anyone. Probably because of their appearance and reputation.

Sure, there was the occasional reluctant mortal, but War Angels attended to the souls of those who understood their own mortality. Soldiers on a battlefield seldom questioned what was happening to them, unlike ordinary mortals whose time had been come up in the middle of some normal daily routine.

A man with a bullet in him and more flying past understood that death was on its way. It was a possibility he'd been made aware of when he signed up for the job.

However, a man struck down by a heart attack in aisle five of the local big-box store was much less likely to give up his soul so easily when his big plan for the day had been purchasing the month's supply of paper towels. Reapers who handled that variety of mortal probably were used to a tussle now and then.

Lucien also felt confidence in the power of the scythe on his arm. Because while Khalid might be jinn and immortal, the only creatures Lucien had met to date that were immune to his scythe were vampires. And that was because they qualified as already dead.

Every reaper's scythe was forged in the fires of Hades and quenched in the river Styx. There was no denying such a weapon's soul-collecting power.

Khalid could fight all he wanted, but the end would come with one swipe of the reaper's blade.

Fortunately for Khalid, Lucien had no intent to keep the man's soul. He would return it as soon as the jinn agreed to let Imari choose her own future. And if Khalid was reluctant to do so, well, a soul was a very good bargaining chip.

He just hoped that Imari's future included him. He knew she had her own life to get back to, but he felt cautiously optimistic that they would stay connected, even if it was only in some small way. They were linked by circumstance now, both of them wrapped up in this event. And even though this was her world, a world he clearly was an outsider in, she wasn't the kind to cut him out of her life because he didn't belong or she no longer needed him. Not after watching her parents cut her from their lives without a backward glance.

She would need time to heal from such hurt. That was a given. And she might want to be alone for that. Something else he would understand. But when she was ready, he would be there for her. In whatever capacity she needed or wanted.

He glanced at her, trying to read her, but he couldn't quite get a handle on what she was feeling. She seemed oddly serene, and yet, he doubted that's how she felt. How could she? Her parents had just made it clear their position in life was worth more to them than their child.

His heart broke for Imari. He couldn't imagine Hattie even thinking such a thing. He reached out and lightly touched Imari's knee to get her to look at him. "Are you okay?"

A smile came and went so quickly he wasn't sure he'd even seen it. "Okay is going to take some time. But I am...dealing with it all." She glanced down at his hand, which no longer touched her, and wrapped her fingers around it. "Mostly I'm worried about you."

He choked back a laugh. "You're worried about me?"

"Yes." Genuine concern shone in her dark eyes. "Khalid is a very dangerous man. He's an ifrit jinn. His job is the defense of the Well of Wishes, but he does that through utter destruction. He's an instrument of chaos. It's his weapon. Fighting him is not going to be like any other fight you've ever had."

He didn't want to tell her he'd never really had any other fights, so he decided to focus on what he knew best. "And I am an instrument of death. He's a fool to challenge me. Especially when I have so much to fight for."

Her smile returned in force then. "You're far too kind to me."

A metaphorical ticking clock sounded loudly in his ears. No matter how confident he was in winning, there was always the possibility that he might not. His time to be honest with her might be running out. He needed to lay out the truth in his heart. "Do you know why I am kind to you? Why I am willing to do everything and anything you need me to do so that you can be safe?"

"Because I make you see color?"

He took a breath, his heart pounding with the life he'd never thought he'd feel again, and uttered the words he never thought he'd say again. "Because I love you."

Imari opened her mouth as she tried to find the right words to respond to Lucien's declaration. There were a thousand things she could say, but none of them she wanted to share with her parents right behind them. She wanted this moment alone with him. A moment where she could be as open and heartfelt with him as he had just been with her. But she wasn't a fool. She knew that moment might never come.

He spoke before she could say anything. "You don't have to say it back. You don't have to say a word, really. I just needed you to know how I feel before I step into the arena with Khalid."

"Lucien, I—I..."

He squeezed her hand. "I know you don't want to be tied to any man. Don't worry. My feelings for you aren't going to turn me into some manipulative monster. This doesn't change anything. You'll have your annulment as soon as it can be done."

"Thank you." Thank you? That was her response to this incredible man? "I mean, I appreciate that." Oh, brilliant. She was really knocking this one out of the park. But she didn't want to lie to him either. She wasn't completely sure she wanted to be married. She cared for Lucien, without a doubt, but marriage was a big step. So was staying married. She had a lot to think about, but right now, she just wanted to focus on keeping Lucien alive.

His smile faded a little. "I hope we can remain friends when this is all over."

"Friends? Are you kidding?" She wanted so much more than that. But how did she explain what she wanted? Should she just tell him she wanted to date him? Dating sounded so...formal after all they'd shared.

The caravan came to an abrupt halt, rocking her and Lucien and bringing their conversation to an end. Ahead of them, Khalid dismounted.

Lucien, his smile now replaced by a stern expression that she took to be his game face, looked around. "Apparently, we've arrived."

She stared out at the arena, dread filling her. "This is it."

The arena probably wasn't what Lucien had expected. It wasn't some open-air amphitheater. Instead, it was a cave. She'd been inside once, briefly. She'd been young and uninterested in the challenge between two of her father's head gardeners. Her most vivid memory of it was how vast a space the cavern was, but other than that, she didn't recall much.

When there was any kind of dispute to be settled here, only those involved remained inside.

It was one way of controlling the chaos that such clashes set free.

"We'll all go in, but only you and Khalid will remain inside."

Lucien nodded slowly as if letting it all sink in. "Then only the victor emerges, is that it?"

"Yes." She studied his face, wanting to sear his image into her head and her heart in case the worst possible outcome happened. Then she made herself smile. "I'll be right here to greet you when you come out."

"I'm glad you have confidence in me."

"I do." But she also knew the outcome could go in Khalid's favor very easily.

"Out," Khalid roared at them.

With a frown, Lucien jumped to the ground and helped Imari from the wagon. Her parents were already off their mounts. She made eye contact with them, thinking they'd say something, but she was met with silence.

So be it. Unless they were going to rescind everything they'd said to her and about her, she had nothing to say to them anyway.

She linked her arm through Lucien's and gave him a bright smile she didn't feel. "I guess we should go in." Then she glanced at Khalid, who was practically trembling with anticipation. Heaven help her, she hoped Lucien wiped the cave floor with him. Not that she wished Khalid dead. She didn't. Not even a little.

She just wanted him taken down a rung, or three. And she needed him to lose. "Are you ready?"

"Yes," her betrothed nuisance growled at her.

She sighed. His whole attitude was so tired. Much like this place she'd grown up in. "Then let's go in and talk to the mediator."

He turned on his heel and marched ahead of them. She and Lucien followed with her parents behind.

The mediator was a rotating position, but it was always filled, meaning there was always someone in the cave to handle disputes. The position could only be held by a marid, the strongest and most powerful type of jinn among them all.

Imari didn't relish being in the presence of a marid. He would judge her for what she'd done, just as her parents and Khalid had, and she hoped that the mediator would still be fair. But that was nonsense. The mediator would absolutely be fair. Anything else could invite chaos, and no jinn in this realm would willingly do that.

They entered the cave. It was a beautiful space, really. Lanterns and torches set around the tiled walls made it quite bright. The floor was dirt, but raked in a spiraling pattern. Order was everything after all.

At the far end of the circular space was the mediator's tower. It allowed the mediator to watch each challenge from the best vantage point.

All of that she remembered, but she was surprised to see the interior wasn't quite as vast as she'd recalled. "I thought this place was bigger."

"It was," her father said.

She turned, surprised he'd spoken.

"The chaos contained within has scarred the walls and thickened them." He looked at her like she was directly to blame for that. Why not? She was apparently the seat of all that was wrong in their lives anyway.

"I never knew it worked that way."

Her mother managed to stop frowning long enough to add, "Jinn magic. It protects us."

Yes, Imari thought. Against dangerous women who want to marry for love, instead of her parents' job security. Perhaps she was being too hard on them, though. Did she really expect them to go against tradition for her? To give up their lives? No. But a little support, a little understanding...that would have been nice.

Although it wouldn't change a thing.

The mediator came down from his tower and walked toward them. He was a small man, but she knew that, like all marid, he had a giant form as well. And his current size in no way spoke to his power. A marid jinn could bend time. No other kind of jinn could do that. Even so, it was extraordinarily rare for a marid to use their power that way, because bending time created the one thing they all strived to be free of.

Chaos.

Instead, marids dedicated their lives to order and peace and maintaining both in the realm they called home.

He bowed. "I am Hammad. You have a dispute?"

They all bowed back.

As expected, Khalid spoke up first. "My betrothed has shamed me by marrying another and trying to break our sworn marriage contract. I have challenged the usurper."

Lucien nodded at the mediator. "That would be me."

The mediator eyed him with curiously. "You are not jinn."

"No, I am not."

"While you are in our world, our rules will still apply to you."

"Fine by me, so long as they don't hamper my ability to defend myself or fight for my wife's honor."

Khalid sneered at the word *wife*, which made Imari smile. If Lucien was trying to rile him up with a little pregame trash talk, it was working. Plus, hearing Lucien call her *wife* gave her a little unexpected thrill.

The mediator continued. "The only rules you must abide by within this arena are thus: You must accept me as mediator. You both must agree to the terms of the challenge. And you must accept the outcome as final."

"I accept," Khalid spat out.

But Lucien wasn't as quick to respond. "I accept you as mediator, and I accept the outcome as final, but the terms of the challenge have not been settled."

The mediator looked at Khalid. "What are your terms?"

Khalid sneered at Lucien. "The winner gets this woman's hand."

The mediator looked to Lucien then. "Do you agree to that?"

"No, I don't."

The mediator seemed confused. "Do you not want to retain this woman's hand? You are married to her, are you not?"

"I am. But the terms I want are that no matter who wins, the decision about Imari's future is up to her. Her choice to be married or not."

The mediator thought that over, then he laughed. "But that would make the point of this challenge moot, wouldn't it? She will choose you, won't she?"

Lucien shrugged. "She only married me to protect herself from the wish merchant pursuing her. She will most likely choose not to be married to anyone. You could ask her, you know. She's standing right here."

The mediator glanced at Imari but shook his head. "No, the terms can only be that the winner takes the woman. It is her betrothed's honorable right, after all, to have the bride he was promised."

Imari's heart sank. That meant that Lucien *had* to win to save both of them.

"That's barbaric," Lucien said.

"She is the one who broke her contract, *jinabi*. She knew our rules when she did it. Order keeps order."

Lucien glanced at her, but she couldn't do anything but offer him a shrug. The mediator was right. She'd known. And she'd pretty much told Lucien how it was going to go down. Just like this.

Lucien seemed to understand. His mouth firmed into a hard line. "One last question before I accept, then."

"Go on," the mediator said.

247

"Who or what determines the winner?"

"When one of you concedes," the mediator said. "Or one of you is dead. Do you accept?"

With one last glance at Imari, Lucien faced Khalid. "I do."

Khalid thumped his fist against his chest. "As do I."

Hammad nodded. "Very well. The challenge begins at the first ring of the bell and ends at the second." He turned and headed back to his tower.

"Prepare to die," Khalid sneered at Lucien. Then he shot a hard look at Imari. "You had better not spend our wedding night weeping over this *jinabi*."

Imari refused to be cowed by him. She crossed her arms and gave him the same glare right back. "The only thing that would make me weep on our wedding night is the thought of how much I would have to teach you and how little pleasure you would bring me."

The corner of Lucien's mouth twitched, like he was trying not to laugh.

The mediator raised his hands. "Then it is settled. The challenge will begin when only the challengers remain in the circle."

Imari's parents bowed and left.

Imari wasn't as quick to go. She leaned up and kissed Lucien's cheek. "See you on the outside."

"Yes," he said. "You will."

She hoped so. In fact, she had to. Because if there *was* a wedding night with Khalid, one of them probably wouldn't live through it.

.

As Lucien and Khalid squared off inside the cavern, Lucien really had no idea what to expect from Khalid. Because of that, he decided to expect anything. And everything. Having no real rules was good, in a way. It removed the possibility that Lucien might accidentally violate a tradition that he'd yet to learn.

And it allowed him to use every weapon at his disposal. The same went for Khalid, but he was, according to Imari, a tool of chaos. That was powerful, to be sure. But Lucien had death on his side, which was arguably the most powerful tool of all.

Then again, Khalid was the captain of many soldiers. Did no rules mean he could call in reinforcements?

Thinking about that while he and Khalid slowly circled each other made him realize he should have asked more questions of the mediator. Was there any time limit on this fight? Were there any loopholes he

should know about? What would he do if Khalid
called upon his soldiers to help?

Lucien certainly hoped he didn't have to figure
that out. Not because the thought of uneven odds
intimidated him, but because he didn't relish the
prospect of reaping more souls out of their time.

He was content to think about that, though,
because it kept him from dwelling on Imari's last
words to him in the wagon. Words that he took to
mean she wasn't sure she even wanted to remain
friends.

It shattered him to think that they might part ways
permanently. But he'd known it had been a
possibility, and he refused to allow it to color his
actions in the ring. He snorted at his own choice of
words.

He would miss color again. But not nearly as much
as he would miss her.

The mediator was climbing the spiral stairs that
led to the top of a narrow turret at one end of the
arena. From there, Lucien imagined Hammad could
see everything. He just hoped that the jinn would be
fair. It seemed logical he would be. To do anything
else would invite chaos, and that was the main thing
it seemed no jinn wanted to do. Not in this world,
anyway.

At last, Hammad leaned over the turret's railing.
He held a fat brass bell by the leather strap that
served as its handle. He raised the bell, then brought
it down sharply, sending a deep peal echoing through
the space.

The challenge had begun.

Lucien tensed. Hades help him, he didn't know if he should attack first or leave that to Khalid. Was it better to be on offense or defense? He decided on the fly to let Khalid make the first move. Then he'd see what the ifrit was made of.

Khalid didn't do anything immediately, however, and the two of them continued to circle each other, shuffling through the dirt covering the floor and blurring the perfect spiral it had been swept into.

The tension in the air hung over them as thick as syrup, but there was no sweetness here. Khalid eyed Lucien with such animosity that, for a moment, Lucien wondered if looks could actually kill.

Slowly, they crept closer to each other. It was a matter of inches, centimeters maybe. But they shrank the distance ever so slightly as they moved. Something had to happen soon.

Khalid must have realized that too. He twirled his staff through his fingers with such nonchalance that Lucien wondered if he was taking any of this seriously. Maybe he thought Lucien was unarmed. A good reason not to call up his scythe yet.

Finally, Khalid spoke. "Do you want me to kill you quickly? Or should I make a game of it? Or will you concede when you realize how little chance you have?"

"I won't concede. And you can't kill me, jinn. You don't have the proper tools." If it was trash talk Khalid wanted, Lucien could do that. But it wasn't going to distract him. That's what Khalid wanted. For

251

Lucien to underestimate him. To get cocky with possibility.

Not going to happen.

"And you don't know how powerful I am." Khalid shrugged. He spun the staff in more intricate patterns, the blade sparkling in the torch light. "I forgive you for that. You're not one of us, *jinabi*, so how could you?"

All this talk was doing nothing to bring an end to this display, but Lucien understood that it was part of the dance.

So he played along. "The Chaos Realm is but one world, jinn. And no, it is not my world. But that doesn't mean I don't understand how to defeat you. What it does mean, however, is that you don't know how powerful I am."

Khalid snorted as if Lucien's power was laughable.

Lucien wasn't interested in games. Imari was outside, waiting to know her fate. And his, certainly. She had to be a knot of nerves, wondering how things would turn out. He didn't want to make her wait any longer than necessary.

He thrust his hand out and called up his scythe. It sprang forth from the tattoo on his forearm, the solid handle forming in his waiting hand. The wood was warm and welcoming, like an old friend. The curved blade hummed in anticipation. It didn't care about the condition of the soul to be reaped, just that there was a soul to be taken. The tool wasn't exactly sentient, but it wasn't without its own sort of needs and responses.

And it had been too long without a soul in its teeth.

He'd never used the scythe in self-defense. He'd brandished it to scare the wish merchant, but that was as close as he'd come.

If he took Khalid's soul, there would be an inquiry. Even if he returned it. That had been the case for Hattie, so there was no reason to think it wouldn't be the same now, especially with a deliberate reaping. But for Imari, he would endure whatever the reaper council put him through.

What was a fortnight of scrutiny and questioning in the name of love? Besides, the council couldn't take anything else away from him. He had nothing left to lose. Nothing but Hattie since Imari seemed to have already made her choice. Although, he hoped that wasn't ultimately what she decided.

Kora, on the other hand, would only miss his money if something happened to him.

Khalid's gaze fixated on the scythe for a moment, then he laughed. "What kind of creature are you? A farmer? In this realm, that is a tool we use to cut grass and weeds."

Lucien hesitated, enjoying the moment. "Some might call me a harvester. I definitely use it to cut things down."

Khalid's chest puffed up as he spun his staff overhead, shifting it to his other hand. "Imari chose a day laborer over a prince. The woman is more fool than I thought."

"You're the fool." Lucien ran the scythe through the air in a slow figure eight, making the blade sing its ethereal song. Khalid wasn't the only one who could showboat. "She's one of the brightest, most wonderful women I've ever known."

Khalid snorted. "You really do love her. You're both fools, then. Love is a reckless emotion."

How well he knew that. "And you think what, that pride is better? Pride is hollow. So is honor without love."

Khalid pointed the staff at him. "Honor is everything. Honoring tradition brings order, and order is peace."

"Not if that peace means you're living a lie." He leveled the scythe at Khalid. "Renounce your claim on Imari. Agree to break the marriage contract, and I'll let you live."

Khalid's brows pulled together in disbelief. "Perhaps the air of my world disagrees with you, as it seems to be rotting your brain if you think you can kill me. I am an immortal. All jinn are. Only jinn can kill jinn."

A speck of doubt slipped through Lucien's confidence. Was it possible his scythe couldn't reap Khalid's soul? His touch had done nothing to Imari after all. But he couldn't think that way, or he'd lose all hope.

He firmed his grip on the scythe's handle. "There is no such thing as immortal, jinn. And it's time I showed you."

254

Imari couldn't stop herself from pacing in front of the cavern. Her slippers were ruined, coated with dust, but all that mattered was Lucien walking out, alive.

What was taking so long?

And why hadn't she told him she loved him?

She made herself stop and take a few breaths. Khalid would want to be sure Lucien knew just how great a foe he was up against. No doubt the ifrit was informing Lucien of where he'd gone wrong choosing Imari as a bride. How Lucien was a fool to go against jinn tradition. How dishonor was worse than death.

Or something like that.

She glanced up to see her mother watching her with a disapproving gaze. Her parents had taken seats under the shade of a stand of palms where there was a small fountain. They seemed content to wait out whatever was happening inside. They were so calm. Like they *knew* Khalid was going to prevail.

Her mother's look stirred Imari's anger. And since she was powerless to do anything against Khalid, she focused on those she could affect. Her parents. After all, things certainly couldn't get worse. She strode over to them, filled with righteous indignation. "You must be so proud at what you've done."

Her father frowned, then looked away, ignoring her.

Her mother arched a brow, then shook her head. "You think I am proud to have such a disobedient daughter?" She shook her hands at the heavens. "Why didn't you give me another girl child?"

"You would really rather I had become the prisoner of the wish merchant than break my marriage contract?"

Farozza hesitated, but only for a second. "Do you think marriage to Khalid would have been a worse fate?"

"Yes."

Her mother pursed her lips. "Where did we go wrong, Zakir?"

"I cannot say."

Imari rolled her eyes. "You went wrong by staying in this world. You should have left like I did. Then you'd know there's more to life than rules." Lucien had certainly taught her that. He lived an unconventional life in an unconventional house with his unconventional grandmother. He'd found a way to exist even when everything he'd known had been taken away from him.

He was proof she could do it too.

"Shut your mouth, girl," her father snapped. "You're the one who's turned her back on life."

Imari stretched her arms out. "This life? Where order is worshipped like a vengeful god? Where chaos is feared more than anything else?" She leaned in. "Not only am I okay with breaking rules, but sometimes, I enjoy a little chaos."

Both of her parents gasped.

The reaction spurred something inside her. "That's right. I drove one of Lucien's cars. Twice. And I exceeded the speed limit. A lot."

Another gasp from her mother and a frown from her father. He turned his head away. "Maybe in the mortal world, that's acceptable, but not in this one and you know it."

"I don't live in this world anymore. I can't. You saw to that by disowning me."

Her mother scowled. "We haven't done it yet. And we won't. Not if Khalid wins. Which he will. Then, if you're lucky, he'll still marry you, and in time, maybe we can forget all this. But you have a long way to go to be the kind of wife a man like the prince can be proud of."

"I will never marry Khalid. And Lucien is already proud of me." Imari looked toward the entrance to the cavern, realizing the truth of her words.

Lucien was proud of her. He'd told her as much. He expected nothing from her. Not even for her to remain his wife.

Suddenly, that didn't seem like such a bad idea after all.

Khalid swung first, but Lucien dodged the staff easily. Khalid had telegraphed the incoming blow with a loud grunt and a slow start.

Lucien whipped the scythe around and used the butt of the handle to force Khalid to his knees, then he spun out of range. He shouldn't have been able to evade the blow of a trained warrior so easily.

Khalid was playing with him.

The jinn got to his feet with a smile on his face, confirming Lucien's suspicions. "Good job, *jinabi*. I wasn't sure you knew how to fight."

Neither was Lucien, but Khalid wasn't going to get the best of him, no matter how well trained the jinn was. If he wanted to keep up the trash talk, so be it. "I don't really know how to fight. It's not what I was trained for."

"Oh?" Khalid seemed genuinely interested. "What were you trained to do, then? To cut grass like a common gardener?"

Lucien brandished his scythe with two hands. "To kill."

The haughty look in Khalid's eyes faltered for a moment, then snapped back. "And again I tell you, I am immortal. You cannot kill me." He spread his arms. "This is not a fight you can win."

"I disagree."

"So be it, but you are still wrong. Let us make a deal. You denounce Imari, go back to your home, and we end this peaceably right now."

"And why would you want to do that?"

Khalid snorted. "It will make my married life easier if I do not have to hear over and over how I killed you. This way, she cannot hold that against me."

"I see. Too bad I don't care about making your married life easier."

Khalid let out a long sigh. Like he'd exhausted himself trying to be the peacekeeper. "I do not understand your desire for another man's wife. Where is your honor?"

"She's not another man's wife. She's *my* wife. You're the one without honor."

A new spark of anger flared to life in Khalid's gaze. "Too far, *jinabi*. Too far." He spun the staff in his hands again. "No more talking. Time to die."

That was Lucien's cue. He shifted into full reaper mode, allowing his reaper form to take over. With the shifting of his bones and the emerging of his skeletal self came the glowing eyes, the robe that billowed around him like a living thing, and the increase in height that made him seem like a living nightmare.

He gave in to the darkness of the form, channeling the memories of the souls that he'd reaped just as he'd done the night he'd first scared the wish merchant away from Imari.

Those memories took on form in their own way. Hands and faces pressed against the abyss of his body, reaching through the gloom as if they could save themselves. It was a parlor trick, a little reaper shock and awe meant to scare and subdue.

Judging by Khalid's horrified expression, it was working. "You're an abomination," he whispered.

"No," Lucien answered. His voice vibrated and rattled like chains pulled over a gravestone. "I am death. And I have come for you."

He lifted his scythe, ready to slice through Khalid and end this challenge once and for all, but Khalid reared back.

The jinn held his staff out like a shield. "You will not take me."

Before Lucien could respond, the jinn seemed to...fall apart. It was as if he was dust. Disintegrating away. No, not dust. Sand.

Piece by tiny piece, the jinn dissolved into a pile of sand on the arena floor.

Lucien stared at it, unsure what to do. Did this mean he'd won? He glanced at the mediator for some kind of response.

The man gave him nothing.

Then a soft, whirring sound filled Lucien's ears. He looked back at the pile of sand. Wind, from where

Lucien couldn't say, was picking it up and spinning it around.

The spiral grew larger. Lucien backed up, at a loss as to what was happening.

The whirl of sand increased in size and height, and the rush of wind tugged at Lucien's robes and filled his ears with a thunderous roar. He struggled against the wind. It tore at him now. Sand stung his face and filled his mouth and nose. It grabbed at the blade of the scythe, turning it and teasing the handle out of his hands.

Lucien squinted against the blast of wind and gripped the scythe's handle more firmly.

Then he heard a new sound mixed into the growl of the wind. A deep, repeating sound that was very much like laughter.

Khalid's laughter.

The sandstorm *was* Khalid. It was another form of his, just as Lucien had become the reaper.

With that realization, Lucien recalculated everything. He couldn't reap the soul of a sandstorm. He needed Khalid to be flesh and bone. The wind whipped harder, tearing at Lucien's body and robe with incredible strength. His options were running out.

He recalled the scythe to his forearm and dismissed his reaper form to retake his human one.

Then he let himself fall to the floor of the arena, as if defeated. His face was toward the cavern entrance. He could only think of Imari and what she must be going through waiting to hear her fate.

The wind died away. The sand fell back to the

ground. Seconds ticked by. Then he heard what he'd been listening for. Soft footfalls behind him, making their way through the dirt in his direction.

Lucien steeled himself. He would have one shot at this and one shot only.

A foot nudged him.

In a single, swift move, Lucien leaped into the air, calling up his scythe and changing back into his reaper form with the speed of a single blink.

Khalid's mouth was still opening in surprise, his eyes still widening in shock.

As Lucien fell back to earth, his scythe sliced through Khalid, hooking the jinn's soul and cleaving it from his body with the efficiency of a hot knife through butter.

Khalid's eyes finished rounding and his mouth came fully open, but the only sound that left him was something between a sigh and a sob.

The last breath. Lucien had heard it many times.

Hattie had once told Lucien that the feeling of her soul leaving her body was like being forced to exhale cold air. Of course, Hattie's soul had been reaped by touch. He imagined having the scythe pass through one's body created an even greater sensation.

Khalid dropped to his knees, then collapsed to the arena ground. A second later, his physical body dissolved away into sand, and what remained of him, a ghost form, arose to confront Lucien. "What did you do to me?"

Lucien plucked the bright tangle of energy off the end of his scythe and held it out. "I took your soul."

"But…how? I'm immortal."

"I am a grim reaper, and I can tell you that no one is truly immortal. And if you have a soul, I can take it."

Khalid stared at his transparent body. "What is this? I don't want this. I want my body back." He glared at Lucien. "I want my soul back."

"Good. I was counting on that."

With a grunt, Khalid swiped at his soul, but his hand just passed through the pulsing ball of light in Lucien's grasp. He sucked in a breath, a purely responsive action at this point, and scowled. "How dare you?"

"This challenge that you initiated was to the death. I've essentially done that." He looked up at the mediator, lifting Khalid's soul toward the man. "I hold the jinn's soul. Is that good enough for you?"

The mediator stared back for a moment, blinking hard. Then he turned and headed down the steps.

"You can't do this," Khalid said. "It's not how things are done. Death is death. This is…I don't know what this is, but you cannot leave me this way."

"I absolutely can. Or I can transport your soul to its final resting place and the form you currently hold will cease to exist altogether. Would you prefer that? Permanent death?"

The mediator shuffled toward them, the fat brass bell in one hand.

Khalid looked horrified. "I want my soul and my body back. You've cheated."

"I don't see how. There are no rules."

The mediator settled in front of them. "You have his soul."

It wasn't a question, but Lucien held his hand out to the man to let him have a better look. "I do. Does that make me the winner of this challenge?"

The mediator frowned. "We've never had this happen before."

"I want my soul back," Khalid bellowed. He grabbed for it a second time and had the same results. He immediately started yelling again.

Lucien was ready to move on. He raised his voice to be heard. "I'll give you your soul back if you agree to my conditions."

Khalid stopped fussing and turned toward Lucien. "You want the woman, you can have her."

"First of all, I want Imari and her parents brought in here so this can take place with them all as witnesses."

"That isn't done," the mediator said.

Lucien narrowed his eyes. "Would you like to see up close and personal how my scythe works?"

Hammad hugged the bell to his chest. "I'll get them."

He made quick time to the cavern's entrance, disappearing through it and returning moments later with Imari and her parents in tow.

Imari's face brightened the moment she saw Lucien. She ran to him. "You're still alive." She put her hands out to hug him.

He stepped back. "Don't touch me. I have Khalid's soul in my hand. The next person I make contact with becomes the owner of that soul."

She stopped short, nodding. "Okay. What's going on, then?"

Her parents kept back a few yards. Farozza kept hold of her husband's arm, and they both watched Lucien with new respect in their eyes. Or perhaps it was fear. Some people only gave respect when they experienced fear. Lucien wouldn't be surprised if Imari's parents were those kind of people.

He held out Khalid's soul. Little sparks of energy traveled through the twisted mass. It was heavier and more tangled than a human's. Khalid had been around a long time. "I reaped Khalid's soul. Now I can either escort his soul to its final resting place, or I can return it to him."

"I want it back," Khalid made clear for the third time.

Lucien gave him a little nod. "So you've stated. But I have demands that must be met first. Hammad tells me this is all highly unusual."

"Highly," Hammad repeated. "It's never happened before."

"Which means," Lucien went on, "that we can establish the *rules* for how such a thing is handled right now."

The mediator seemed to ponder that a moment, then he nodded vigorously. "Yes. I will allow that."

"Good." Lucien turned his attention to Khalid once again. "You will renounce your marriage contract, setting Imari free without strings of any kind."

"Yes. Fine." Khalid crossed his arms and glared daggers at all of them. "I renounce our marriage contract and proclaim it null and void." He leaned toward Imari. "I never wanted to marry you anyway."

She snorted and rolled her eyes.

Hammad raised his brows. "I will see that you're allowed to choose another bride, my Prince. One a little more to your liking."

"Good," Khalid snorted. As much as a ghost could snort.

Lucien looked at Imari. "What else would you like?"

She hesitated like he'd caught her off guard. "For all jinn to be able to choose their futures. For marriage contracts to be abolished."

A look of pure horror overcame the mediator. "Oh no, that would never do. Marriage for love is very unorderly. Love doesn't last. It creates chaos! Contracts, however, are forever. Your request is denied."

She frowned. "Then I want one last trip to the Well of Wishes."

"No," her father spat out. "She is banished. She may be freed from this marriage contract, but that is all. You must both leave immediately."

"Hammad?" Lucien kept his eyes on Zakir.

The mediator cleared his throat. "Vice-Minister Zephara, I will allow it. One final visit."

"Chaos," Farozza whispered.

Imari spun to look at her parents. "Is that all you're worried about? You're never going to see me again."

A solemnness settled over their faces that Lucien

hadn't expected, but then her parents turned and put their backs to her. It felt very final.

Imari's lower lip trembled, and her eyes went liquid, but she lifted her chin as she spoke to Lucien. Her voice was strong and clear, and it filled him with pride for reasons he couldn't name. "That's it. No more demands. Just the visit to the well."

"All right." Lucien made sure Hammad was paying attention. "By your word, this is final and settled?"

The mediator nodded. "Return Khalid's soul to him, and I will declare you the winner of this challenge. Imari will be free of the marriage contract and will be granted one final trip to the well. Then you both must go."

"You won't get an argument from me." He pinned Khalid with his gaze. "Hold still." Then Lucien thrust his hand into Khalid's transparent form and released the soul, yanking his hand free with supernatural speed.

With a shudder and a painful sob, Khalid's body stiffened and became whole again. He collapsed to the floor of the arena, his eyes rolling back in his head.

Lucien wiped his hand on his robe. "By the way, there's a little adjustment period. You'll be fine in a day or two." He raised his brows at the mediator. "It's done. Anything else you need from me?"

"No." Hammad gave the bell a ring, sending one sharp peal through the cavern. "This challenge is settled." He headed back to the tower.

Lucien extended his hand to Imari. "Shall we go?"

She watched Khalid a moment longer, then without a word, took Lucien's hand and nodded.

They walked back into the sun that way, hand in hand. Lucien savored the feel of her palm against his. He couldn't imagine what was going to happen next between them, but at the moment, he was filled with a bittersweet joy.

He'd freed Imari. He'd done exactly what he'd set out to do. And yet...she hadn't said anything. She had to be overcome with emotion. She was about to leave her home and her parents for good. No doubt that was enough for her to deal with.

He glanced at her anyway, mostly to be sure she was all right.

Her eyes were still filled with unshed tears and emotions he couldn't read. "Are you okay?"

She nodded, then faced him and put her hands on his jaw. "You did it. You freed me. I owe you everything."

"You owe me nothing."

She shook her head. "No. That's not true."

"I didn't do it because I wanted anything from you."

"I know." She smiled, and a single tear slipped down her cheek. "I know."

His dear Imari. He hated to see her hurting. "Are you ready to visit the well?"

She looked back at the entrance to the cavern for a second. "Yes. Then I'm ready to go home."

Her last glimpse of her parents. Her last magic carpet ride. Her last visit to the well.

Her final one thousand wishes.

It was a lot to process. Too much for the moment, really. She'd probably have a good cry when she returned to Nocturne Falls, but for now she had to concentrate on the present. That was the only way to get through this.

The carpet landed near the Well of Wishes, and she and Lucien got off. The carpet rolled itself up and kept rolling across the sand until it came to rest on a pile of rugs.

She stared at the well.

"Do you need me to do anything?" Lucien asked.

"No. This won't take long."

He nodded and took a step back, like he was giving her space.

She appreciated that. He seemed to know what she

needed and when. How different he was than Khalid. In so many ways.

The water in the well was crystal blue and inviting. The surrounding guards, not so much.

She approached the edge of the well. The guards eyed her, but didn't move. She let out the breath she'd been holding. They weren't going to try to stop her.

The well maidens rose to greet her. "Sister," they said in unison.

"Sisters," Imari greeted them in return. They didn't feel like sisters to her, but what did it matter? She'd never see them again.

She stepped up onto the stone edging and stared down into the water. From here, the steps that led into the well were visible.

One last replenishment. One thousand wishes more.

That might seem like a vast quantity to most people who weren't immortal, but a thousand wishes could be used up incredibly fast if a genie wasn't careful.

Fortunately, she knew how to be careful with such things. She'd already been careful for many, many years, guarding her one last wish.

The water rippled as a faint breeze crossed the surface. No point in waiting.

She stepped into the water and went down the steps until she was completely submerged. The water was cool on her skin, just like she remembered it. She lingered a second longer, then she came back up and walked out, leaving the well behind.

The water evaporated off her as she went. It was

magic, of course, bespelled so that no water would leave the well with her.

By the time she stepped back onto the stone edge, she was completely dry again, right down to her hair.

It was done. And it couldn't be undone even if the mediator changed his mind.

She smiled. Having her wishes refilled almost made her giddy with the excess of it all. A thousand wishes. It felt like a windfall. Like she'd won the wish lottery.

But she knew better. She'd still have to guard each one, making a studied decision before using a wish. Because there would be wishes used.

Lucien deserved a big handful of them, although she wasn't sure he'd want any.

She rejoined him.

"That's it?" he asked.

"That's it."

"Hmm. And you're already dry."

"It's jinn magic. No water can leave the well."

"Why does that not surprise me?" His brows lifted for a second, then narrowed in concern. "Are you ready to go?"

She stared up at him, overwhelmed by all she was feeling. "Yes. Ready."

"How do we get back? I have no idea how to return to Nocturne Falls from here. Although I suppose I could take a crack at it. My powers do allow me a kind of teleportation."

"No, I've got it." She smiled at him. Surprisingly, she didn't even have the urge for one last look.

271

She slipped her hand into his and wished them home.

They reappeared outside of Elenora Ellingham's estate.

Lucien seemed surprised as he looked around. "This isn't where I thought we'd end up."

Imari pointed at the Lamborghini still parked in the drive. "The car is here, so I figured you'd want to get it home."

"Good thinking." He paused a moment, looking at the bottle in her hands. "So that just appears and reappears as you travel? Because it wasn't with you in the other dimension."

"Something like that. It's jinn—"

"Magic. Right?"

"Right." She laughed and tucked the bottle under her arm, a little less concerned with the bottle now that it wasn't as important. As long as she was married, no one could command her wishes but Lucien. And it couldn't take her home anymore. Her parents would put the magic in place to prevent that very soon. If they hadn't already.

He held up the keys. "You want to drive home?"

"No." She had too much on her mind. Too much to deal with. She was afraid her head would wander, and she'd end up damaging the car.

"Okay." He unlocked the car, opening the passenger door for her. He waited until she was in, then shut it and joined her on the other side.

The vehicle rumbled to life.

He pulled out and got them on the road. Neither of them spoke for a few minutes, then he broke the silence. "I'll call the sheriff when we get back. Make sure everything's in order with the wish merchant. I'm sure they'll want a statement from you, but that can probably wait until tomorrow."

She nodded, half with him and half lost in thought. That wasn't fair. Lucien deserved her full attention. "Thank you for everything. You've just been amazing. Without you…" She laughed softly. "I owe you a lot."

"You owe me nothing."

"Lucien, you can say that all you want to, but it doesn't change the facts. Without you, my life would be a prison. Instead, I have my freedom and my happiness. And I no longer dread my future. I owe you, plain and simple."

"You don't—"

"Stop it. Or you're going to make me mad."

He smirked. "All right, then. But I don't want you to feel obligated to me."

"I don't feel obligated. Just very, very thankful. More than I can express with words."

"You're welcome."

She leaned over and kissed his cheek. "I guess I owe Greyson, too. Without him, I never would have connected with you."

Lucien slanted a look at her. "Technically, we'd already met."

"True. But I had no idea who you were."

He seemed to think about that for a second. "Why weren't you afraid of me? Everyone else has been. Even my ex-wife was when I first met her."

Imari shrugged. "I'm immortal. And I'm old. Wish merchants aside, there's not much in this life that scares me."

"Marriage to Khalid."

"Yes. Ugh. Can you imagine?" She shook her head. "That was truly terrifying. Say, is he going to be like Hattie now? A kind of ghost? Or something else?"

"No, he should be completely himself again. I reaped his soul with my scythe. Hattie's I took by touching her, something I didn't know was possible until it happened."

"That's good. He'd be extra cranky if he was a ghost."

When he spoke again, his voice was quiet, more solemn. "Are you going to miss your home?"

She didn't hesitate. "No. This is my home now. Has been for a while. What my parents did to me hurts, a lot. No one wants to think that their family would choose wealth or status over them."

"Hattie would happily adopt you, you know."

Imari laughed. "I might take her up on that. I love Hattie." She looked at him, her heart nearly bursting. "And I love you, too."

The words settled over Lucien with such warmth and honesty that, for a moment, everything else fell away. The car, the world outside, the troubles of his life. "You do?"

"I do. How could I not? You are the perfect man."

"My ex would argue with that."

"Well, she's an idiot."

He choked on a laugh. "When we were in the caravan and you laughed about being friends, I thought...that was the end of it."

"I laughed because I couldn't believe that's all you wanted. But we got interrupted and I couldn't say everything I wanted to." She shook her head. "You still fought for me."

"Yes. That was never going to change. I'm a man of my word."

"You are that. And you love me, too, right?"

He nodded. "I do. I never wanted to love anyone again. I never wanted to risk myself that way. But you

275

are just amazing." He looked over at her. "I know we have an annulment to get through, but after the paperwork's done, I'm hoping we can start over. Date. To the extent that I can go out, which isn't much, as you know."

"Date?" She stared at him, open-mouthed. "Is that really what you want?"

He started to tell her the truth, that he would love to stay married, but then he closed his mouth, pressing his lips together in a firm line. This had to be her decision. "I want whatever you want."

"Are you sure about that?"

He gave her a curious glance. "Yes. Why?"

"Because I'm pretty sure I want to stay married."

The car jerked to the right, then he straightened it out and pulled over onto the shoulder. "Say that again."

She unbuckled her seat belt and twisted to face him. "I want to stay married. I mean, if you do."

"To me. You want to stay married to me."

She laughed. "Yes, to you. Unless you don't want to."

"No, I, yes, that's good. No, definitely yes." He pressed his hand to his head for a second. "I feel like I missed something. What did I miss?"

"Look, I'm going to be completely upfront here. Being married to you, a man I trust and respect and love, is the best way for me to protect myself. That wish merchant? He's not a one-off. There are others out there. And I have no way of ever getting more wishes, so I need to be more protective of them than ever."

He nodded. "I see."

"But I don't want you to think that I'm just using this marriage for my own protection. It's not just that. It's how good life is with you. How easy and comfortable and fun and just...good. You like me for me. Not for what I can offer you. That's been a rare thing in my life. Sure, I've dated some nice guys before, but never one I had these kinds of feelings for. So why should we stop being married? We love each other, but we can still take things slow. Get to know each other."

"Okay."

"So why end this marriage until we have a reason to?" She chewed on her bottom lip nervously. "I mean, what if...we never have a reason to end it?"

He went from looking at her to staring out the windshield, his grip on the wheel tight and unyielding. Life had made him a realist. "But what if things don't go as well as we think they will? What if ending it is the only solution? It will hurt that much more."

She put her hand on his shoulder. "I have never, in my long life, wanted to be married. Now I'm telling you I don't want to *not* be married. To you. And you told me you'd never wanted to be married again, and yet here you are, married to me. In love with me."

"True." He took a breath. "Plus, you are the only person I seem to be able to touch without killing."

"Another resounding reason to stay hitched." She winked at him. "Not to mention, Hattie won't scold us if things get...conjugal."

A small, choking noise came out of his throat, and an unfamiliar rush of heat swept over his face.

"Hey, I didn't know reapers could blush."

"I'm not."

She tipped her head. "Um, yeah, you are. And it's adorable." She twisted back around in her seat and fastened her seat belt. "All right, husband. Take us home."

The remaining few minutes of the drive were lost to Lucien. His head was otherwise occupied with the unexpected and overwhelming news that his beloved Imari wanted to stay married to him.

He wasn't quite sure how to process it, really. He'd never felt joy like this, other than the day his daughter had been born and the very early days with Pavlina. But those memories had become more bitter than sweet in the past few years, and he hoped his relationship with Imari wouldn't follow the same path as his relationship with Pavlina had.

But that wouldn't happen. He couldn't let himself think that way. He and Imari were good together. Really good. Great, actually. And Imari was nothing like the flighty and fickle Pavlina.

He parked the Lamborghini in its designated spot, then got out and went around to get Imari's door.

He would show her just how perfect a husband he could be. He knew he was subject to moods. He'd work on that. Be less broody. Happier. Easy to do with Imari around. After all, she was proof that he could still be happy. She *was* his happiness.

He'd spoil her with things, if she wanted things. Trips were harder, given how dangerous it was for him to be around people, but he'd find a way. Maybe rent out an entire resort somewhere.

That gave him an idea. If she wanted a date night, he could do the same thing. Buy out one of the restaurants in town for the night. That would be romantic, wouldn't it? He'd ask Hattie. She'd know.

He offered Imari a hand out of the car.

She took it and kissed his mouth as she went by. He grabbed her and pulled her close, kissing her back. Showing her just how happy he was. Kissing her now felt so different because she was his and he was hers. It was a kiss filled with love and promise and hope for the future. And as he held her in his arms, a feeling of completeness came over him.

When the kiss ended, she smiled blissfully up at him. "This is going to be fun."

"Fun." He shook his head at the idea. "That's going to take some getting used to."

"Well, I hope it never gets old. I don't want it to."

"Me either."

She flattened her free hand on his chest. "I'm too wound up to sleep. You want to watch a movie or something?"

"We could get dressed up and go into the club."

Her eyes brightened. "Yeah?"

"Yeah."

The brightness faded. "I don't really have anything clubby to wear."

"You realize I own the place. You can wear a

bathrobe if you want. We'll sit in the VIP section and people-watch. If you want to."

She gave him a coy smile. "Can we dance up there?"

"I don't dance."

"C'mon, Lucy, it'll be fun…"

He rolled his eyes with great playfulness. "Is this my life now? Do I really live with two women who insist on calling me by that dreadful nickname?"

"Dreadful? I think it's cute. Not as cute as you, but close."

He laughed softly. "You know I will do anything you want. If it's dancing, so be it. Just don't say I didn't warn you about my ability. Or rather, lack of."

"Maybe I can show you a few moves." She wiggled her hips in the most enticing way before letting go of him to hook her arm through his. "Let's lock my bottle in the safe first, okay?"

"You got it. In fact, I'll teach you the combination."

He closed the car door, then they headed for the entrance to the house.

Imari leaned into him a little as they walked. "I could eat something, too."

"I bet Hattie has some leftovers for us."

"Perfect."

As they entered the house, Lucien sensed something odd. It was just an instinct and not anything he could name, but something felt off.

Hattie materialized in front of them. She hovered above the floor, her expression tense. "You're home. Good. Everything all right?"

"Yes," Lucien said. "Everything's really—"

"Good," Hattie interrupted. "Because I have to tell you something."

He braced himself. "What happened?"

Hattie glanced behind her before answering. "Kora's home."

"That's right," a female voice called out. Kora walked into the mudroom. She ran her tongue over her fangs. "Hello, *Daddy*."

"Hello, Kora. What brings you here?" He could feel Imari tighten up. He understood. Kora was intimidating. Statuesque, icy blonde, and beautiful in a severe kind of way. Tonight she was dressed head to toe in black leather. Her short dress and matching jacket showed off her long legs, and the stilettos on her feet only made her taller.

Kora leaned against the mudroom wall and jerked her chin at Imari. "Who's this? And how is she still alive if you're touching her?"

Hattie clucked her tongue and frowned. "Kora, mind your manners."

"Mémé, you seem to forget. I don't have any." Kora moved away from the wall and closer to Imari, passing right through Hattie as she walked. "So? Who are you? Don't tell me dear old Dad found himself a girlfriend."

"Girlfriend isn't the right word," Imari said.

Lucien put his hand on Imari's arm. "You don't have to explain anything to her. I'm sure my daughter is just here because she's run out of money."

Kora laughed. "Maybe that's why your girlfriend

is here too, huh?" She waved her finger at Imari. "Are you on the clock? Or is it a set fee? I don't know how you girls work."

Lucien stepped between his daughter and his wife. "You will not speak to Imari that way, do you understand me?"

Kora backed up, hands in the air. "Touchy. Wow. Okay, I get it, you like her." She shrugged. "Cool with me. Like I care anyway."

"I will ask you one more time, Kora." Lucien exhaled, trying to calm himself. "Why are you here?"

Her friendliness disappeared. "I need an advance on my allowance."

"You don't get an allowance."

"I should, seeing as how you're the reason my mother's dead." She leaned around him to look at Imari. "Did he tell you that part? How he's the reason my mother killed herself? If not, you're welcome. Feel free to split if that's too much for you."

"I am *not* the reason Pavlina faced the dawn."

"Seriously," Kora said, still looking at Imari. "You should go before you get in too deep. He's bad news."

Imari narrowed her eyes and came to stand next to Lucien. "I'm not going anywhere."

"Hey, no shame in quitting. I ditched him. It's easy."

Imari looked up at Lucien, her eyes filled with love and questions. She smiled at him. "I'm not about to walk away from the man who saved my life."

Kora snorted. "Oh, brother. You should marry her, Luce. She might be your only chance."

"For your information," Imari said, "we're already married."

Kora's mouth came open. "Are you kidding me?"

Lucien hadn't been ready to let Kora in on that, but he wasn't going to be anything but proud of Imari and his relationship with her. "Kora, wait for me in the living room. Imari and I have a little business to take care of before I deal with you. Hattie, is there anything to eat? Imari and I are both hungry."

Hattie nodded while Kora looked on, her mouth still agape. "I'll heat some leftovers up right away."

Lucien took Imari's hand, and together they walked away, leaving Kora in the mudroom. Lucien didn't stop until they were in his office with the door closed. "I understand I have a lot of explaining to do."

"Not a lot," Imari said. "Whatever you feel comfortable with is fine. After what you just saw of my family, I'm certainly in no position to judge."

"That's very fair of you, but you still deserve an explanation." He slumped against the door for a moment. "First of all, I'm sorry for how Kora spoke to you. Everything she does is designed to get a reaction."

"I sort of figured that based on her whole look. But nothing she says is going to change the way I feel about you."

"I appreciate that. I'm sure you'd still like a little background."

Imari took a seat on the big leather sofa, curling her legs under her. "I wouldn't mind. She seems…hurt."

He joined her on the sofa, pulling one knee up so he could sit facing her. "Hurt? She's just a willful, spoiled child who's never grown up."

"But something has caused all that anger in her. Most likely this belief that you're somehow responsible for her mother's death."

He pondered that. "She can't really think that."

"Then why did she say it? You said it yourself to Khalid that the mouth speaks what the heart is full of. Some part of her must believe it."

He sighed. "Maybe you're right." He narrowed his eyes. "How do you know so much about children?"

"I don't think I do. Jinn just have an innate gift to read people. And Kora comes off as hurt. That's what makes a lot of people defensive and prickly. Pain. And the desire not to feel it again." She drew circles around one of the upholstery nails on the back of the couch. "It's why you were so reluctant to get involved with me. Right?"

He studied her, taking in her beautiful face. "Right. I was…afraid. It sounds so foolish now."

"No, it doesn't. How could you have known what the outcome would be?" Her smile was gentle. "I'm sure that's what Kora's going through too. So what happened between you and her mother? And why did your ex choose to end things in such a permanent way?"

Lucien rolled his shoulders, the weight of his past already heavy on him. "It's a long story."

"We have time. And I don't think Kora's going anywhere until she gets what she wants from you, so…" Imari shrugged. "Tell me."

He took a breath. "It all started when I took my sabbatical from being a reaper…"

The pain in Lucien's eyes made Imari hurt for him. She listened intently as he explained what had happened.

"All reapers take a sabbatical. It's more than a recommendation, it's scheduled. The council believes it helps those of us in the especially difficult divisions to balance out the work we do. You can opt out, and some do, but I didn't."

His gaze went to a distant place. "I wanted a family. I wanted to bathe myself in life. To remember that there was something good in the world. I saw so much destruction and carnage, I needed the other side of the coin."

She nodded, unable to imagine how hard his job had been. "I would have too."

"I'd already met Pavlina. She was a wild creature. I was captivated by her. She was a vampire, but she was more alive than anyone else I knew. She lived life in such a big way. By her own rules. If she wanted something, she took it." The faintest hint of a smile bent his mouth. "That's how she ended up with me."

"She pursued you?"

"No." He laughed. "But she whipped me into such a frenzy that I went after her like nothing else mattered. And it didn't. I was under her spell. We married two weeks after we met. The day I began my sabbatical, actually."

He shook his head like he was trying to rid it of memories. "Everything was such a whirlwind. The courtship. The marriage. Kora."

Imari thought about that a moment. "I don't mean to be indelicate, but I didn't think vampires could procreate with any other kind of supernatural, so how did Kora happen?"

His gaze had slipped to some random spot on the cushion between them. He raised his head to look at her. "Reapers are a loophole, you might say. We're so closely associated with death that we're one of the few supernaturals compatible with vampires. In *that* way. Our powers don't pass on, only the vampire's do. That's why Kora is so much her mother's daughter."

"I see." For a second, Imari wondered if Pavlina had known that. And had possibly sought Lucien out for that purpose. But she didn't know the woman or her motives, so Imari didn't want to speculate. "Were you happy at all? You must have been at some point if you married her."

"I guess I was. Caught up in her whirlwind is more like it. When Kora was first born, things seemed

287

perfect. A happy little family." His expression darkened, underlining how that happiness hadn't lasted.

"So what happened? How did it break down?"

He sighed, a deep exhale of breath that roared out of him like a storm of emotion. "Pavlina had a short attention span. Everything and everyone was attractive to her. She wanted it all. Having a child only temporarily slowed her down."

"What do you mean she wanted it all?"

"The attention I gave her wasn't enough."

"She...cheated?"

"Repeatedly. I lost track, actually. I stayed for Kora's sake."

Of course he had. Because that's who Lucien was. A good man with an incredible heart. She couldn't help but think he must have been an amazing father. The very idea got her maternal instincts all hot and bothered. Could a reaper and a genie have children? It was something worth finding out.

He rubbed his hand over his face. "It's a terrible thing to feel betrayed by someone you love."

She sniffed. "Don't I know it."

He looked stricken. "I'm sorry. That was insensitive of me. Of course you know how it feels."

"Don't apologize. It's something we share now. An awful something, but that kind of understanding makes for a good bond." And because he understood that feeling, he'd think long and hard before betraying anyone himself. Not that she thought he would betray her. But it was like extra insurance.

He smiled. "Thank you."

"You're welcome. Now, tell me the rest."

"Pavlina. She did what she wanted. Disappeared for weeks on end. Ignored both of us. Lived, essentially, like she was single again. And somehow, despite all of that, I became the bad guy in Kora's eyes. In fact, the older Kora got, the more distant she became with me. She wanted her mother. But her mother was rarely there. And when Pavlina was there, she was never engaged. Never the doting mother Kora wanted her to be."

Imari tapped her fingers on the back of the couch. "I'd guess that what Kora wanted was not only her mother's attention but her mother's approval. She saw her mother treating you badly, so she thought that was how to get it. She followed in Pavlina's footsteps."

"Yes. That's exactly how it was. She had anger toward her mother, too, but she took it out on me. Maybe because I was usually the only one there to take it out on." His gaze shifted away again. "I'm as much to blame, though. I thought I could win her affection with things and leniency."

"What parent wouldn't feel that way?"

His laugh was bitter. "You see how that worked."

"No one would blame you."

"Kora does. For everything."

"Why? How are you responsible for Pavlina's choice to meet the dawn? At least, I'm assuming that's what she did."

"It is. And I don't know."

"You must have some suspicions. What has Kora told you?"

"Nothing. She refuses to talk about it."

Imari lifted her brows. "And yet you continue to fund her lifestyle?"

"I...yes." He closed his eyes for a moment. "I've been afraid that if I stop, I'll never see her again." He looked away, a battle of emotions raging on his face. Then his jaw tightened. "She's still my daughter."

"And you love her."

"I do." His voice was strangled when he answered, thick with pain.

Imari went to her knees and leaned forward, cupping his face in her hands. "I'm so sorry."

He bent toward her so they were forehead to forehead. "I have to be firm with Kora. I know that. And with you in my life, I can be."

It thrilled Imari to know she gave him that kind of courage. "I'll do anything I can to help."

"Thank you. But my conversation with Kora is probably best had alone."

She kissed his forehead before sitting back. "Whatever you think."

He sighed, sounding very much like the most exhausted man in the world. She felt for him. For everything that weighed upon him. She hoped she could ease those burdens a bit. Maybe not with Kora. That relationship wasn't Imari's to get involved with unless Lucien asked. But surely there were other aspects of his life she could help with.

She could, at the very least, bring him some fun

and joy and lightness. The balance of his life was sorely lacking in that area.

He got to his feet. "I should go talk to her now. No point in putting it off."

Imari stood up next to him, then picked the bottle off the side table where she'd put it before sitting down. "Can we put this in the safe first?"

"Yes, of course. I forgot all about that."

"With good reason."

He walked over to the Klimt painting and opened it like a door, revealing the safe behind it. "Watch now and I'll show you the combination."

"You don't have to do that, you know. I trust you."

"And I trust you. Which is why you should have the combination. It's your bottle, after all. You should be able to access it whenever you want."

"Thank you." That was quite a statement coming from the man who'd been so closed off when they'd first met.

He punched the numbers into the key pad.

She watched, memorizing them. "Do those numbers mean anything, or are they random?"

His smile was melancholy. "Kora's birthday."

Her heart clenched at that. How sad that the petulant woman-child in the other room was so blind to her father's love. "That's sweet."

"That's one word for it." He opened the safe door. "I am aware of how much of a weakness she is for me."

"I think daughters are that way for fathers." She thought of her own father. "Most of them, anyway."

She put the bottle inside, then stood back, lost in the thought of her parents' betrayal.

Lucien closed the door and reset the lock, then he pulled Imari close. "Don't let it eat you up, or you'll end up as bitter as I am."

She shook her head, a little too choked with emotion to answer. She cleared her throat and found her voice. "I won't. I'll go see what Hattie's rustled up for dinner while you talk to Kora."

"Perfect. I'm sure you'll hear the yelling just fine from the kitchen."

"You think it'll be that bad?"

"When I tell her she's cut off? Absolutely. But if she wants anything from me, she's going to give me some answers."

She slipped her arms around his waist. "Are you prepared for her not to say anything? For her to walk away and not look back?"

He hesitated. "She won't do that. She'll yell and scream and carry on, but at some point, she'll give in. She's relied on me too much."

For his sake, Imari hoped he was right.

They walked out to the living room together. Kora was settled on one of the couches, scrolling through her phone.

She didn't look up when they came in. "Took you long enough."

A dark cloud seemed to appear around Lucien.

Imari squeezed his arm, then excused herself to the kitchen.

Hattie was hovering, nervously. The table's surface

was covered in dishes. "There you are." Hattie's smile didn't quite reach her eyes. "I got the leftovers out."

"I see that," Imari said. "Thank you." She picked up a plate and started helping herself to the food that was laid out. "It all looks great."

"It's just leftovers. I could make you something else."

"I love leftovers." Imari knew how concerned the woman must be. Maybe she should ask for something else just to give Hattie a task to be distracted with.

"What's he going to tell her?" Hattie whispered.

"That she's got to talk to him if she wants any more money," Imari whispered back.

Hattie's brows rose. "That's not going to go—"

The crash of something ceramic interrupted them, followed by some yelling. Kora's yelling.

Hattie flew to the kitchen entrance, but didn't go any farther. She spun around to face Imari again. "Should I go in there?"

"I don't think so. He wanted to do it alone. But I'm sure if he needs you, he'll call for you."

Hattie sighed. "I'm sure you're right. I just wish they could get past whatever it is that's keeping them apart." She hovered back by the table, twisting her hands together. "He loves her, you know. He really does."

"I know." Imari took a seat at the table. Her appetite had waned since returning, but eating gave her something to do. She picked up her fork and was about to take a bite when Lucien walked into the kitchen.

He looked at Imari, the most desperate expression on his face she'd ever seen. "I need your help."

Imari got to her feet. "Anything. Just tell me what you want."

A second of silence passed before he spoke again. "I have a wish I want granted."

Lucien appreciated very much that Imari hadn't hesitated at his request. Instead, she and Hattie had followed him back to the living room. Back to Kora.

Hattie gasped when she entered and saw the victim of Kora's outburst shattered on the fireplace hearth. "My vase! Kora, how could you?"

The faintest hint of remorse passed through Kora's eyes, but it was quickly replaced by cold indifference. "It's just a vase. And not even a nice one."

"It was a *very* nice vase," Hattie huffed. She materialized and started gathering the pieces.

New anger wound through Lucien's bones. He was utterly done with this child of his and her atrocious attitude and endless disrespect. She might be an adult, but she certainly didn't act like it. "Kora, apologize to your great-grandmother."

She rolled her eyes, then sniffed out a, "Sorry" that seemed anything but.

Hattie set the pieces on a side table and went back to her ghost form.

Lucien turned to Imari. "It seems my daughter has been fed a lifetime of lies about me from her mother. Kora believes that I cheated on her mother incessantly, that I abused Pavlina physically and emotionally, and that I never wanted a child to begin with. Thanks to her mother's influence and inability to tell Kora the truth, I cannot convince her otherwise. I need your help."

Confusion danced through Imari's gaze. "Sure. What do you want me to do?"

"How do your powers work on time?"

Her mouth bunched to one side before she answered. "They don't. I can't change what's happened in the past."

"I don't need you to change it. I just need Kora to *see* it."

A light came on in Imari's eyes. "Like Dickens and the Christmas ghosts."

The reference pleased him. "Something like that, yes."

Kora snorted and crossed her arms. "I'm not letting your girlfriend perform magic on me. I don't trust her."

Lucien snapped his head around to glare at Kora. "Imari is my *wife*. And her magic is perfectly safe."

"Surrrre it is," Kora said. "What else are you going to say about step-mommy dearest?"

"I can prove it's safe," Imari said. "If Hattie will indulge me."

"Whatever you need, dear," Hattie said, hovering closer.

"Thank you." Then Imari looked at Lucien. "What would your one wish for Hattie be?"

He swallowed, pondering the question while he looked at his grandmother. Imari had to know what his answer would be, had to be anticipating what he'd ask for. He hoped he wasn't wrong about that and that his wish could be granted. If not, this was all going to fall apart in a very bad way. "I would wish for her not to be a ghost anymore. For her to have her body back as solid as you and I. Wouldn't you wish for that too, Mémé?"

Hattie nodded slowly, almost reluctantly. "Sometimes, I do wish for that. But I'm fine the way I am, Lucien. I have you, and I'm happy."

"But you would be happier to be your old self again, wouldn't you?" Lucien understood her reluctance. She didn't want to hurt his feelings. But that's not what he needed right now. "Tell the truth, Mémé. Please. It's okay."

She looked down at her hands and uttered a soft, "Yes."

"Right," Kora said. "You're just going to wish her back into being. Even getting her soul back couldn't do that. Good luck."

Imari ignored Kora and smiled up at Lucien. "All you have to do is ask."

A breathless hope filled him. Could it be this easy? "I wish Hattie had her mortal form back without the mortal consequences or the possibility of having her soul reaped again by my unreliable powers. Can you do that?"

Imari's smile widened. "You're a smart man. Most people need a few wishes to get things right." She turned toward Hattie and nodded sharply.

The thin shimmer of glitter sparkled in the air.

Then Hattie materialized in front of them, dropping from where she was hovering to land squarely with her feet on the floor. "Oof."

Lucien rushed to grab her arm and steady her. "Are you okay, Mémé?"

"I think... Oh my." She patted herself down. "I'm real. I'm *really* real." She looked at Lucien. "I didn't do it, either. This doesn't feel like my version of real. It feels much easier than that. This isn't taking any effort on my part." She gasped as she lunged forward to hug Imari. "Did you really do this? Did you make me whole again?"

Imari laughed. "That's the incredible power of jinn magic."

Hattie squeezed Imari even harder. "You wonderful woman. What did this family do to deserve you? I cannot thank you enough."

Lucien stared, unable to believe what Imari had done. For years, he'd relived the awful day he'd accidentally taken his grandmother's life and in a single moment, Imari had restored Hattie's physical body, erasing his mistake and lifting a burden that had weighed so heavily upon him.

It was staggering. He almost wept with the joy of it. "Thank you."

Imari looked up from the hug that Hattie still held her in. "You wished for it. That's how it works."

Hattie finally let Imari go to hug Lucien. "Isn't it wonderful?"

"It is, Mémé. It truly is." As he kissed the top of her head, his gaze wandered to Kora. She seemed taken aback. It wasn't often she looked anything but cynical.

"Now then," he said as he released Hattie. "Time for my second wish."

"I'm ready when you are," Imari said.

"I wish for Kora to see the truth about her mother and about me and about her childhood."

Kora's eyes rounded. "Don't touch me."

"I don't need to, just like I didn't need to touch your great-grandmother," Imari said. She approached Kora. "Where would you like to start?"

"Nowhere. Get away from me."

"Aren't you interested in the truth?" Imari asked.

Kora sneered. "I know the truth."

"I don't think you do." Imari looked over her shoulder at Lucien. "What should I start with?"

He chose a memory that was still sweet to him, but one Kora probably had little recollection of. "The day of her third birthday party. Apparently, I was away with my girlfriend and unable to attend."

Imari nodded. "Done." She spread her hands through the air, and a scene appeared like a movie playing. The edges glittered as if Imari had opened up a magical dimension. Which, maybe she had.

Lucien recognized the scene instantly. It was his

and Pavlina's apartment in Paris. "Do you remember that place, Kora? You should. We lived there until you were thirteen."

But Kora didn't answer. She seemed transfixed by what was unfolding. It was her party. There were only a handful of other children there, and all were from the very special, paranormal daycare that had taken him an age to find.

She looked like an angel and his heart ached for those days. She would still willingly climb into his lap then and let him read to her. She wore a pink and white dress with an enormous bow on the back and two playful kittens embroidered on the front.

Lucien had found the dress in the Galeries Lafayette, an old and very famous department store. The frock was a little too big. He'd guessed at the size and had missed slightly. Kora hadn't cared. "You loved that dress so much you wouldn't let me take it back to get the right size."

Kora still didn't answer. She just stared.

Lucien appeared suddenly, carrying a pink and white cake with three candles. The children and the parents all sang Happy Birthday, in French of course, and the candles were blown out with help. The cake was eaten. Presents were opened. The children ran wild through the apartment, burning off the sugar they'd ingested.

And not one sign of Pavlina.

"Enough," Kora said.

But Lucien wasn't sure one example really was enough. "Show us her high school graduation."

"You weren't there," Kora snapped, finally looking at him. "I know you weren't. You can't fake that."

"Do you really think your mother forbidding me to come would stop me?"

Imari spread her hands through the air again, wiping out the last scene and replacing it with a new one. The magical camera panned through the crowd until it came to the last row of the audience where it was standing room only.

Lucien was there, by the door, smiling with pride.

"No," Kora yelled. She jabbed a finger at Imari. "You're doing that. He wasn't there."

"I cannot change the past," Imari said.

Lucien thought one more example might do it. "All Saint's Eve. Seventy-five years ago. And the last time I saw Pavlina alive."

"That will prove nothing," Kora said.

"You claim your mother told you we fought that night so horribly that I tried to stake her. I think the truth will prove quite a lot."

Imari changed out the scene one more time.

The new apartment unfolded before them, a more modern one. Lucien and Pavlina stood in the kitchen. Pavlina was dressed for the evening in a red cape and matching satin mask. Lucien was in trousers and a white dress shirt, sleeves rolled up. He had a dish towel over his shoulder.

"She was going out to a party. I asked her to stay because Kora was supposed to stop by to visit." Lucien remembered the night vividly as he looked at his daughter. "You never did stop by that night."

"I was out with friends," Kora spoke softly. "Halloween is a big night for vampires, you know."

"I know. Your mother used those exact same words with me that evening."

Kora turned back to the screen. Watched her mother scream and yell and argue. Watched Lucien stand there and take it.

He knew what was coming next. He kept his eyes on his daughter to see her reaction.

She flinched as Pavlina slapped him hard enough to draw blood. Then Pavlina stormed out in a huff. As if Lucien was to blame for her outburst.

"Enough?" Imari asked.

"No," Lucien said. "Play it out some more. Speed it up a little, though."

She nodded and let it go.

Before them, Lucien, now all alone, finished the dishes, then retired to the living room. He read the paper and watched the clock. Time passed, but still he remained. Every once in a while, he put the paper down to glance toward the door.

"What were you doing?" Kora asked. "Did you think she'd come back?"

"No." He shook his head. "I was waiting for you."

Kora swallowed but said nothing.

On screen, time continued to pass. The early morning hours approached. Lucien got up, a little frantic. He put his coat on and left. The camera followed him out to the street.

"Where were you going?" Kora asked quietly. "Were you looking for Mom?"

He had a feeling she already knew what he'd been doing, but needed to hear it from him. "No. I was looking for you. I was afraid the sun would find you before I did."

Kora sat down on the couch, her head and shoulders low.

"Do you need to see anything else to prove once and for all that I had nothing to do with your mother's end? To prove that everything she's told you about me was a lie?" He prayed that she'd seen enough. He did *not* want her to suffer through watching her mother meet the dawn.

Kora shook her head. "No. I don't want to see anymore. Please."

Imari looked at Lucien. He nodded, and she brought her hands back together. The scene faded to black and disappeared.

The silence in the room was palpable.

Then Kora put her head in her hands and started to cry.

Hattie rushed to her, putting her arm around her. "Oh, honey, let it out. It's okay. Your daddy and I love you very much."

Kora leaned into Hattie, and the crying turned into deep, wrenching sobs.

Imari put her hand on Lucien's arm. "Go to her. She needs her father. I'll be in the kitchen."

"Thank you," he whispered.

She nodded as she left, smiling.

He went to Kora, sitting on the other side of her. Gently, he laid his hand on her shoulder. "I'm sorry for what your mother did to you and made you believe."

Through sobs, Kora managed to speak. "I've been so mean to you and Mémé. I've been awful. I'm so sorry."

He brushed a strand of hair off her cheek. "I'm willing to put the past behind us if you are."

"How can you still love me after the way I've treated you?"

"Because you're my daughter and my love for you is unconditional."

With another loud sob, she threw herself into his arms. "I'm so sorry."

He held her close, kissing the top of her head. "I know. It's okay. We'll get through it."

After a few more minutes, she leaned back to look at him. Her makeup was a mess, but she was still beautiful to him. "Would it be okay if I stayed here for a while?"

"Absolutely. But there will be ground rules. And if you're not kind to Imari—"

"Are you really married to her?"

"I am."

"Do I have to call her Mom?"

He laughed. "No."

"Does she make you happy?"

"More than I have words for."

"I'm glad to hear that." Kora got up. "I need to go apologize to her."

"She's in the kitchen."

Kora headed in that direction, but paused before leaving the room. "I love you. Both of you."

Hattie sniffed, still a little teary herself. Lucien understood. In the course of a few short hours, their lives had changed dramatically for the better. And they had Imari to thank.

He just hoped that having Kora under his roof wouldn't do anything to jeopardize his relationship with Imari.

Hattie put her hand on his arm. "You need to get her a ring."

He made a face. "What kind of ring does Kora need?"

"Not Kora, Lucien. I'm talking about your wife! You married her, and she's agreed to stay married, but because of how it happened, you never got her a ring. Maybe that didn't matter when it was just for her protection, but now that it's for love, things have changed. And your adult daughter is moving back in. You not only need to get Imari a ring, but you need to make it a good one."

"Hades, you're right." He shoved to his feet. "I need to call Willa immediately."

"That's the spirit." Hattie smiled.

"I'll call from my office. Then I think we should all have a nice family dinner. What do you say? Even if it's just leftovers."

"I can whip something up, no problem. And I'd say that would be amazing."

"Good. Tell Imari and Kora, will you? I'll be out as soon as I'm done with my call."

Hattie nodded. "Perfect."

He went to his office as Hattie headed for the kitchen.

But his office wasn't empty. Imari stood in front of the Klimt painting, her bottle in her hands. "Hey," she said softly.

"Hey. Everything all right?"

She looked at the bottle she was holding. "I was just thinking."

"About?"

"How I should probably go home."

Imari hadn't expected Lucien to be so shocked by her announcement.

"You're leaving?"

She nodded. "You need space to reconnect with Kora." It wasn't how she'd pictured things going, but she wasn't going to hinder Lucien and Kora repairing their relationship. That was far more important than her desire to stay with Lucien. "And I need to get back to my apartment at some point. And then there's my job."

"But you said you wanted to stay married. I thought…that you'd stay here, too."

"I don't want to get in the way of you and Kora. I love you, Lucien. This doesn't change that." She did love him, so very much. "And I do want to stay married, but we already knew we couldn't go from zero to sixty. We need to get to know each other properly. Gradually. You know, the way it usually works. And we've got all kinds of time to do that. Right now, Kora needs you."

"Imari, I need you, too."

She smiled as she walked to him. She liked seeing him as a father. It suited him. "And I need you. I didn't mean to imply I didn't. But again, I don't want to get in the way of you and Kora figuring out your new relationship."

She leaned into him, the bottle safely tucked against her side. "Don't look so sad. This isn't the end of anything. Really, it's just the beginning. Of you and Kora. And of us. There is so much good yet to come."

He sighed, but the exhale ended in a thin smile. "I can't lie, I don't like it. But I know you're probably right that Kora and I could use this time together. It's very understanding of you."

She shrugged. "After what I just went through with my parents, could you expect me to think any other way? You're so lucky to have this opportunity."

"You're the one who made it happen."

"That reminds me." She set the bottle on the small table by the couch. "Isn't there another wish you'd like to have?"

"I have everything I need."

She cut her eyes at him while offering him a coy smile. "Lucien. Come on, now."

"You mean being able to see color?"

She'd already planned on giving that ability back to him, but it wasn't what she was talking about. "I mean fixing your abilities."

He seemed shocked by that. "You can fix my reaper powers?"

"I told you, jinn magic is strong stuff."

"That would mean...I wouldn't have to separate myself from people anymore."

"Isn't that what you want?"

He was quiet for a moment, the muscles in his jaw working. "Yes, of course. But I didn't think such a thing was possible. You've already done so much for me, and I know your wishes are limited—"

"Lucien." She gave him a stern glance. "You saved my life. And risked your own doing it. I owe you."

"You owe me nothing. After what you did for Kora? We're square."

"Then consider these wishes my wedding present to you."

He smiled. "You are gift enough. But I am not so foolish that I would turn down the chance to be whole again." He put his hands on her shoulders and kissed her, then pulled her in close. "Thank you."

She held on to him, savoring the feel of him in her arms. All her life, she'd thought this kind of happiness was for other people. People who were able to make their own choices. People who'd been born to a different path than she had. And now, here she was, with the love of a good man.

And thanks to Hattie, and potentially Kora, she had a new family. One who would never decide their station in life meant more than their relationship with her.

"Just say the words," she whispered. "Wish for what you want." She felt him take a breath.

"I wish I could see color again. And I wish that my reaper powers were fully mine to control again."

She stepped back and summoned her wishes. The familiar spin of possibility washed through her with a happy buzz, and she imagined the things that he'd asked for. Then, with a nod and a small shower of glitter, she made them reality.

He sucked in a breath. She imagined it was because the color had returned to his sight.

"Better?" she asked.

"Perfect." He shook his head. "I can't believe you fixed me so easily."

"Jinn—"

"Magic," he finished with a laugh. Then his mood shifted back to a more serious tone. "I could wish for you to stay, couldn't I?"

"You could." She already knew he wouldn't. He wasn't the kind of man who would force his will upon her.

"But that would make it my choice and not yours." He kissed her. "I do wish you'd stay, but I also understand you probably need some time to process everything that's happened to you, too."

"I do." She kissed him back. Her husband. How odd. And wonderful.

"I do hope you'll still be here often, Imari. Your presence will always be welcome. And I actually think it will help Kora."

"You think so? How?"

"Kora could use the example of us together. She

needs to see what a happy relationship looks like. Besides that, Hattie loves you."

"But she has her granddaughter now."

"Doesn't mean she doesn't still want you here. She does."

Imari smiled. "I'll be around."

He glanced toward the kitchen. "Good. Because I just hate the thought of you not being in this house. Of not having you in the same room. Or being able to touch you. And kiss you. And hold your hand. Whenever I want."

She slipped her arms around his waist again. "Then you'll probably want to take me out on dates. Especially now that you can go out in public without the fear of accidentally doing someone in."

His smile returned. "I like the thought of being out with you in public very much."

"Good. Then it's settled. I'll move back to my place for a little bit, and we'll all get to know each other better. That will give me some time to get to know Kora as well. Without the pressure of us all being in the same house together."

"Agreed." He glanced around the room like he was seeing it with new eyes, which in a way, he was. "This house is odd, isn't it? Living underground like this. It's not what most people do."

"No, it isn't. But then, most people aren't generally trying to hide from the rest of the world. Nor do they have a reason to."

He nodded slowly. "I think it's time to make some changes."

"Like what?"

He just smiled and shrugged. "You'll see."

A week later and Imari still wasn't sure what kind of changes Lucien had been talking about. So far, nothing new had really happened.

Well, outside of everything that was already new. He and Kora seemed to be moving forward in a healthy way. Hattie had joined the Nocturne Falls gardening club, despite the fact that she had no garden.

And Imari was back at work.

Which was a little strange. Because as much as she loved her job, she missed being at Lucien's.

Her apartment seemed so empty without Hattie in the kitchen, or Lucien's weighty presence.

And she'd been over to his place twice. Both times for dinner, which had been lovely, but since being back at work for three days, their schedules hadn't lined up. She'd been too tired after the first day of work, then he and Kora had made plans to do something, then her girlfriends had insisted on a night out to catch up. The bottom line was she missed him. A lot. Text and phone calls were great, but they weren't Lucien in the flesh.

And he was going to be away again, soon. He had to face the reaper council to discuss why he'd reaped and then returned Khalid's soul. She'd asked to go with him for that. Seemed only fair after what Lucien had done for her. But he'd said that wouldn't sit well with the council.

She leaned against the hall that divided the spa rooms. Dwelling on how much she missed Lucien wasn't helping get her through the day. Time to focus. Her next client was already waiting for her. A new client. She had a lot of new clients today. Wasn't that unusual. This was a tourist town, after all. But she hoped this one, a Mr. Black, wasn't creepy. Sometimes with the guys, you never knew what you were getting, although the spa did a pretty good job of weeding out the weirdos.

She put on a smile and knocked softly on the door of the Oasis room. "Mr. Black, it's Imari, your massage therapist. Are you ready for me?"

A muffled grunt answered her. She took that for a yes and opened the door.

Lucien leaned against the massage table, smiling. "Hi there."

She almost squealed. She shut the door behind her so as not to disturb the spa's quiet. "Lucien! What are you doing here?"

He shrugged. "I missed you."

She threw her arms around him, which was totally not appropriate therapist-client behavior, but whatever. "I missed you too. It's been too long."

He nodded and kissed the edge of her jaw. "Too long. But I know we've both been busy."

This was the first time she'd seen him out in public since everything that had happened. She knew it was a big step for him, even with his powers mended. She hooked her arms around his neck. "It was really sweet of you to come by."

"I had to see you. To touch you." He pulled her closer and trailed kisses toward her ear. "And do this."

Her breath shuddered with the waves of pleasure his kisses were causing. "You, uh, know they're going to charge you for this massage."

"Who cares? I can afford it."

"I know, but I would have given you one for free at your house. Or mine."

He stopped kissing her. "I didn't come here for a massage. I came here to spend an hour with you."

She backed up and rubbed her hands together. "Oh, you're getting a massage." She'd been wanting to give him one for a while. For someone who'd been unable to touch or be touched, this was going to be an amazing experience for him.

"I am?" He looked skeptical.

"You are." She pointed behind him. "Drop the robe and get on the table under the sheet, face down in the ring at the end."

He straightened, putting his hands on the robe's belt. "I should warn you, I don't have anything on under this robe. That's what they told me to do when I got here. Get undressed. So I did. I was afraid they wouldn't let me back here if I didn't."

She turned around to give him some privacy and to hide her quickly heating cheeks. "Yep, that's standard procedure. Under the sheet."

She heard a soft rustling behind her. Lucien. Getting naked.

314

Heat swept her from head to toe. How was she going to do this? She'd massaged people from all walks of life, all body types, all varieties of supernatural, and always kept it strictly professional.

But this was Lucien, the only one she'd ever wanted in a very unprofessional way. And he was her husband.

"Ready."

She swallowed and took a breath. She could do this. Fifty minutes of the best massage she'd ever given. Easy.

She turned around. The sheet covered him completely, but even in the soft light of the Oasis Room, it was impossible to ignore the incredible shape of the man beneath that sheet.

Professional, she reminded herself. Yeah, right.

"Okay, I'm going to start with your back." She pulled the sheet down to his waist. Next she held her hand beneath the automatic warmed oil dispenser, then rubbed the oil between her palms. "Just relax and let yourself go. It's okay if you fall asleep."

He grunted. "The woman I'm in love with is about to put her hands on my naked body and you think I might fall asleep?"

"Massage is very soothing." Sure it was. That's why her lady parts were making wishes of their own.

Lucien hadn't come to the spa for a massage, but when Imari's warm, oiled-up hands caressed his back, his mind lost track of the real reason he'd come here.

Forget the wishes and the flying carpets and glitter in the air. Her hands were the real magic. The long, slow strokes she worked over him made him feel blissfully drugged. He'd never been touched like this, never wanted to be.

But then, he'd never known it could feel like this.

He might have been flying on that magic carpet again as weightless as he felt. He sighed, eyes closed, world around him forgotten.

Except for the woman touching him. There was no way he could forget her. "You are amazing."

Her soft laugh answered him. "I told you you'd like it."

"If we were not already married, I would propose." The last word reminded him why he was

316

here. He'd brought her a gift, and it was currently in his robe pocket.

More soft laughter as her hands slipped lower. Then lower still.

His body responded in a new way. A way that he hadn't expected. A way that filled his head with ideas that should not be acted on in Imari's place of employment.

He yanked the sheet around him and scrambled into a sitting position.

"Whoa." Imari backed up, her eyes on the ceiling. "You all covered up there?"

He checked. He was. Mostly. He adjusted the sheet. "Yes, but we are married, you know. It's not like you can't look if you want to."

She did now, smiling sheepishly. "I know, but we aren't at that stage of our relationship. Yet."

But maybe soon, was what her tone implied. He was fine with that. He was ready when she was. Maybe more ready. Or too ready. He cleared his throat and tried to think about other things. Like Hattie. And Kora. That helped ease him away from the edge of no return.

"Did you not like the massage?"

"I liked it very much. So much we probably shouldn't continue until we're at *that* stage of our relationship."

"Oh. *Oh!*" She snorted, then pressed her lips together in a wobbly smile. "Yep, good. I'm in agreement there." She crossed her arms. "So I guess we could talk until your appointment is up."

"I have a better idea. I brought you a present. It was somewhat impulsive, but I promise that if you don't like it, I won't be offended or upset."

She frowned. "Now I'm worried."

"Don't be." He hopped off the table and dug into the pocket of his robe, pulled out a small black box. He held it out to her. "Hattie said I should get you a ring."

Her frown lessened. "Oh, that's sweet."

She opened the box and looked inside. Then she glanced up at him, puzzled. "Is that...a key ring? I'm not sure that's what Hattie meant—"

"I know it's not the kind of ring she meant. But this key ring holds a key. To a house. That I bought for us."

Her mouth hung open for a moment. "You bought a house?"

"Yes, I know it was impulsive, but I spoke with Pandora Williams—isn't she a friend of yours?"

Imari nodded, still looking a bit shocked.

"Well, I spoke to her about the idea of buying a new house, and she told me the house two blocks from the Victorian her fiancé owns was about to come onto the market, but I might be able to scoop the sale if the offer was good enough. Apparently, it was because the owners accepted right away."

"You bought a house. Above ground."

He nodded, completely unsure what to think about her reaction. "I thought it would be good for us to have a space that's...a new beginning." Especially if there was any chance they might start a family.

Children needed a yard. And Hattie wanted a pet.

"What about your underground house?"

"Kora will live there. It's perfect for her since she has to avoid daylight anyway. Plus I'm training her to take over some of my responsibilities at the club. Hattie would like to live with us, though, if that's all right with you. The house is plenty big enough, I assure you. Very large yard, too."

"Oh, Lucien. I don't know what to say."

"Are you happy or upset? I can't tell." He hoped with everything in him she wasn't upset.

She laughed, and her eyes sparkled with tears. "Happy. I can't believe you bought us a house. And yes, Hattie can live with us. I would love that."

He exhaled in relief. "Would you like to see it? Pandora said it will need some work. Enough that it might take a few months. The owners haven't updated it since they bought it in the '80s, but you can change it however you like. The only thing I ask is that you use lots of color. And let Hattie decorate her own space."

"Of course, she can do whatever she likes in her— wait. Are you telling me you bought a house two blocks down from Pandora Williams boyfriend's house? On ritzy Shadows Drive?"

"Yes."

"But those are all big, fancy, *expensive* Victorian mansions."

He nodded. "Yes, they are. And the house is quite large. Pandora said three floors. I think Hattie would like an elevator. Sadly, the garage only holds four cars, but I'll find a way to manage that."

"Why do you keep saying Pandora said? Haven't you seen the house?"

"Not yet, no."

She let out a little laugh-sob combination, then put her hand over her mouth. "You're kind of nuts, you know that? Who buys a house that was undoubtedly a lot of money without looking at it first?"

He lifted one shoulder. "I do, I guess. I promise I won't always be this impulsive. I know how you genies like order."

She threw her arms around him. "No, don't change. I love you just the way you are. I think order is overrated."

He hugged her to him. "There is one more thing. An actual ring. Two, really. You need one and I need one. I don't want any question that we're married."

She nodded. "Yes, rings. We need those."

"Good. Let me get dressed and we'll go shopping."

She tilted her head at him. "I have a job, remember? And I am booked with clients for the rest of the day."

"You do have a job. Remodeling our new house."

She made a face at him. "Funny. No, I mean my current job."

"Ah yes, and all those clients waiting for you. Mrs. Crabapple is right after me, followed by Ms. Simmons, then Mr. Franklin—"

"How do you know the names of all my clients?"

He smiled broadly, rather pleased with himself. "Because they're all me. Well, all appointments made by me. And no pressure, but if you would rather not be employed here, that's fine with me too. Now that I'm no longer a danger to anyone, I would love to travel again. With you."

Her chest rose and fell with a single breath. "Are you offering me a life of leisure?"

"I'm offering you whatever kind of life you'd like. What would make you happy?"

"More time with you." She shook her head. "Wow. I guess I'm going to quit."

"You don't have to decide right now. You can think about it while we're ring shopping." He winked at her. "Willa is expecting us."

"She is?"

He nodded. "And then I thought we could go to dinner at Guillermo's, the Italian place in town. Willa said it's very romantic."

Imari put her hands on his face and kissed him. "How did I get so lucky to have you for a husband? I never thought I'd have a man so wonderful, never dared to think my life could turn out this way, and yet, here I am. It's like…a dream. Except you're real."

He smiled and kissed her back. *Dream* was a good word. "I feel the very same way. When I told you I had everything I needed? Everything I've ever wanted? I was lying."

Her face fell a little. "You were?"

"Yes. But I can say that now and it's the truth. Imari Dupree, you're *my* wish come true. I love you."

Her smile returned, and she laughed as she leaned into him. "I love you, too, Lucien. I never would have thought I'd spend the rest of my life with a grim reaper, but for a guy who's basically death, you're pretty perfect."

He gave her a sheepish look. *Perfect* was not a word that had ever been used to describe him. It was a lot to live up to. "I hope you still think that when you realize how hard I am to live with."

"Hard to live with? I'm a genie. You saw the house I grew up in. Now you're offering me a life of leisure? I might turn into a spoiled brat."

"I would love to spoil you." The idea thrilled him, actually. "Nothing would bring me greater pleasure."

"You sure about that?" Her brows lifted and the light in her eyes took on a spirited gleam. "That's quite a bold statement right before we go ring shopping."

"Absolutely." He hoped she picked out the biggest rock in the store. "In fact, I say bring it on. Show me what you've got."

"Really?"

"Really." He could tell she didn't quite believe him. She'd learn. "See if you can give Elenora something to be jealous of."

She pursed her lips before bursting out laughing. "Be careful what you wish for."

THE END

Want to be up to date on new books, new audiobooks & other fun stuff from Kristen Painter? Sign-up for my newsletter at www.kristenpainter.com. No spam, just news (sales, freebies, and releases, you know, all that jazz).

If you loved the book and want to help the series grow, tell a friend about the book and take time to leave a review!

Other Books by Kristen Painter

PARANORMAL ROMANCE:

Nocturne Falls series:
The Vampire's Mail Order Bride
The Werewolf Meets His Match
The Gargoyle Gets His Girl
The Professor Woos The Witch
The Witch's Halloween Hero – short story
The Werewolf's Christmas Wish – short story
The Vampire's Fake Fiancée
The Vampire's Valentine Surprise – short story
The Shifter Romances The Writer
The Vampire's True Love Trials – short story
The Dragon Finds Forever
The Vampire's Accidental Wife
The Reaper Rescues The Genie

Can't get enough Nocturne Falls?
Try the NOCTURNE FALLS UNIVERSE books.
New stories, new authors, same Nocturne Falls world!
www.http://kristenpainter.com/nocturne-falls-universe/

Sin City Collectors series:
Queen of Hearts
Dead Man's Hand
Double or Nothing
Box set

Nothing is completed without an amazing team.

Many thanks to:

Cover design: Janet Holmes
Interior formatting: Author E.M.S
Editor: Joyce Lamb
Copyedits/proofs: Marlene Engel/Lisa Bateman

About the Author

USA Today Best Selling Author Kristen Painter is a little obsessed with cats, books, chocolate, and shoes. It's a healthy mix. She loves to entertain her readers with interesting twists and unforgettable characters. She currently writes the best-selling paranormal romance series, Nocturne Falls, and the cozy mystery spin off series, Jayne Frost. The former college English teacher can often be found all over social media where she loves to interact with readers. Learn more at her website:

www.kristenpainter.com

Printed in Great Britain
by Amazon